D0713221

BULLET
HOLE

BULLET HOLE

a novel by

Keith Miles

1817

HARPER & ROW, PUBLISHERS, New York

Cambridge, Philadelphia, San Francisco, Washington
London, Mexico City, São Paulo, Singapore, Sydney

A HARPER NOVEL OF SUSPENSE

FIRST U.S. EDITION

Library of Congress Cataloging-in-Publication Data

Miles, Keith.
  Bullet hole.

  I. Title.
PR6063.I3175B8   1987   823'.914   86-45670
ISBN 0-06-015764-X

87 88 89 90 91 RRD 10 9 8 7 6 5 4 3 2 1

For Rosalind
with love and thanks

'The only way,' I said to Alexander, 'of really finding out a man's true character is to play golf with him. In no other walk of life does the cloven hoof so quickly display itself.'

P. G. Wodehouse: *Ordeal By Golf*

Chapter One

Carnoustie headed north towards St Andrews. God was in his heaven and David Jacobs was on the radio. Cruising along at a steady fifty-five, I had the chance to look around me. And sigh.

The motorways of Britain are depressingly honest. They tell the truth about people. There is no better place to learn the full details about the darker side of the human psyche than on the M1 on a sunlit Sunday morning in July. It is not only a major thoroughfare: it is a mass confessional with periodic lane closures. Sin is everywhere.

Put the average man or woman behind the steering wheel of a motor vehicle and you turn them into demons. They race, bully, bicker, impede, distract, show off and generally torment. They blind you with their headlights, deafen you with their horns, intimidate you with their proximity, mesmerise you with their nodding dogs, terrify you with their recklessness and appall you with their complete disregard for the basic courtesies. They also abuse their machines cruelly and court disaster as if they had nine lives.

The M1 is the high road to damnation.

Carnoustie hates it as much as I do. It brings out the worst in both of us. Instead of going on a dignified and unhurried journey to our destination, we are forced to compete, to jostle, to bear malice, to seek revenge. At any moment, our comfortable cruising speed could be reduced to a juddering twenty by a coach lurching out of an access road or increased to a teeth-rattling seventy-five when a removal van we try to overtake decides to respond to the challenge. Hazards abound. You end up becoming one yourself.

So why do we always use this route? I wish I knew.

The rasp of an exhaust jerked me out of my reverie as a high-powered motorcycle shot past us, illegally and dangerously, on the inside lane. Bent low over the handlebars, a leather-jacketed figure swung his machine out in front of us and accelerated away, his white scarf streaming, his black helmet glinting. When I flashed angry headlights at him, he caught their glare in his mirrors and gave us a gloved V-sign over his shoulder. We surged forward in pursuit but there was no hope of catching him. With all her virtues, Carnoustie is no speed merchant. The chase was soon abandoned and we fell back to a more sensible pace.

Pylons rose up to disfigure the landscape. As we passed beneath overhead cables, the honey-smooth voice of David Jacobs became a hoarse gargle. The interference then cleared and we were into the overture to 'Mack and Mabel'. Carnoustie felt soothed. She almost purred.

Carnoustie is a motor caravan. To be more exact, she is a T-registered Bedford Adventura CF250. She boasts four-berth sleeping accommodation and has a complete kitchen with full gas cooker, refrigerator, stainless steel sink with two drainers, and a constant source of hot and cold water pumped electronically. She is especially proud of her shower unit which, with the portable toilet, makes her independent of organised sites. Fitted with underfloor freshwater storage tanks, she also has a waste water tank which enables us to choose the point of disposal.

Among the many extras which a loving owner has added are a stereo radio and cassette player, a colour television, mains electricity, vinyl flooring, a Viking Petite catalytic heater and a set of golfing prints framed in rich brown to match the teak-effect furniture.

For most of the year, Carnoustie is my home. She has everything.

Bra-a-a-ark! Bra-a-a-ark!

Including a telephone with an aggressive ring.

Bra-a-a-ark! Bra-a-a-ark!

With one deft movement of the hand, I killed off 'Mack

and Mabel' and lifted the receiver. It was Fiona. She sounded peeved.

'Alan?'

'Welcome to the day!'

'I've just woken up and . . . you're not in bed with me.'

'Full marks for observation!'

'Where *are* you, Alan?'

'On the M1. Somewhere in Derbyshire.'

I could see her lips pouting. 'But I want you *here*.'

'No can do, Fiona. I told you I had to be off first thing this morning. Duty before pleasure, my darling.'

'You might have said goodbye,' she complained.

'I did. When you were asleep. I kissed you on the forehead.'

'Thanks a bunch. I'm rationed to kisses on the forehead now, am I?' Her tone softened immediately. 'You should have woken me, Alan. For a fond farewell.'

Fiona specialised in fond farewells. The first time I tried to say goodbye to her, it took two and a half days. At one and the same time, she can send you on your way and deprive you of all urge to go. If ever she gave up her job at the hospital, Fiona could make a career out of the fond farewell. She could teach the subject at night school and set up weekend courses for advanced students.

'Are you still there, Alan?'

'No. I've just popped out for a run on the hard shoulder.'

'Very funny.'

'Thanks for ringing, anyway . . .'

'Hey, don't hang up on me, you bastard. Or I'll jump in the car and drive up to St Andrews after you.'

'Don't you dare!' I yelled.

'Why not?' she teased. 'I might bring you luck.'

'Fiona, you *promised*.'

'But I want to see you play.'

'Watch me on the telly.'

There was a long, ambiguous silence at the other end of the line, then a warm whisper caressed my ear. 'Alan . . . I'm lying on the bed. I've got nothing on. I'm all yours, sweetie. If you were here right now—'

3

Instinct made me slam down the receiver and switch on the radio again. The mere thought of a naked Fiona was enough to make my palms sweat. I had to put temptation firmly behind me. It may be different for other golfers but sixteen traumatic years on the professional circuits have taught me that self-denial is a vital part of my game. I could never begin to concentrate on my shots with the Mistress of the Fond Farewell in the offing. During the week of the Open, I must not even have heard of a blonde physiotherapist called Fiona Langley.

Bra-a-a-ark! Bra-a-a-ark!

'I'm not at home.'

Bra-a-a-ark! Bra-a-a-ark!

I grabbed the receiver and bellowed a few obscenities into it. Fiona giggled. I took a deep breath. 'Look, do us both a favour, will you? Stay out of my life.'

'I miss you.'

'Go back to sleep.'

'I love you.'

This time it was Fiona who hung up. I smiled, forgot all about her, put down the receiver and eased Carnoustie past an articulated lorry. David Jacobs started talking about Rossini.

When I had set out from Northampton, I had reckoned that I would stop only three times – at Woodhall Services for light refreshment, at Washington Services for some fuel, and at an unspecified point between Carfraemill and Dalkeith for lunch. St Andrews, in short, was a par four.

The beauty of a vehicle like Carnoustie is that it ensures privacy. You can be blissfully lonely in a crowd. When I pulled into the car park at the Woodhall Service Area, the place was bursting at the seams. The world and his wife had descended on Yorkshire. Instead of having to queue interminably for a cup of over-priced, lukewarm coffee, then battle for table space in order to drink it, I was able to step into the parlour and get out the perculator. Safe inside my own four walls, I ran no risk of being recognised by the idiot public. Being a sporting celebrity is a mixed blessing. You become a sitting target for complete strangers who think they have some sort of claim on your attention. I do not suffer fools gladly any more.

Restored by coffee and biscuits, I set off on the second leg of the journey. The M1 seemed busier than ever and I was grateful to be able to leave it and join the Great North Road. Traffic was still heavy but Carnoustie maintained a much more even pace.

I allowed myself some first thoughts about the week that lay ahead and the enormous task that confronted me. By the time we reached Wetherby I had almost completed my practice round on the Old Course, testing its defences and relearning its subtleties. My mind was all slashing drives and bold approach shots and delicate putts. Fiona was not even a hazy memory. She was strictly out of bounds.

Braking hard to avoid collision with a wayward oil tanker, I realised that I was back on a motorway again. Demons came out to play all around me and I automatically lapsed back into the bad behaviour that passes for good driving. Washington Service Area beckoned with a blue sign and I drove straight to the petrol pumps.

The old man at the pay desk obviously recognised me but could not put a name to the face. He delayed giving me my change while he worked on the problem. Eventually, he got there and it produced the usual half-witted grin of triumph.

'Hey, I know who you are,' he announced, thrusting my money at me. 'Alan Saxon! Yeah, that's it. Alan Saxon.' The grin was commuted to a smile. 'Didn't you used to play golf or something?'

It was an all too familiar question and I have still not found a suitable answer to it. So I nodded politely, turned on my heel and walked quickly away. I wanted my anonymity back. Leaping into the driving seat, I switched on the ignition and set Carnoustie in motion.

Only then did I become aware of my passenger.

'Hello,' she said, familiarly.

'Who the hell are you?'

'I was hoping for a lift.'

5

Carnoustie came to a halt but my temper gathered speed.

'You can't just climb into somebody's vehicle like that! Of all the bloody nerve! Now get out before I throw you out.'

'But I'm going to St Andrews,' she explained, calmly.

'I don't care if you're going to the sodding Hebrides. *Out.*'

She sat there happily and made no effort to move. I put her age at twenty but she had the languid confidence of a much older woman. Resting on her knees was a nylon haversack. She unzipped it, took out a small, leather-bound book, flicked through the pages, then held one open for me. I stared down at my own autograph in red biro.

'Last year. At Royal Birkdale.' She put the album away. 'I did well there. My name is Janie, by the way.'

'It's been nice knowing you, Janie. Now disappear.'

'But I'm on my way to the Open.'

'I never give lifts,' I insisted. 'On principle.'

'That's why I got straight in. It was my only chance. If I'd tried to hitch, you'd have driven right past me. I read somewhere that you're obsessively shy. You have this fetish about travelling alone.'

'I am not obsessively shy!'

'Okay – desperately insecure, then. Amounts to the same thing. According to this article—'

'*What* bloody article?'

'The one that said you tend to fly off the handle.'

The humour in her eyes stifled my explosion. I sat back and appraised her more carefully. Her face was interesting rather than attractive but the shoulder-length black hair was beautiful. Though she wore only a check shirt, denim jeans and white trainers, she managed to look almost elegant. But the most striking thing about her was her composure. She was poised, relaxed, completely at ease.

Curiosity slowly got the better of common sense.

'Who are you?'

'I told you. I'm Janie.'

'But where are you from? What do you do?'

'I'm a student.'

'Of what?'

'Psychology. At Bristol.'

'And you like golf.'

'I like golfers.'

She looked at me with a mixture of innocence and provocation that rang all the alarm bells. I knew that I should heed their warning and put the girl out. She was an invader. A distraction. A threat. She was another Fiona. If I let her stay, I would be jumping out of the frying pan into the fire. Out of physiotherapy and into psychology. Out of the fond farewell and into the familiar hello.

She deserved to be kicked out at once. Without mercy.

'I'll take you as far as Coldstream,' I heard myself say.

'Thanks. That'll do for starters.'

Carnoustie eased forward again and we rejoined the traffic on the last short stretch of motorway. Janie stowed her rucksack beside her feet and took sunglasses from her breast pocket. As she put them on, she tossed her hair and I felt it brush my shoulder.

I drove in silence and tried in vain to justify the fact that I had offered her a lift. She had conned me and I had been a willing victim. She had aroused my interest and made me break my golden rule. Torn between resentment and fascination, I became more and more uneasy and resolved that I would get to Coldstream as quickly as possible. For this raven-haired student of psychology, that was very definitely the end of the line.

We came off the motorway and a golf course soon appeared to our left. Sunday morning sportsmen were enjoying leisurely contests in the bright sunshine. People were playing golf for the sheer fun of it and the sight lifted my spirits. Janie, however, ignored the spectacle completely. I could not understand why.

As we plunged into the Tyne Tunnel, she broke the silence.

'I do like that,' she said, pointing to the little figure that hung from the driving mirror. 'Is it a lucky charm?'

'Sort of. My daughter gave it to me.'

'It's very sweet.'

Without bothering to ask permission, she unhooked it so that she could examine it. The silvered golfer was made out of die-cast metal and he was in the act of driving from the tee. Lynette had bought it for me because she thought it looked like a miniature version of her father. For that reason alone, the object had special value for me.

Janie was intrigued by it and pinned it to her shirt.

'I'd love to have it,' she declared. 'As a memento.'

'Sorry.'

'I'm ready to pay for it.'

'Not for sale.'

'But your daughter could get you another one,' she persisted. 'Then I could have this. How much was it?'

'I wouldn't part with it for anything.'

Janie did not give up easily. 'Where did she buy it?'

'Haven't a clue.'

'Then ask her,' she urged, indicating the telephone. 'Ring her up right this minute and ask her.'

'I can't,' I told her. 'Lynette is abroad.'

'Where?'

'School trip. A coach tour of six countries. They're in the middle of France today, I think.'

She fumed quietly and considered her next move. We were not really talking about a miniature golfer. We were engaged in a battle of wills. Janie seemed determined to have her own way and was annoyed that she was meeting so much resistance. She cleared her throat and returned to the attack.

'Ring your wife, then. She may know.'

'My wife and I are divorced. We speak to each other as little as possible. Besides, why should I go to all the trouble simply to satisfy a whim of yours?' I tapped the driving mirror. 'Put it back where I can see it, please.'

She was not done yet. 'Is there *no* way I can persuade you, Alan?'

I had never been propositioned quite so bluntly before and I needed a moment to absorb the impact. Then I tapped the mirror again. Reluctantly, she hung the figure back in its place.

Out of the corner of my eye, I watched the tiny golfer swaying gently to and fro. There was no way that I would ever surrender him. When you see your only child as rarely as I do, and love her as deeply, and miss her as painfully, any present from her takes on an added significance. Of all the funny little gifts that Lynette had sent me, the golfer was my favourite. It travelled everywhere with me. I wore it on my sweater during every tournament and I had developed an almost superstitious reliance on it. Apart from that, Lynette always asked after it in her letters.

How could I tell a twelve-year-old girl that I had given her star present to a hitch-hiker in return for services rendered?

Coldstream got its first mention on a signpost and this seemed to bring Janie back to life. I thought she had been sulking but her tone was amiable and her manner forthright.

'It would be marvellous if you won the Open again.'

'Yes,' I agreed, modestly.

'You'd be the first British player since the war to take the title twice. That would be fantastic!' She gave a short laugh. 'You'd have to buy another motor caravan and call it St Andrews.'

'I'll stick with Carnoustie,' I told her. 'That was the big one for me. The first time has got to be the best. Not that I'd say no to a second time, mind. Or a third, or a fourth, if it comes to that. But Carnoustie will always have pride of place.'

'What was it like, actually *winning*?'

I shrugged. 'A lot better than losing.'

'When exactly was it?'

'A long time ago, Janie. A long, long time ago.'

It was fourteen years but it felt more like a century.

'How do you rate your chances at St Andrews?'

'Ask me next Sunday.'

'I'm asking you now.'

9

'No comment.'

'Why are you afraid to talk about it?'

'I'm obsessively shy. Remember? And desperately insecure.'

'In other words, I can mind my own business.'

'Look,' I stressed, 'I offered you a lift not an interview. Now there must be a thousand and one other things we can chat about – the weather, the price of fish, the state of the nation, what a nice girl like you is going to do with the rest of her life. Choose any subject. Except golf. On that I keep my own counsel. I discuss it with nobody.'

'Fair enough,' she conceded. 'Let's talk about your marriage.'

'Janie—'

'Why did it break up? For the usual reasons?'

'Listen—'

'Or did your wife get pissed off because she wasn't allowed to mention golf either? I bet you were a barrel of laughs to live with.'

'Shut up!'

'First you tell me to choose a subject. Now I've got to belt up. Have you always had this trouble making up your mind?'

I pulled on the steering wheel, mounted a grass verge and brought Carnoustie to a halt. Janie and I stared at each other. For several minutes there was no sound except the panting of the engine. Her gaze was steady and challenging. She was daring me to put her out. And while that had been my firm intention when I stopped, I could not find the words to do it. There was something about her which deprived me of my usual sense of purpose. She knew it.

The more she irritated me, the more drawn I became to her.

'How old were you when your hair went grey?'

It was such an odd thing for her to ask me at that particular moment that I laughed involuntarily. She laughed too, then repeated her question.

'I must have been about your age.'

10

She touched my head with soft fingers. 'I like it.'

'I don't,' I confessed.

'Is that why you always play in a baseball cap? Oh, sorry!' she corrected herself. 'Forget I said that. I didn't mean to talk about golf again. But I do like it, honestly. A full head of grey hair makes a man look so distinguished. And sexy.'

'I don't feel either just now.'

She glanced through the windscreen, then turned to smile at me. 'It's not all that far to Coldstream, is it?'

But we both knew that I was taking her all the way now.

We had a picnic lunch just outside Dalkeith. It consisted of a salad washed down with white wine and followed by a selection of fresh fruit. The glorious sunshine persuaded us to eat in a field and I spread out a tartan blanket for the occasion. Janie devoured the meal as if it was the only one she was likely to get for a while. For the first time, I sensed a vulnerability about her.

She was good company, chatting happily, compliment-ing me on the food, teasing me because I diluted my wine with Perrier water, behaving as if we were old friends at a reunion lunch. When the meal was over, she insisted on clearing everything away and washing the dishes in the sink. I stayed in the field and watched the sheep on the distant hillside, picking their way past outcrops of rock as they climbed to higher grazing. It was a restful scene. I could have enjoyed it for hours. But Janie reappeared and strolled towards me.

I started. Janie had taken off her trainers, socks and jeans and undone the front of her shirt. As she walked barefoot over the grass, I could see the white triangle of her pants peeping out from beneath the shirt. Her legs were long and thin and she moved with the grace of a dancer. Kneeling beside me, she slipped off her shirt to reveal a slim, smooth body with small, rounded breasts.

'Thought I'd improve my suntan,' she said, lying on her back and arching up so that she could ease off her pants. I put a hand out to stop her. 'What's wrong? Nobody can see me here.'

11

'*I* can see you, Janie.'

'So?'

I stood up. 'Maybe it's time we pressed on.'

'Failure feelings? Or have you taken a vow of chastity?'

She arched up again, pushed her pants down over her thighs, then sat up so that she could remove them completely. Rolling over on to her front, she stretched herself full length on the blanket. All at once the sun became oppressively warm.

I was thankful that I had put so much Perrier into my wine. 'I'll wait for you,' I said and strode off, not daring to look back again. As I climbed into the cab, I congratulated myself on what I saw as a fine recovery shot.

When Janie rejoined me, she had put on her pants and buttoned up her shirt. She threw the tartan blanket over the back of her seat, then struggled into her jeans. I put us back on the road once more.

'Why not?' she asked, casually.

'Lots of reasons.'

'Somebody else?'

'That's one of them.'

'Because I'm so much younger than you?'

'That's another.'

'And what's the main reason?'

'I have an appointment to keep in the Auld Grey Toon.'

She dismissed the topic with a shrug and leaned forward to flick the little golfer with her finger, making him swing crazily from side to side like a hanged man in a fierce crosswind. As I steadied him, I shot her a look of reproof. By way of a reply, she began to put on her socks and trainers.

A couple of miles beyond Dalkeith we picked up signs for the Forth Road Bridge. Ten minutes later we were approaching Fairmilehead and looking for the turn on to the ring road.

The Edinburgh ring road is a cruel misnomer. Newcomers expecting to find a circular route around a major city are severely disappointed. Instead, they are forced to twist and turn and loop and zigzag for mile after mile along a road that is closer to a Gordian knot than a ring. Roundabouts punctuate the route every now and again and a great deal of sign-reading and lane-changing are required.

It was at one of these roundabouts that we came to grief. Whether I was driving too fast, or distracted by Janie's conversation, or simply very careless I do not know, but I suddenly found myself only yards away from the side of a large green van that had come into the stream of traffic from the right. I braked instantly and the speed of my reflexes probably saved us from a serious crash but Carnoustie still screamed and skidded and clipped the rear of the van.

Since Carnoustie is so much more than a mode of transport for me, I was outraged when I jumped out and saw the damage. Her offside front wing had been viciously dented, her bumper bent and one of her headlights smashed. My anger conveniently hid from me the fact that I had been responsible for the accident and I charged across to the now stationary van to bang on the side. The driver, a short, wiry middle-aged man in dirty overalls, got out to face my ire.

'What the fuck do you think you're doing?'

'Your fault, mate,' he retorted, bristling.

'You pulled out in front of me!'

'Look where you're going next time.'

'And you.'

The argument quickly escalated to the stage of wild gesticulation and outright abuse. Though I was a foot or so taller than him, he was in no way abashed and turned out to have a far more fluent command of ripe language than I. Other drivers stopped to join in the debate and those who claimed to be witnesses all sided with my adversary. Together with the fact that his vehicle had come out of the collision more or less unscathed, this only served to enrage me further. It was inevitable that somebody in the crowd would recognise me and equally inevitable that the van driver hated golf. When a comedian suggested that I should shout 'fore' as I came up to a roundabout, everyone laughed.

By now, of course, we were holding up a long line of

traffic and impatient horns were playing a symphony of annoyance. It was time to go. After ridding ourselves of a few more accusations, the van driver and I traded names and addresses and agreed to let our respective insurance companies punch it out by correspondence. He reserved the right to have the last word.

'I hope you drive better from the bloody tee.'

The laughter was even more mocking. I pushed through the crowd and stalked back to the battered Carnoustie. Bumper and wing could wait but the headlight had to be fixed and that would mean a search for a garage that could do the job. Even not counting the brief pause on the grass verge when I had tried to eject my passenger, I would still be making two unscheduled stops. After carefully aiming at a par four, I would be arriving in St Andrews with a double bogey.

It was a bad omen.

There was worse to come. When I got back into the cab in need of sympathy, Janie had vanished. And so had the miniature golfer that hung from the driving mirror.

I felt sick.

Chapter Two

If you have any golfing instincts whatsoever, the first thing you see when you come into St Andrews along the Guardbridge Road is the Old Course. It surfaces on your left as if by magic and makes the other elements in the prospect totally invisible. You ignore Madras College playing fields and do not notice the first tee of the adjacent Eden Course. You look straight through the imposing modern hotel and don't even take in the sweep of the bay beyond. What monopolises your attention and sets your blood racing is nothing less than the most famous golfing venue in the world.

The Old Course of the Royal and Ancient Golf Club.

The home of the game.

As usual for an Open Championship, the course was fringed with tents, dotted with television cameras and splashed with grandstands but even in its occupied state it still had the power to stir my soul when I got my first glimpse. There is a reassuring permanence about the Old Course. It is something immovable in a shifting world.

I felt a surge of gratitude. I was safe.

When buildings rose up to obscure the view, my eye went as ever to their chimneys. They are enormous and are surmounted by well over a dozen pots. I was reminded once again that I had come to a city that needs to keep its home fires burning in the winter, a place where square, solid houses of distinctive grey stone are built to withstand the wild mischief of the climate. Central heating has made some of the chimneys obsolete but they remain as silent witnesses to low temperatures and high winds and ferocious storms that blow in off the sea. For all this, the keen air and the surprisingly good sunshine record make St Andrews a very healthy place in which to live.

15

The Old Course makes it heaven.

Bent, blemished and feeling very sorry for herself, Carnoustie turned into Golf Place and rolled towards the competitors' car park behind and to the right of the R. & A. Clubhouse. It had been a long, tiring, taxing journey. We found a space between a Range Rover and a Jaguar, and both breathed a sigh of relief. We had finally arrived.

The ball was dead at last.

After switching on the burglar alarm, I got out and locked the door behind me. It was good to feel the hallowed ground beneath my feet once more. I was steadied immediately.

'Hello, Alan. Welcome to the Open.'

'Thanks.'

'Nice to see you again.'

'And you.'

Gordon Reeman greeted me with a firm handshake and an over-warm smile, then gestured towards Carnoustie. 'Prang?'

'Maniac in a van on the Edinburgh ring road.'

'But *you* weren't injured in any way?' he said with concern.

'No, I'm fine.' I did not mention the damage to my self-esteem.

'Good, good!'

I had never liked Gordon Reeman. He was a big, burly, well-groomed man in his fifties with a pencil moustache underlining a broken nose. Immaculate in a lightweight blue suit, he wore gold cufflinks on the sleeves of his white shirt and sported an R. & A. tie. Gordon was head of the security team at the Open. His firm had been entrusted with official security at the event for over a decade and Gordon had first appeared on the scene at Muirfield in 1980. He was the sort of man who got himself known very quickly.

He looked me carefully up and down. 'Hit form recently, Alan.'

'The luck's gone my way,' I said, modestly.

'Oh, come on now! There's more to it than luck. Alan Saxon is in fine fettle at the moment. Admit it.'

'If you insist.'

'I do,' he beamed.

Gordon had the unmistakeable tone, stance and brisk

affability of a military man. As the son of a policeman, I had grown up with a deep distrust of all uniformed authority and although it was some years since Major Reeman had retired from the army, I could still see the uniform very clearly.

'Daresay you'll want a first look at the course.'

'How is it playing?' I asked.

'I think it will test you. Tremendous amount of work been done. The chaps have beavered away for ages to get it just right. Trouble is, there's been no significant rainfall up here for ten weeks so the greens have had to be irrigated. But,' he added, wagging a finger at me, 'I'm told that the course will examine the finest golfer – especially when that wind starts to blow.'

I nodded ruefully. My two previous visits to an Open Championship at St Andrews had been turned into nightmares by the capricious winds. Play the Old Course on a calm day and it seems almost benign; tackle it in gusts of seventy miles an hour and every hole becomes a trial by ordeal. The weather is the Old Course's main defence mechanism. It can shred the strongest nerves and introduce the most self-possessed player to the seductive notion of suicide.

'Plenty of people about,' I noted.

'They've been arriving in droves all weekend, Alan. According to the Information Centre, there isn't a spare bed to be had within twenty miles.' He indicated Carnoustie. 'Just as well you brought your own.'

'I always do.'

'Of course, the hordes will really descend on Thursday when the first round gets under way. The one certain prediction you can make about this Open is that it will draw record crowds.'

'We had 142,000 at Royal Birkdale last year.'

'I reckon we can beat that figure by forty or fifty thou.'

'That'll keep you security bods on your toes,' I suggested.

'Oh, we're ready for anything,' he said airily. 'It's all been planned down to the last detail. I have a team of more

17

than sixty men and I've briefed them very thoroughly.' Before I could stop him, he slipped into his standard lecture. 'There are three prime areas for us, you see – control of access on to the course, cash protection, and night guarding of the property. The bigger the crowds, the greater the problem of making everyone pay for the privilege of watching the golf. Very difficult to monitor every single access point on a course like this, and you'll always get those who'll try to sneak in without a ticket.' He chuckled grimly. 'We'll nab most of them, don't worry. Then there's cash protection. Vital function when there's so much money involved. A ticket for any day from Thursday to Sunday costs £8. Multiply that by the sort of numbers we're expecting and it's a whole lot of money. As for guarding the property at night . . .'

'I'm sure you'll do it very well,' I observed, trying to bring his lecture to a close.

'We don't want a repeat of last year, Alan. Vandalism on one of the greens. The sacred turf must be protected. And everything that's been erected around it. Major undertaking for us.'

I subdued the irony in my voice. 'I don't know what the Open would do without you, Gordon. We're all very grateful.'

'We're a specialist team for a specialist job. My chaps can handle any situation. And, naturally, there'll be a massive police presence as well.' He smirked. 'At a massive cost, I may tell you. British bobbies don't come cheap. Not even the Scots variety.'

A vision of my father flashed into my mind. I shuddered.

'Yes,' he continued, 'I'm relying on my men to run things like clockwork. That way, *I* can manage to watch a bit of golf.'

'One of the perks of your job.'

'I intend to take full advantage of it, believe me.' He gave another grim chuckle. 'Well, I must be off. My wife is expecting me for tea, then I have to come back here. No peace for the wicked, is there? For the next seven days I'm

18

on duty around the clock. The eye that never sleeps.' He patted my shoulder. 'Goodbye, Alan.'

'Cheers.'

He marched towards a Vauxhall Carlton and got in. I was glad that I was not a member of his security staff. Beneath all that reflex bonhomie there lurked a real martinet. I was reminded once more of my father and that is never a pleasant experience.

There was another factor which linked Gordon Reeman with my father. Both men resented my ability to make a living as a professional golfer. Gordon's resentment was more carefully concealed than my father's but it was there nevertheless. In his view, we were paid far too much. If we won. And *he* was there to protect our money. It rankled.

'Hey, Alan! Alan!'

'Good luck, mate!'

'You can beat the Yanks this year!'

Though garage attendants at motorway services may take time to identify me, the combination of my steely grey hair and unusual height makes me instantly recognisable in golf circles. I was being hailed by a group of young men up on the Scores, the road that runs along the sea front behind the clubhouse. They sounded as if they had had a very enjoyable and very alcoholic lunch. One of them was carrying a small Union Jack, another was studying me through binoculars, a third was trying to focus his camera for a long shot of me. It was encouraging to know that I still had some fans and I acknowledged them with a wave as I headed for the exit.

Gordon Reeman overtook me in the Carlton and gave me a bland smile of farewell. Nods and greetings came from all directions as I left the car park but there were already too many police uniforms about for my comfort so I did not pause. After the setbacks of the day, I needed the tonic of a closer look at the Old Course.

Members, officials and early arrivals among the players were milling around and I had to run a gamut of welcomes to get to the terrace in front of the clubhouse. The sight which met me was breathtaking. Directly ahead of me was the first tee and to my left was the huge, inviting eighteenth green. Stretching out before and flanked on the left by a file of houses, shops and hotels, were the broad acres of the double fairway, crisp, undulating turf in prime condition that was sliced in two by Granny Clark's Wynd, a narrow public roadway some 130 yards or so away, which ran on down for almost twice that distance to Swilcan Burn, the snaking stream at the edge of the putting surface.

Because there is no rough to be seen, some commentators have criticised the Burn Hole and the Tom Morris Hole as being too easy a start and finish, respectively, for a championship course. They are quite wrong. It is impossible to stand on the first tee and not feel the sheer weight of tradition exerting its pressure on you and when you reach the eighteenth tee you find yourself staring history in the face. You look down the long avenue of spectators to the clubhouse itself, an imposing, dignified stone building of Victorian solidity, which is the headquarters of golf and which houses many of the game's most precious relics. Past and present coexist at St Andrews and lend the Old Course a timeless quality. If you compete in the Open there, you soon discover that there are no easy holes. Too many ghosts play alongside you.

'Well, what's the verdict, Alan?'

'Amazing.'

'We like to think so.'

Ian Calloway had joined me on the terrace and his blue eyes shone behind his horn-rimmed glasses as he gazed down the fairway. As Secretary of the Royal and Ancient Golf Club, he carried vast responsibilities on his shoulders but they seemed to sit there lightly. Ian was a friendly, unassuming man of middle height and years with a quiet passion about the game to which he had devoted his life. The bald head and the permanent frown of concentration made him look more like a research scientist than a golf administrator.

'We've gone for difficult pin positions, cultivated the

rough and varied the speeds of the greens,' he explained. 'Our links supervisor reckons that we've stiffened our defences very well.'

'Not too well, I hope.'

'There's nothing to disturb a player of your class, Alan. After all, you tamed Carnoustie when it was at its most frightening. If you can do that, you can master any course.'

What I liked most about Ian was the way that he always referred to my one moment of glory as if it were a recent achievement that could be repeated instead of treating it as did most people, including friends, as a freak event in the distant past. Like the Tay Bridge disaster.

'I owe you a big vote of thanks, Ian,' I told him.

'Why?'

'For changing the rules so that I could be here.'

He laughed. 'I can't pretend that we did it specifically to help you, Alan, but I'm pleased that you got the benefit.'

'You may live to regret it,' I joked. 'Means that you'll be seeing me at the Open for at least the next quarter of a century.'

'It wouldn't be the same without you,' he grinned.

Earlier in the year, the R. & A. had amended the qualifying rules for the Open Championship to give all former winners under the age of sixty-five exemption from qualifying if they were not otherwise exempt. Hitherto, only winners from the ten previous Open Championships had been granted automatic entry and this had caused problems for more than one of us. Embarrassing headlines pursue ex-champions who fail to get into the supreme event in the golfing calendar.

'You left it a bit late last year,' Ian recalled.

'State Express Classic. Week before the Open. I scraped in by the skin of my teeth as the last of the ten qualifiers.'

'Then you came straight up to Royal Birkdale and shot a marvellous 64 to lead at the end of the first round!'

It was typical of Ian Calloway that he remembered the best of my contribution at the previous Open. He omitted the fact that I had had an indifferent second round followed by a calamitous third round and had failed to make the cut for the final day. I was not used to anyone being so generous and tactful about my game.

21

'By the way, I have a message for you, Alan.'

'Oh?'

'From Dubby Gill. He'd love to see you.'

'I'd intended to see him, anyway. I rely on him for my inside tips. Nobody knows the Old Course as well as Dubby. How is he?'

His face darkened. 'Go as soon as you can,' he advised.

'Is it that bad?'

'Another stroke. The doctor's not too hopeful.'

'I'll get round there this evening,' I promised.

Dubby Gill and I had known each other for almost twenty years, since my first, inglorious appearance at St Andrews as a callow amateur. The Old Course had crucified me. I managed to find a bunker with almost every other shot and I went to pieces completely at the notorious Road Hole. At the end of the day, I felt as if I never wanted to see a set of golf clubs again. Then Dubby Gill sought me out, introduced himself as the head greenkeeper, told me he had been watching me, and believed he could help me if I was willing to listen. I was. He pointed out where I was going wrong with my drive and gave me some basic advice about how to tackle the course.

Next morning before breakfast, I put that advice to the test and shaved twelve strokes off my previous score. Dubby Gill had saved me when I was about to drown. We became firm friends from then on.

Ian Calloway excused himself as he was called away to take a telephone call. I was very grateful to him. With a major tournament to mastermind and control, he had still found time to pass on a message to me from a now retired greenkeeper. He was that sort of man.

I chatted for a few minutes with other friends, then went off to arrange a practice round for the following morning. After a final look down the fairway, I slipped back to the car park, winced again at the sight of Carnoustie's wounds, made myself a light meal, ate it, cleared away, then had a wash and shave.

It was still early evening when I arrived at Dubby's cottage.

'Oh, come on in, Mr Saxon,' cooed Beth Gill, opening the door.

'Hello, Mrs Gill. I had a message to—'

'Yes, yes. He can't wait to see you. Talked about it all day.'

'How is he?'

'Fine, in himself. But he rambles, Mr Saxon. Sometimes the poor dear just loses his way. You'll have to be very patient with him.'

'I'll try.'

Beth Gill was a short, stout, bustling woman in a flowered dress and slippers. She had a kind, rolypoly face with silver hair that was brushed back neatly and tied in a bun. Born and brought up in the Lake District, she had somehow kept all traces of a Scots accent at bay even though she had spent most of her life north of the border.

She ushered me down the passageway and into the tiny but cosy living room. Dubby was slumped in his favourite armchair by the fireplace. He was wearing pyjamas and dressing gown, holding an empty pipe in his right hand, and staring at a religious programme on the television. He did not hear us when we came in and only looked up when his wife stepped across to switch off the set.

'Whit ya doin', woman?' he croaked.

'You've got a visitor,' she explained, softly.

'It's me, Dubby.'

'Alan!' His eyes watered and he dropped the pipe into his lap so that he could shake hands with me. His grasp was weak. 'Guid tae see ye, man!'

'How are you keeping?'

'Great, Alan! Just great.'

'I'll make a nice pot of tea,' offered Beth, moving towards the kitchen.

She got no thanks from her husband. 'Away ye go and gie's peace,' he called after her, then retrieved his pipe so that he could use it to motion me to the sofa. When I sat down, he let out a wheezy cackle of satisfaction. 'Aye, ye're lookin' grand, Alan!'

It was more than I could say for him. Dubby was clearly

23

unwell. He seemed to have shrunk since the last time I had seen him and deep corrugations had put another decade on his features. Pale, wasted and panting slightly, he bore little resemblance to the strong, ebullient little man I had known, and I was disturbed to notice that his left arm was paralysed.

I hid my concern behind a cheerful comment.

'I was hoping you'd be able to take me round the course and show me what they've done to toughen it up.'

'Ach weel, man!'

'You know it like the back of your hand by now.'

'Tomorrow.'

'We'll see, Dubby.'

'Tomorrow, Ah'm tellin' ye!' He chewed on the stem of his pipe. 'Who's your caddie?'

'Nairn MacNicol.'

'Drunken bugger!'

'I'll sober him up,' I assured him. 'When he's off the bottle, he's a first-rate man to have in your corner. He may have his quirks, and a lot of people can't bear him, but I'll stick with Nairn. Never let me down yet.'

Beth's head popped out of the kitchen. 'Can I tempt you to a slice of Dundee cake, Mr Saxon?' she asked.

'I've not long eaten.'

'Just a small piece then,' she ruled, and the head vanished.

Dubby snorted and aimed a look of hatred at the kitchen door. I was surprised. He had never been an over-attentive husband and had liked to rule the roost but he had always shown his wife a gruff, grudging affection. They got on well together. My visits to their stone cottage in the oldest part of the city had invariably been happy occasions, full of warmth, welcome and good-humoured banter. Things had changed. In the short time I had been there, I sensed a rift. Beth was very much on the defensive and Dubby was treating her with an irritation that bordered on hostility. It saddened me even more.

'Pass that tin, Alan,' he said, using the pipe as a pointer again and jabbing it towards the sideboard. 'Ah've a few photies tae show ye.'

The large, square biscuit tin dated back to pre-war days and the endearing rural scene painted on its lid had been scuffed and dented by the passage of time. It felt quite heavy and I placed it gently in Dubby's lap. He gestured for me to remove the lid, then thrust his pipe back into his mouth. The tin was packed with photographs, letters, golf programmes and assorted odds and ends.

'This'll interest ye,' he promised, taking out a sepia snapshot. A small boy in short trousers was standing on a tee, addresssing a ball with a hickory-shafted club. 'A photie of *me!*' he cackled.

'I thought it was Bobby Jones winning the grand slam,' I teased.

'Now *there* was a golfer, Alan! Out of this worrld!' His right hand scrabbled among his souvenirs. 'Ah've a progie somewhere. With his autograph.'

'Let me find it, Dubby,' I volunteered. With two hands to use, I soon located the treasured relic, a fading, tattered programme from the 1927 Open Championship at St Andrews. 'Here it is with Bobby Jones's signature across the front. Must have been a great event to watch.'

'It was, Alan, it was. He took the title with a 285, six strokes clear of Aubrey Bloomer and Fred Robson. Six strokes, man. How many champions dae that?'

'Very few. *I* won it by a single stroke.'

'Ah was in Carnoustie tae see ye,' he affirmed. 'Aye, and Ah'll be doon the Auld Course tae watch ye win the Open again!'

'It's a bargain.'

But I feared it was one that neither of us might keep.

Dubby burrowed into the tin again, came up with a handful of cherished mementoes and was soon lost in a tangle of pleasant memories. I let him chunter away, though I had heard many of the anecdotes before and he kept repeating or contradicting himself. The main thing was that he was much more animated now and there was a hint of colour in his cheeks. I was ready to listen to him all evening.

When his wife brought in the tea things, he was so engrossed in a tale that he did not even see her. Taking

25

care not to interrupt him, Beth put down the tray, poured tea for the three of us, then cut some cake. After serving me, she placed her husband's cup gingerly on the arm of his chair.

Dubby was still fifty years away, talking about a ladies' amateur championship he had watched at Gleneagles and arguing that it was 'nae game for lasses'. His hand plunged back into the tin and yet another dog-eared programme was fished out. As he lifted it up to read it, a snapshot fell out from between its covers and he glanced down. His manner changed abruptly. Eyes blazing, he grabbed at the photograph, dropping the programme and knocking his tea off the arm of his chair. Beth's reaction was equally surprising. With a cry of pain, she leapt forward to retrieve the photograph from his grasp and knocked the tin and its contents flying.

He yelled, she sobbed and the souvenirs were scattered everywhere. Beth took the photograph and ran into the kitchen in tears. His anger pursued her all the way.

'Get out, woman!'

'Take it easy, Dubby,' I advised.

'Get out my road and stay out!' he shouted after her.

When he struggled to stand up, I eased him gently back into his chair. 'Look, calm down, will you?'

'Leave go of me!'

'Dubby—'

'Take your hands off!'

'Then don't get yourself into such a state. What's all the fuss and bother about?' He glared at me defiantly, then sank back into the cushions. 'Now, relax. Okay? Do yourself a favour and relax!'

But he was no longer listening. Breathing heavily and holding his right hand to his chest, he had lapsed back into a private world and shut me out. I surveyed the damage. Cup and saucer had landed safely but the tea had left an ugly stain on the rug.

I quickly gathered up the fallen items from the tin and set the cup back on the tray. Then I went into the kitchen where Beth Gill was still sobbing her heart out. She controlled herself when I came in and dabbed at her eyes with a lace handkerchief.

'Oh, I'm terribly sorry, Mr Saxon. It was all my fault.'

'Why?'

'I should have thrown it out years ago. I thought I had.' She still held the snapshot in one hand. 'Is he all right?'

'I hope so, Mrs Gill. I hardly need tell you that someone in his condition just shouldn't get worked up like that.'

'I know, I know,' she whimpered, biting her lip.

'If it's not a rude question, why did the photo upset him?'

She sighed and handed it to me. 'I'm to blame, Mr Saxon.'

When I looked at the snapshot, I still couldn't understand why. It showed four men doing some rough clearance on a golf course. One of them was swinging a pick, a second was bent double to pull something out of the knee-length grass, a third, wearing a hat, was busy with a rake while the fourth had paused from his labours to glance up at the camera. In the foreground, sitting on its haunches beside a discarded greatcoat and watching the men with serene interest, was a white dog with black ears and markings.

'That was Gip,' she explained. 'Desmond worshipped that dog.'

'Desmond?' It took me a split second to remember that Beth alone called her husband by his real name. 'What happened to Gip?'

'He disappeared. Desmond was certain that . . . ' She bit her lip again and sniffed. 'Desmond believed that one of the Germans killed him. They were prisoners of war, you see. Helping to clear the Old Course.'

'Was Gip never found?' She shook her head. 'When was this?'

'1946. First Open Championship after the war.'

'And Dubby—' I checked myself. 'And Desmond can get into a lather over a lost dog after all this time?'

'Gip was very special to him, Mr Saxon.'

'What made him think the animal had been killed?'

27

'I don't know,' she said with a shrug.

'Are you sure, Mrs Gill?' I pressed.

She blushed and lowered her eyes. I didn't have to wait long for the truth. 'Desmond hated those men. That's why he blamed them. Both his brothers had died in the war and it – it made him so bitter, Mr Saxon. He *hated* all Germans. Still does.' She took the snapshot from me and glanced at it. 'He loved Gip. This reminded him how much.'

'It would have been wiser to destroy the snapshot.'

'I know. And I will.'

I recalled something else. 'If you give me a wet cloth, I'll see what I can do about that tea stain.'

'Oh dear, I'd forgotten that,' she exclaimed, turning at once to the sink. She put the snapshot aside, ran water into a bowl, tipped Persil into it, then dropped a dishcloth into the suds. 'I'll take care of it, Mr Saxon. Tea stains can be a problem.'

'Perhaps it might be safer if—'

'He's gone quiet now. I doubt if he'll start up again.'

She went back into the living room with the bowl. I took the opportunity to look at the snapshot again. Two things had escaped my notice the first time. The prisoner facing the camera was smiling broadly and on the reverse was a scribbled message in pencil, now so faded that it was impossible to read.

As I put the snapshot down, a question troubled me. Dubby had grabbed viciously at it and scrunched it right up. If his wife really meant to destroy it, why had she gone to the trouble of smoothing out the worst of the wrinkles?

The rest of my visit to the Gill household was short, quiet and uneventful. Dubby had more or less clammed up on both of us and sat there brooding as we drank our tea and munched our cake. I was soon thanking them for their hospitality and moving to the door. Beth saw me out and I had a final question for her.

'Who took that snapshot, Mrs Gill?'

She thought about it, then owned up. 'I did.'

As soon as I climbed back into Carnoustie, I was

reminded of an earlier outrage. The miniature golfer was not in his place on the driving mirror. For a few moments, quiet panic set in as I wondered how I could account for the loss to Lynette. She would be badly hurt. Unless I could buy another figure just like hers. Or track down Janie and reclaim the one she had stolen.

It had been a dreadful day. Against all promptings of caution and common sense, I had picked up a hitch-hiker, squandered the chance of any mental preparation for the Open, been involved in a road accident and abused the innocent party, damaged my travelling home, lost the most valued gift my daughter had ever given me, arrived at St Andrews to be met by one of the people I liked least, been reminded of my father, learned that a close friend of mine was desperately ill, then witnessed a distressing scene between him and his wife.

All in all a catastrophic day.

I would have been far better off staying in Northampton with Fiona and playing bedroom golf. It was a game she had invented, refined and patented. Though it might raise a few eyebrows among purists at the R. & A., it captured the spirit of the game and had one feature that I found irresistible. Whenever I played it with Fiona, I ended up as an Open Champion.

Fiona, Janie, Lynette, the van driver, Gordon Reeman, my father, Dubby and Beth Gill. Enemies to my concentration. Saboteurs of my pre-tournament plans. It was time to bury them along with the day and start afresh in the morning.

A short drive took me to another run of terraced cottages where I left a note for my caddie, Nairn MacNicol, with his landlady. It was a terse communication, telling him at what time I expected him on the first tee and warning him, if he intended to roll up anything but stone-cold sober, to inform his next of kin before leaving.

Carnoustie and I then turned our thoughts to bed and left the city on the Anstruther Road. I had arranged to stay at a small farm some four or five miles off. It was tucked away up a side road and offered us fresh water, waste disposal facilities, a cable that fed us mains electricity and a two-acre field all to ourselves. It was short on chambermaids and there would certainly be no shoe-cleaning service, but it seemed like perfection to us right then.

We found our demi-paradise, met its dairy herd and its goats, went through the civilities with our hosts, adjourned to the luxury of our own field, hurried the necessary bedtime rituals and brought Sunday to an early close.

Nairn MacNicol was waiting for me next morning as I swung into the competitors' car park. My note had frightened him into sobriety for the first time in months and he blinked in astonishment as he rediscovered the real world. Nairn was a short, slight man in his forties with a boyish face that belied his age and long, brown hair that was Brylcreemed into submission, then swept up at the front into a tidal wave. I gave him my clubs, barked another warning about the demon drink, then clapped him on the shoulder by way of greeting. He was relieved.

Though it was only eight o'clock as we walked to the first tee, numbers of people were already about. Other golfers had made even earlier starts and we could see some of them in the distance. Fans were starting to arrive and I noticed a few golf writers lurking around on the principle that the best time to assess form is during morning practice sessions early in the week. I felt like a racehorse going out for a gallop under the eyes of the tipsters.

A huge hand reached out to pump mine.

'Hello, Alan. Lovely to see you again.'

'Hi.'

'How's the world treating you?'

'That's what I've come to find out.'

'Chocks away, then!'

My playing partner was Body Beautiful and he was exuding his usual manic enthusiasm. If tournaments were won solely on zeal for the game, Body Beautiful would be invincible. As it was, he had the kind of record of consistent failure or near-misses that would plunge any other golfer into terminal pessimism. Not him. Having scraped into an Open yet again, he had the unassailable faith that he would finally come good and win.

One glance at Timothy Quentin told you how he acquired his nickname. He was a big, blond, superbly-proportioned athlete with handsome features that made him the definitive model for golf wear. Timothy had been 'a player of great potential' for so long that it was difficult to believe he was still not yet thirty. Immensely popular with everyone, he had a public school eagerness that spoke of pillow fights in the dormitory.

Body Beautiful was a type. He exists in all sports. In boxing, he comes to the centre of the ring, poses magnificently but fails to land a telling punch. In cricket, he is an impressive figure as he strides out to the crease and rehearses a few graceful cover drives, only to succumb to a yorker in the first over. In athletics, he thrills the crowd with his warm-up routine but fades badly in the race itself.

He has promise, talent and a burning love for his sport but somehow he never actually wins. England has been known to field eleven of him in football internationals at Wembley.

'Good shot!'

'Thanks.'

'Well played!'

I had just managed a par on the Burn Hole and been given the standard congratulations as I sank my putt. Body Beautiful sized up his own shot, tapped the ball purposefully and missed the cup by those vital few inches that had separated him from success throughout his career.

'Tough,' I murmured, borrowing his own favourite word.

His second putt was a mere formality. 'One over for the Championship!' he grinned.

His caddie retrieved the ball and replaced the flag.

After the Burn Hole, the course swings round to the right, runs on down to the River Eden, loops back on itself like a glorified fish-hook, then retraces its steps along the great double fairways. It was from the second tee onwards that Nairn really came into his own. Seen from the air, the Old Course bears a marked similarity to the surface of the moon, all mounds and depressions and craters. From ground level, however, it looks very different. It ripples out in front of you in endless waves. Mounds, ridges, dips, swales, gulleys, bunkers and plateaux are everywhere, fringed in gorse or dressed in heather. Some of the worst hazards are the most cunningly concealed.

Nairn was my guide dog for blind shots. He could read distance with pinpoint accuracy and he knew the exact location of hidden bunkers and invisible rough. With club selection, too, he was a master. What made him even more of a paragon among caddies was his brevity. He imparted his wisdom in a few words and left me to play the shots. In sharp contrast, Body Beautiful's caddie went in for long discussions about which line to take and how to play out of sand.

Though the weather was mild and the breeze low, the Old Course still put up a strong fight. The Dyke, Cartgate, Ginger Beer, Hole o' Cross, Heathery Hole and High Hole granted us no favours, and while we had definite glimpses of birdies in the loop at the eighth, ninth and tenth, we were soon back to more challenging terrain. Always a stern test for any golfer, the eleventh, twelfth and thirteenth had lost none of their wiles, and the Long Hole which followed them posed its regular quota of problems. Body Beautiful drove out of bounds over the wall and I had the frustration of hooking a shot into the middle of Hell Bunker.

Cartgate, going home, rewarded me with an unexpected birdie but I promptly dropped a shot at the treacherous sixteenth, the Corner of the Dyke. We walked to the seventeenth tee to face the ultimate examination of our skill and nerve.

The Road Hole on the Old Course is one of the most

celebrated in golfing history. Attempts have been made to recreate some of its features on other courses but it defies imitation. Over the years it has become a graveyard of hopes and reputations, and it always has a casting vote in the selection of a new Open Champion. The fact that three large grandstands had been erected beside its green showed that it was expected to yield its traditional harvest of drama, misadventure and comic humiliation.

To the right of the tee and looming over it like a concrete colossus, is the Old Course Hotel, an unlovely example of modern architecture that affords its guests a view in a million. It is all too easy to misjudge your drive and send those same guests scurrying away off their balconies. An additional obstacle between tee and green this year was the replica of the old coalsheds that disappeared in the 1960s when the swift axe of Dr Beeching fell on the railway station.

Since the fairway turns right beyond the sheds, the question that you have to answer is how much, if any, of the corner should you cut off?

Encouraged by Nairn to take a bold direct line, I drove close to the hotel and went safely over the angle to the fairway beyond.

'Good shot.'

'Thanks.'

'Well played!'

Body Beautiful did not try to emulate me. He drove further left and skirted the rough. It was unambitious, perhaps, but free from taint. He went bouncing off down the fairway in search of his ball.

At 461 yards, the Road Hole is only just below regulation par-5 distance and so my drive, though powerful and true, had left my ball a long way from the green. I looked respectfully at the infamous tract of grass. Set diagonally across the shot, it is built up into a plateau some four or five feet above the fairway. It is elongated from left to right but narrow from back to front. At the left-centre is the hungriest bunker on the course, its mouth wide open to swallow any titbits. I had been told that it had been slightly remodelled this year to make it less voracious but it still looked as keen as ever to gobble up anything it could. So deeply does the Road Hole bunker bite into the green that there are putting surfaces either side of it. By placing the pin behind the bunker, maximum terror is assured.

Nairn's advice coincided with my own judgement. I would play my second shot deliberately short, as close as possible to the front-right corner of the green. To aim for the flag itself would be to risk landing in the bunker or, even worse, overshooting the green altogether and finishing up on the road. And a golfer who ventures on to that road is, literally, the victim of highway robbery.

I got reasonably close to my target area with my second shot and watched while Body Beautiful played a fine shot to put his ball within yards of mine. Both of us then chipped on to the green and took two putts. We were well pleased with ourselves as we filled in our scorecards. Road, bunker and mortification had been avoided.

We had now been playing for well over three hours and had walked the best part of four miles. I felt invigorated. To be on the Old Course once more and to be matching its challenge was an exhilarating experience. I had put the upsets of the previous day behind me and was completely absorbed in my golf. I had been made whole again.

Then we strolled to the eighteenth tee.

A sudden cheer to our left made us look across to the first green. Ulrich Heidensohn had just begun his practice round with an incredible eagle, as I learned later, at the Burn Hole and was holding his club aloft in jubilation. Beyond the ropes that protected the fairway was a sizeable knot of spectators, mostly teenage girls, acclaiming their hero. It was the entourage of a rising superstar. The West German player was the darling of the galleries. Wherever he went, Ulrich had a devoted following.

My eye raked casually over the delighted fans until it fell on the figure of a tall, thin girl in check shirt, jeans and trainers. Even before I was certain it was Janie, I broke into a run.

'Where are you going, Alan?' gasped Body Beautiful.

But I had no time to stop and explain.

Janie spotted me heading diagonally across the fairway towards her and immediately took to her heels. She had a good start on me and showed a surprising turn of foot but the combination of longer legs, greater fitness and a fierce determination helped me to close the gap. The chase caused interest and amusement on all sides. It is not often that a former Open Champion is seen sprinting towards the clubhouse in pursuit of a female student. Hundreds craned to watch the phenomenon. I didn't mind. To get my daughter's present back, I would have raced through the streets of London after Janie during the Lord Mayor's procession.

They call it pure behaviour.

She had reached the exit and rushed out into the road before I caught her, and she was panting feverishly. I grabbed her by the arm and swung her round, ready to demand the return of the miniature golfer. Before I could speak, however, she let out a piercing scream and slapped me hard across the cheek. I released her at once and she vanished into the crowd. When I started after her, a policeman blocked my way.

'What seems to be the trouble, sir?'

'Oh . . . nothing. Nothing at all.'

'Was the lassie causing you some bother?' he asked in a tone that suggested he believed the exact opposite. 'Who was she?'

'It doesn't matter. I was – probably mistaken.'

'Yes, sir. You probably were.'

Further chase was impossible now. The policeman pursed his lips and eyed me with disapproval. I had seen that look before. I had suffered it on a daily basis for seventeen years until I finally left home for good. My father had been an expert at that slow, censuring, demoralising stare. A twinge of pain accompanied the memory.

I disentangled myself from the policeman and pushed through the ring of bodies. Public opinion was not behind me.

'Poor girl!'

'What on earth was he trying to *do* to her?'

'Take no for an answer next time, mate.'

'It shouldn't be *allowed*.'

As I went back to the clubhouse, I had to fend off a flurry of questions from journalists who had flocked out of the press tent. It was an amazingly long and agonising walk back to the eighteenth tee, where a bemused Body Beautiful still waited with our caddies. Apart from anything else, I had caused a breach of course etiquette. Ulrich and his playing partner would be quite entitled to lodge a complaint about the way I had interrupted their game, and a less forgiving soul than Body Beautiful would have had some harsh words for me.

The West German and his opponent had driven from the second tee by now, so I did not dare to interfere with their game again, but made a note to apologise to them later on. I silenced Body Beautiful with profuse apologies and asked if we could complete our round. He was his usual amiable, obliging self.

'Fire away!'

'I will.'

'Oh – and the drinks are on me this morning.'

'Thanks.'

'Just one thing, Alan. That girl.' He stepped closer and his voice became a stage whisper. 'Someone you knew?'

I was glad when it was all over and I could flee from the keen scrutiny of onlookers. News of my chase had clearly spread and it had brought several people out on to the clubhouse terrace. After refusing the drink, I repossessed my clubs, told Nairn when I would next need him, shrugged off further questioning and fled to Carnoustie for sanctuary. Under the circumstances, I might have been quite pleased with a score of 72, par for the course, on a first outing. As it was I simply wanted to get right away from the place and forget all about the morning's work.

Lunch was a toasted cheese sandwich and a glass of orange juice in the privacy of our own field. I was starting to feel much better about things when the telephone rang. It was Clive Phelps.

'How are you, Alan?'

'Bearing up. You?'

'Shagged out, old son. We came up on the sleeper last night and played cards all the way.' He yawned. 'I lost.'

Clive Phelps was a good friend. As well as being one of the few journalists with whom I had not at some time or other had a vendetta, he was an excellent golfer. With less smoking, gambling and womanising he might even have made the grade as a professional. But he would have stopped being Clive Phelps.

'Where are you hiding?' he asked.

'It's a closely-guarded secret.'

'Even from the press?'

'Especially from them.'

'That's my story, then,' he chuckled. 'Alan Saxon Goes to Ground. World's Golfing Press Join in Manhunt. It's a great angle. If you could come up with a microfilm in a hollow putter, I could turn this into a rewrite of *The Thirty-Nine Steps*.'

'What do you want, Clive?'

'What I always want, old son. A noggin and a natter.'

I sighed. 'Does it have to be me?'

'Of course. Home-grown Open Champions aren't too thick on the ground. You're one of a dying species, Alan.' He gulped something down, then belched discreetly. 'Take pity on a struggling scribe. I have a lot of column inches to fill. I want to feature you in my preview. Let's say this evening at nine.'

'I'm tied up.'

'You know where to find me.'

'Clive, I won't be able to—'

'You'll have all the hock and Perrier you can drink. Oh, and by the way, I've stopped smoking those nasty fags you always complain about. See you later, old son.'

He rang off and the meeting was fixed. Clive had done me too many favours for me to refuse. We usually had plenty of laughs together and it occurred to me that lively company for an hour or so might take me out of myself. Besides, no other journalists were likely to feature me in an article. They would be too busy interviewing the superstars like Horton Kincaid and Jeff Piker and Ulrich Heidensohn.

And I was no longer in that league.

When I arrived at his room in the Scores Hotel that evening, Clive was sitting in a thick fug doing a crossword. The smoke made me cough.

'I thought you'd given up cigarettes?'

'Taken up cigars instead. More manly. Like one?'

'No,' I said firmly, 'and *you* can leave them alone while I'm here. If you want to start a cancer factory, do it when I've gone.'

I crossed to open both windows wide. The room was on the top floor and looked out over the bay. Below me and to the left was the R. & A. Clubhouse and my stomach turned as I saw the spot in the road where I had caught up with Janie that morning.

'Before we go any further, Alan,' he said, handing me the drink he had just poured, 'let me tell you that I've got a fiver riding on you this week. How's that for confidence?'

'If you can only spare five quid for me, who have you put the really big money on? Kincaid? Devereaux? Tanizaki? Heidensohn?'

'You know me, old son. I always back Britain.'

We drank together and caught up on each other's news. Clive was shabbily dressed, of medium build with dark curly hair and a large moustache that might have been inherited from a Victorian poisoner. He was about ten years older than me and had the finest collection of golf stories and jokes I have ever heard. Again, he was loyal to his chosen friends.

Time slipped by very pleasantly as we talked golf over some bottles of chilled Piesporter. I was drinking too much too fast but it seemed to be doing the trick. Clive was getting enough material out of me for a dozen articles and I was slowly seeing my problems in a softer focus. More important, I was boosted by the fact that Clive genuinely believed I had a good chance of winning the Open.

'Take it or leave it,' he repeated, slapping his thigh, 'that's my forecast. Saxon, Kincaid, Piker. One, two, three.'

'No Heidensohn?'

'Ully will be there or thereabouts but his game is not really suited to links courses. He's a target golfer, which is why he's done so well on the US circuit. Wait till the wind starts to howl. It'll play murder with those lofted drives of his.' He remembered something else and grinned. 'Then, of course, there's his little weakness. They don't call him Herr Superstud for nothing.'

'He seems to thrive on it.'

'There is a limit, Alan. I mean, I'm all in favour of a quick bang to settle your nerves before you go out to play but Ully takes it to extremes. Bang bang chitty chitty bang bang! He's at it day and night.'

'They *are* supposed to be the master race.'

We laughed and finished off the dregs of the last bottle. Clive was all for ordering more but it was almost midnight and I had already drunk far more than I had intended. He saw me down in the lift and out to the front steps, then he went off in search of a drinking school. I inhaled the night air and reflected on what he had said.

Saxon, Kincaid, Piker. Britain, America, Australia.

It was a wonderful fantasy and it carried me all the way to the car park. Clive Phelps had revived me in more ways than he knew. I had gone into the hotel feeling jaded, uncertain and angry with myself and he had sent me out in a happy and positive mood.

The car park was more or less deserted and Carnoustie was tucked in the corner in splendid isolation. I fumbled for my keys and allowed the names to slide through my mind once more.

Alan Saxon. Horton Kincaid. Jeff Piker. In that order.

As I unlocked the door and climbed into the cab, I mentally rehearsed my victory speech, holding the trophy in both hands and luxuriating in my triumph. Open Champion for the second time. History in the making. A decisive end to my years in the golfing wilderness.

My celebrations were short-lived. As I jabbed my key into the ignition to start the engine, something hard and vicious struck me on the back of the head. I plunged forward into darkness.

Chapter Three

At first, only sound intruded. A distant telephone. The jingle of keys. Windows being opened. Tea being poured. The squish of tyres over a wet road. A girl's laughter. A woman's sobbing. Hymns. Cheers. The click of a camera. Cows being milked. Zips. Rain. Hotel lifts. The screech of a skid. Metal pounding metal. A dog barking.

Next, a long time after, I became aware of movement. I was falling forward, sitting up, being lifted and dragged. I was jerked from side to side and thrown against something solid. I was lifted up again to an enormous height, then dropped.

Light came slowly into the darkness. It was weak and patchy yet it burned my eyes. Glimpses. Shadows. Phantoms. Heads with no faces. Uniforms with no bodies. Buildings with no doors. Motorways with no vehicles.

As if a switch had been thrown, sound, movement and light all ceased. They came back with equal suddenness, louder, rougher, brighter, merging with each other then separating, merging once more to form new patterns, then disintegrating before I could identify what they were. Pain blocking all sensations.

When it finally eased, I was in a bedroom with Fiona. She was stretched out on the bed, inviting me to join her but I was buried up to the waist in a bunker. I dug with both hands but there was no escape and the bed began to recede further and further away with Fiona beckoning wildly until she was no more than a speck on the horizon. The bunker tilted sharply at an angle and I let out a soundless cry of torment before waking up.

I was in bed with Fiona after all. She was naked, I was fully clothed and the two of us were lying at a rakish angle. When I touched her cheek, her head rolled over

41

affectionately towards me and her long hair fell across my face. I nestled up to her for love and comfort and reassurance. I began mumbling to her about my dreams when a great hot needle lanced right through my brain.

Fiona had short, curly hair.

I pulled away so abruptly that I fell to the floor and banged myself against a cabinet. Carnoustie seemed to be parked at a crazy angle and it was difficult to stand up. My arm flailed around in the dark until I found the light switch. I had to shield my eyes against a searing pain and it was minutes before I was able to withstand the glare enough to be able to look at the pale figure stretched out on my double bed.

It was Janie. She was quite motionless and looked younger than I had remembered. The bottoms of her feet had a greenish hue and there were marks on her legs and arms. When I shook her to wake her, the head lolled over the other way and tossed the black hair against the pillow to reveal the slender neck. It was covered in dark bruises.

My mind was spinning and I swayed about unsteadily in the confined space. As I fought off the urge to vomit, I sank to my knees and leaned against a cabinet. Something was against my leg and I grabbed it when I saw what it was. Her rucksack.

I tore back the zip on impulse and emptied everything on to the floor, groping after the smaller items as they rolled down the slant. There was a tee shirt, two pairs of pants, some socks, a toilet bag, a book, an autograph album, a cheap camera, some postcards and a couple of Biro pens. Janie had believed in travelling light. Though I searched again, there was no miniature golfer.

With no warning, the vomit rose inside me and spewed out furiously over the floor. I closed my eyes and lapsed into a half-sleep, dropping across the angle of the bed and losing all control over my movements. The vomit had spent itself but its stink remained to disgust and accuse me. My stomach was ablaze, my heart was thumping, and my head seemed to have grown larger and to be made of some kind of metal. Strong fists were hammering on my skull.

'Is anybody in there?'

'This is the police! Are you all right?'

'Can you open this door?'

The hammering intensified and brought me out of my doze. They were trying to force their way in. Carnoustie had suffered enough damage and humiliation as it was and I had to protect her.

'I'm coming!' I yelled, grabbing for the nearest curtain and yanking it back. 'Stop hurting her like that.' The beam of a torch hit me and I had to turn away. 'I'm coming,' I murmured.

While I struggled to unlock the stable door at the side of the vehicle, my two visitors peered in through the uncurtained window.

'Jesus Christ, Andy! Look at that!'

'Is she dead, man?'

'I'm calling the station right now.'

While one policeman ran back to the patrol car, the other came round to the door. He was just in time to catch me as I pitched forward in a faint.

The interview room at the police station was small, bare and devoid of character. It had a table, three chairs, and light fixtures set in the ceiling. A metal ashtray stood on the table and a mug of hot, dark tea had been brought in for me but one sip was enough to dissuade me from drinking it. The uniformed policeman who kept me company had the look of a man who did not enjoy night duty. I could sympathise with him.

They had brought me back to St Andrews, cleaned me up and had me examined by a doctor. Detectives had taken a statement but they had given me the impression that it was very much a preliminary interview to mark time until a more senior CID officer could be brought in from outside to take charge of the murder investigation.

Being inside a police station had activated all my old fears and prejudices; I saw my father behind every door. Like the prospect of execution, it concentrated my mind wonderfully and I had worked out exactly what I would say under questioning as well as what I was not going to say. My brain had cleared and my defences were up.

I waited for almost an hour in the interview room, watching my tea go cold and counting the number of times my companion shifted his feet. The door then opened and the two detectives who had taken my statement came in with two other men. There were brief introductions and I was left alone with Detective-Superintendent Tom Ings and Detective-Inspector Lucas Robbie.

When I saw Ings I understood a muttered reference I had heard earlier to someone called Ginger Tom. It had to be him. Tall, angular and thin to the point of being cadaverous, he had a shock of ginger hair that glowed under the lights. His colleague, by contrast, was short, stocky and almost completely bald. Both men were in their fifties.

Ginger Tom shook me with his first question.

'I believe your father is a policeman, Mr Saxon?'

'Yes.'

'Then I daresay you'll know the ropes a bit. With regard to our procedures, I mean. That should help.'

He was not a native Scot. There was a hint of a regional accent at the back of his voice but I couldn't place it. While Inspector Robbie sat opposite me and took out his pad, Ginger Tom remained on his feet and waved some sheets of paper.

'I've only had time to glance through your statement, Mr Saxon. Perhaps you'd be kind enough to go through the main points again? For our benefit.'

'Of course.' I was certain that he had read the document very carefully and was double-checking its contents. 'Where shall I begin?'

'Where else? The beginning.'

'Right,' I said, inhaling deeply. 'Here goes. I was invited to the Scores Hotel last night by Clive Phelps, a friend of mine, who wanted to feature me in an article he's writing for his newspaper. I got there around nine. Carnoustie – that's my motor caravan – was parked nearby in the competitors' car park. The hotel bar was heaving and since I'm not much of a one for crowds, the interview took place over a drink or two in Clive's room. We also chatted about good times we'd had together in the past and gossiped generally about the golf scene. I'd only meant to stay an hour but it was nearly midnight when I left. Clive saw me down to the front entrance of the hotel, then went back inside. I crossed over to the car park, which was pretty empty, and made for Carnoustie. I unlocked the door, got in behind the driving wheel, and was hit on the back of the head by the statutory blunt instrument.'

'How are you feeling now?' asked Ginger Tom.

'Much better, thanks.'

'I saw the medical report. It was a very nasty bang. You must have an unusually thick skull, Mr Saxon.' He shrugged apologetically. 'But I'm interrupting your story. You got as far as the blunt instrument. What happened then?'

'I went out like a light.' The bump on my head corroborated the fact by starting to throb again. 'Next thing I knew, I was waking up on a bed in pitch darkness. I became aware that someone was beside me. I put the light on, saw Janie lying there, tried to wake her, realised that she'd been strangled, and promptly threw up all over the floor. That's when the police car arrived. Apparently, someone had seen Carnoustie in that ditch and rung here to report the accident.'

Ginger Tom nodded, flicked through my statement, then paced up and down the room. I noticed that the trousers of his tweed suit were inches too short. He was wearing fawn socks.

'Why do you call the deceased "Janie"?' he asked.

'That was her name.'

'She told you?'

'Yes.'

'When?'

'On Sunday. When I gave her a lift.'

'Are you in the habit of giving lifts to young women?'

'No, I am not,' I asserted.

'So why did you pick up this particular one?'

'I don't know.'

'Oh, come on, Mr Saxon. You can do better than that.'

'It's the truth, Superintendent, I don't know.'

'Let me rephrase the question, then. Why would most people in your position stop to pick up a groupie?'

'I did not pick her up,' I insisted. 'In either sense of the word. While I was paying for petrol at the Washington services, she got into Carnoustie. Without any invitation whatsoever.'

'And why should she choose you?'

'Because she knew I was going to St Andrews, I suppose.'

His eyes twinkled. 'Or because she knew that you had something of a reputation as a ladies' man?'

'I resent that suggestion,' I snapped.

'You shouldn't,' he said, easily. 'It was meant as a compliment.'

A signal passed between them and Robbie took over.

'I believe you played a practice round yesterday, Mr Saxon?' His voice was deep and melancholy with a gentle Scots burr. 'How did you find the Old Course?'

'In excellent condition.'

'As guileful as ever?'

'I thought so.'

'How long is the Ginger Beer Hole on the championship card?'

'463 yards.'

'And the Tom Morris?'

'354 yards. Why do you ask?'

'Purely in the spirit of enquiry, sir. What distance would you expect to get with your pitching wedge?'

'Between 80 and 105 yards. In normal conditions, that is.'

'What about a 5-iron?'

'Somewhere around 175 yards.'

'That's well beyond *my* range with a 3-iron,' he admitted. 'Golf is such a precise game at the top level, isn't it? Why is it that someone like you who is so exact about yardages can't even count the number of drinks he has with a friend?'

'One or two glasses, you say in your statement,' resumed Ginger Tom. 'And a moment ago you said that the interview with Mr Phelps took place over "a drink or two". In three *hours?*'

'Journalists usually soak it up better than that,' added Robbie.

'Look, what are you getting at?' I demanded.

'The fact that you'd had a skinful,' said Ginger Tom, bluntly. 'Even when it's diluted with Perrier water, wine can get to you after a while. I'm suggesting that when you left the Scores Hotel last night, your judgement was seriously impaired by drink and that the kindest construction we can place on it all is that you were about to commit an offence by driving a motor vehicle while under the influence of alcohol.' He perched on the edge of the table and looked down at me. 'The two officers who found you had the impression that you had been drinking heavily and the medical report confirms that impression. We shall have to wait for the results of the blood test before we know for certain, of course, and we will naturally check at the hotel to see how many bottles of Piesporter were sent up to Mr Phelps's room.'

I was beginning to feel as if I was buried up to my waist in a bunker again. 'You can't prosecute me for drunken driving when I didn't actually drive Carnoustie,' I argued.

'We don't intend to prosecute you for that, sir,' said Robbie. 'You weren't given formal warning and you weren't breathalysed.'

'Then why are you trying to catch me out?'

They exchanged a glance, then Ginger Tom was on the move again.

'There is another possibility, Mr Saxon,' he said, 'and I emphasise that it is only a *possibility*. But one we must consider.'

I braced myself. 'Go on.'

'You might have driven that vehicle, after all. You might have got back to it, found the young lady inside,

47

taken her to bed, found that things got out of hand, struggled with her, not realised, in your condition, that you were strangling her, then flew into a panic when you saw that she was dead.'

The sand in the bunker was now up to my neck. 'That's bloody ridiculous! How do you account for this lump on the back of my head?'

'It might have been sustained when you crashed. You could have left the car park, driven off in search of a quiet place in which to dispose of the body, lost control of the vehicle in that lane, plunged into the ditch and been thrown against the door.'

'I thought you'd only had time to glance through my statement,' I said with an edge of sarcasm. 'How come you've got to the stage of a fully-fledged hypothesis?'

He sat in the empty chair. 'Did you murder that girl?'

'No.'

'Are you quite certain?'

'Why should I want to kill Janie?'

'For the same reason that you chased her yesterday morning.' He smiled at my discomfort. 'Policemen are only human, Mr Saxon, as you well know. They like to gossip the same as anyone else. That story was all round this station by lunchtime. Now I don't *know* that it was the same girl and we'll have to wait for the officer involved in the incident to come on duty before a positive ID can be made, but I suspect that it might have been this "Janie". Was it?'

'Yes.'

'Why is there no mention of the incident in your statement?'

'It didn't seem relevant.'

'Pull the other one, Mr Saxon.'

'Okay, I forgot.'

'Selective memory. A lot of people I interview suffer from that complaint.' He leaned forward towards me. 'So why did you chase her?'

'Because I thought she'd stolen something from me.'

'What?'

'Some money,' I lied.

'When was this?'

'On Sunday.'

'While you were giving her a lift?'

'Yes. I was involved in a minor accident on the Edinburgh ring road. I got out to speak to the other driver and a slight argument developed. It must have been all of ten minutes before I went back to Carnoustie. Janie had vanished.'

'Along with your money?'

'That's what I believed.'

'How much was it?'

'About twenty pounds. I'd left my wallet on the dashboard.'

'Was the wallet taken as well?'

'No. Just the money. It wasn't a large amount, I know, but it niggled me. The idea of being robbed, I mean. By someone who was getting a free lift off me all the way to St Andrews.'

'So when you saw her again, you just went for her?'

'Yes. It was my first instinct.'

'Do you always obey your first instincts, Mr Saxon?' asked Ginger Tom. 'When something niggles you, do you always over-react like that?'

'The girl pinched my twenty quid. I was entitled to get it back.'

'Did you mention the theft to the officer who obstructed you?'

'No.'

'Why not?'

'Because I didn't want to get bogged down in explanations. There was a fair old crowd watching by that time. I just wanted to get away.'

'The presence of the crowd didn't deter you from grabbing her in the first place,' he pressed. Without looking at him, he sensed that his colleague had a question. 'Inspector Robbie?'

'Did you report the road accident to the police, sir?'

'No,' I sighed. 'It was . . . trivial.'

'Then why did you argue the toss with the other driver for ten minutes?' he said.

I shrugged wearily. 'You know how it is with road accidents.'

'Yes,' agreed Ginger Tom. 'People get niggled and over-react.' He took out a packet of cigarettes, flipped it open and offered it to me. I shook my head. He put a cigarette between his lips, found some matches in his pocket, and lit up. 'Have you never smoked, Mr Saxon?'

'Never. I think it's a filthy habit.'

'So I've heard. Inspector Robbie gave it up last Christmas, didn't you, Lucas? Since then he's put on over a stone and spent a fortune on boiled sweets. True or false?'

'Too bloody true,' confessed the other.

Ginger Tom got to his feet again and walked away. 'So you don't keep any cigarettes in your motor caravan?'

'Of course not.'

'What about the girl? Did she smoke?'

'Not while she was with me.'

'Tell us about her.'

'Janie?'

'What sort of a girl was she? Pleasant company? Lots of laughs? Did she have much conversation? Why had she got hooked on golfers?'

I measured my words carefully. 'She was a nice enough girl. Very self-possessed. Older than her years. We chatted about this and that. She was well up on the gossip around the golf scene. She obviously kept an eye on the sporting press and mentioned some article she'd seen about me. That's about all I can tell you, Superintendent, except that she was a student at Bristol University. Psychology.'

'I'm sure she was a student of psychology, after her own fashion, but I doubt very much if we'll find her enrolled at any university.'

'Why should she lie to me?'

'To impress you, I should imagine. Being an undergraduate sounds a lot better than being a drifter.'

'But she told me about her course when we stopped for

50

lunch. She was really enjoying her studies. Last term apparently, she spent six weeks on attachment to some hospital in Bristol. Observing and so on. Janie went into great detail. How could she make all that up?'

'Where did you stop for lunch?' probed Ginger Tom.

'Oh, just south of Dalkeith.'

'Why didn't you mention the fact in your statement?'

I took refuge in silence. My head was now one solid ache and my body felt drained but I still had sufficient control to protect myself. I had deliberately omitted any reference to the episode in the field. Under the circumstances, to admit that I had seen Janie naked once before would be to deepen suspicion all round. Neither the ginger hair nor the bald head would believe the truth.

'Well?' resumed Ginger Tom after a long wait.

'It slipped my mind.'

'Ah, we're back to the selective memory act.'

'Superintendent,' I said, holding my head in my hands, 'it's been a pretty harrowing night for me one way and another. I go out for a drink with an old friend and I finish up being grilled in a police station. As I see it, I'm an innocent victim in all this and yet you're treating me as if I'm a prime suspect.'

'That isn't the case at all, Mr Saxon,' he replied, adopting a more soothing tone, 'and I'm sorry if you're finding this interview too oppressive. I promise that we won't go on much longer. Er, is there anything you'd like? Aspirins? More tea?'

'I'd just like to get it over with, that's all.'

'So would we.' He rested his cigarette in the ashtray and took something out of his pocket. 'Have you ever seen this before?'

'It's Janie's autograph book.'

'Did she show it to you?'

'Yes. She turned to the page with my own autograph on to prove that she was a fan of mine. I can't recall actually signing it. I had dozens of books thrust at me during last year's Open.'

'Open the front cover,' he said, handing it to me. I did

as requested and was taken aback. 'Read out that name and address, please.'

'Peter Vane, 14 Florence Street, Huyton, Liverpool.'

'So it doesn't belong to her.'

'It could be her brother,' I guessed.

'Hardly! What parents in their right mind would christen a child Jane Vane? Besides, autograph books are highly personal things. You don't loan them to anybody, least of all to sisters. No, I think that she may have stolen it.'

'Stolen it!'

'Don't look so shocked. The girl stole your money, didn't she?'

'Well, yes, but—'

'Look at that childish handwriting. That lad is no more than ten or eleven. Kids of that age are fanatical about the sports they follow. If he lives in Liverpool, then he would have been able to get to Royal Birkdale very easily to hunt for autographs. And having gone to that trouble, I don't think he'd have wanted to be parted from his book.'

'There is another point,' added Robbie.

'Inspector Robbie is our golfer,' explained his colleague.

'I hope you won't be offended, sir . . .'

'Why should I be?' I wondered.

'The names in that book are people like Kincaid, Hume, Devereaux, Brymer, Nicholson, Tanizaki and yourself. Not really the golfers who are the main targets for groupies. The pin-up boys are players like Jeff Piker and Tim Quentin and Ulrich Heidensohn. If the book belonged to the girl, those are the sort of autographs I'd expect to find.'

'What happened to my reputation as a ladies' man?' I asked.

All three of us laughed. It eased the tension considerably.

'Well, that just about wraps it up for now, Mr Saxon,' said Ginger Tom, retrieving his cigarette for a last puff before stubbing it out. 'You must try to get some rest now. We shall need to take a further statement from you in due course but that can wait.' They were both on their feet and about to move away. 'Oh, one last thing.'

'Yes?'

'The girl's rucksack. It was in your motor caravan.'

'I know.'

'Did you search through it?'

'No. Why should I?'

'To try to find the money you thought she'd taken from you.'

'I didn't touch the rucksack, Superintendent. When I came to, it had been emptied out all over the floor.'

'Strange that there was no purse. And a great pity. Purses have some kind of ID in them as a rule. I'd like to know who that girl really is. And we will do in time. In time.'

'Could I ask *you* a question, please?'

'Ask away.'

'Do you really think that I killed Janie?'

There was a long pause as he explored my eyes. 'No, I don't.'

'Thank you.'

'But I'm keeping an open mind on it.'

'Someone's got it in for me,' I urged. 'I was set up.'

'Have you any idea why, Mr Saxon?'

'Because that someone doesn't like me.'

'I gathered that,' he said with a grim chuckle, then turned to his companion. 'As a golfing man, Inspector Robbie has an alternative theory.'

'More of a gut reaction than a theory,' explained the other.

'Go on, Inspector.' I was keen to hear him.

'You're a threat, sir. Over the last few months, you've regained your best form. Somebody thinks you have a strong chance of winning the Open and wants you out of the running.'

The idea had simply never occurred to me. I was still reeling as the two of them walked out of the room.

*

53

It was still only 7 a.m. by the time I had washed, shaved and tried to force down the full breakfast that was made for me. Though I was not being detained in custody, I had little choice but to stay there in the short term. There was nowhere else to go. Carnoustie had been impounded and was, in the standard phrase, helping police with their enquiries. Rescued from the ditch and brought back to St Andrews, she had been parked in the courtyard at the rear of the police station, photographed more times than a reigning Miss World and was now being searched from top to bottom. I was tortured with guilt at the indignities I had brought upon her and wondered if our relationship would ever be the same again. I was also horrified at the thought that my home had been taken over by a team of experts who were sifting through my belongings, my secrets, my private life.

Posthumously, Janie was telling the police all that *she* knew.

Her death was a flame-thrower inside my head. The memory of it made my brain sizzle and brought sweat oozing from every pore. It had been such a brutal and unexpected murder and I could not rid myself of the fear that I was in some measure responsible. If I hadn't given her a lift, she might now be alive. If I hadn't chased her from the Old Course, she might not now be lying on a slab somewhere and suffering the crudities of a post mortem. Her association with Alan Saxon had marked her out as a murder victim.

All animosity I had felt towards her had now vanished in a wash of pity and remorse. In retrospect, my rage over the theft of the miniature golfer seemed petty and unnecessary, and when I recalled how I had searched through her rucksack while she lay dead beside me I was racked with self-disgust. Janie had not deserved to die. The one positive thing that came out of my agonising was a resolve to track down her killer. How I could even start to do such a thing I did not know, but the decision had been made.

I owed it to Janie.

The more I thought about her, the more conscious I became that I knew very little about her. Had she really been a student at Bristol? Why had she been drawn to the golfing fraternity? What had happened to her after she had disappeared on the Edinburgh ring road? Who *was* she? I had a vision of distraught parents arriving to hound me over my involvement with their daughter.

I imagined how I would feel in their place. With Lynette.

The only way I could exonerate myself was by taking active steps to find the murderer. Leaving the task entirely to the police would not be good enough, even if they were successful. *I* had to do my share. Alone. I had to win back my self-respect. I had to atone.

'Enough to eat, sir?'

'Yes, thanks.'

'P'raps you'd like to follow me, then.'

'Oh – right.'

Leaving the half-eaten breakfast, I went down a corridor with the uniformed sergeant and listened to the squeak of his boots. He conducted me into the room where I had been examined by the doctor some hours earlier. It contained a raised bed, a desk, a few upright chairs, a sink unit and an array of locked cabinets. The curtains were drawn and the only light came from the Anglepoise lamp on the desk. The sergeant pointed towards the bed.

'All yours, sir.'

'Thanks.'

'You won't be disturbed for a while.'

He went out and I braced myself for the clang of metal and the turning of a key in the lock. Instead, the door was shut quietly and the only sound I heard was the squeak of the boots as they marched off down the corridor.

There was no hope of my sleeping but I took off my shoes and lay on the bed to rest. I pulled one of the grey woollen blankets up to my waist, put my hands behind my head and stared at the ceiling. The idea that I was somehow under restraint kept nudging at me.

Less than eight hours ago I had been sharing a drink

and a laugh with a good friend, who had achieved the impossible by sending me away with renewed confidence in my ability as a golfer and the feeling that I was, after all, happy to be back in St Andrews. Now I was in the middle of a murder investigation that would both sully my image and jeopardise my chances in the Open. Alan Saxon was in for a lot of bad publicity and Clive Phelps was about to lose his fiver.

I thought back to the moment when I had last seen him.

After shaking hands with Clive and watching him go back into the hotel, I had come down the steps, turned left into the Scores and then right into Golf Place for the short walk to the car park. There were a few people about but I had been too preoccupied to pay much attention to them. What I did recall, however, was the fact that the lights had been on in the R. & A. Clubhouse as I passed. Carnoustie had been in the corner of an almost empty car park. When I entered the vehicle, I had been struck on the head from behind.

It infuriated me that someone had been able to get into my home. Because I carry so many valuable items – not least my golf clubs – I have gone to much trouble to make Carnoustie secure against the car thief. Special locks have been fitted to the doors and the stable door on the side is double-bolted on the inside, top and bottom. I even got the coachbuilders to strengthen certain panels and put in reinforced windows. As an additional protection, the vehicle is fitted with two security devices. One sets off an ear-splitting alarm when the ignition key is turned and, if that is de-activated, the second cuts out the engine completely. The switches controlling the two devices are carefully hidden under the dashboard.

Whoever got into Carnoustie was a professional.

The key question was whether or not Janie had been in the vehicle as well. It was difficult to believe that someone had managed to get a dead body into a motor caravan at some time between 9 p.m. and midnight. The car park was overlooked from the Scores and I myself had seen Carnoustie down below when I had opened the windows in

Clive's room to let out the smoke. Had Janie been taken into the vehicle and then murdered? Again, it seemed unlikely. She had made noise enough when I had grabbed her arm and she would not allow herself to be throttled without a violent struggle and a lot of commotion.

A professional would not take risks.

I came to the view that Janie had not been in Carnoustie when I was knocked unconscious. It was more probable that my assailant had driven us out in Carnoustie to a quiet spot in the countryside and picked her up there. When the patrol car found us, we were in a secluded lane about two miles beyond Leuchars.

The time of Janie's death was critical. If it was before midnight, I was in the clear with an alibi named Clive Phelps: if it was after I had left the hotel, then there could be real problems for me.

I went through it all time and time again and reached the same conclusions. Out of a welter of impression and guesswork, I felt that I could establish certain facts about the murderer. He knew about my association with Janie. He was a practised car thief. He was deliberately trying to stop my bid for the Open Championship. And he was the anonymous caller who had rung the police to report that Carnoustie had crashed into a ditch.

I was looking for a killer with a flair for stage management.

My mind focused on Janie again. Where had she spent Sunday night? With whom? Why was she part of the Heidensohn fan club when he went out for his practice round? As I replayed the incident on the Old Course, I was distressed that the last time I had seen her alive she had screamed up at me and slapped my face. In my brief relationship with the girl I had contrived to get almost everything wrong.

I closed my eyes, got into Carnoustie and drove her into the Washington service area again. I agreed to give a lift to a girl in check shirt, denim jeans and white trainers. I replayed our conversation as accurately as I could in the hope that it might contain some clue to her identity. Then

I crashed into a van on the Edinburgh ring road and she ran away from me. Why?

I was still groping for the answers when the door opened.

'Mr Saxon?' whispered a voice.

'Yes?' I sat up at once.

'Ah, you're awake,' said the uniformed sergeant. 'Good. You have a visitor, sir. If you're up to seeing him, that is.'

'Who is it?'

'Mr Calloway. From the R. & A.'

'Send him right in, please.'

When Ian Calloway walked in, I had just finished putting my shoes back on. He came over to me in concern and took me by the shoulders.

'Are you all right, Alan?'

'I've spent more enjoyable nights,' I admitted.

'It was on the news this morning. I came as quickly as I could to see if I could be of any help.'

'Thanks, Ian.' I was touched.

'I also gave Gordon a ring to ask him to get over here. He knows how to deal with the police. Talks their language.' He gave me a reassuring smile. 'I want you to know that we'll do everything we can for you, Alan.'

'Then the first thing you can do is to accept my apology.'

'For what?'

'For landing you with just the sort of headlines you don't need. Sex Killing at Open. Nude Body in Golfer's Motor Caravan. You know the way the papers go to town on these stories.'

'It's not your fault,' he said.

'I'm glad someone around here thinks that,' I joked.

'There's no question of a charge against you, surely? As I understand it, the girl was found dead in Carnoustie and you semi-conscious.'

'They're working on the theory that I drove her to some lonely spot, had my wicked way with her, strangled her and then knocked myself out with a 9-iron to make it look as if I'd been attacked.'

There was a pause. 'Would you care to tell me what *did* happen?' he asked, quietly. 'It would help my position a lot. The press are going to be hounding me for comments.'

I sympathised. The organisation of an Open Championship takes well over a year, costs a fortune and involves the employment of thousands of people. Ian had controlled the arrangements at every stage and just as all that corporate effort was about to bear fruit, murder had taken place on the doorstep. He had a right to know the truth and I needed moral support from a friend.

I went through the night's events as quickly and accurately as I could. He listened intently and didn't try to interrupt. His expression didn't change when I told him about the chase after Janie down the first fairway of the Old Course. When I had finished my story, I was almost out of breath.

'That's it, Ian. And I swear it. I didn't kill her.'

'I believe you,' he said simply.

I shook his hand in gratitude.

There was a tap on the door and the sergeant showed in Gordon Reeman. The latter was as anxious about me as Ian and was keen to know how I had been treated by the police.

'Ginger Tom can be a bastard when he wants to be,' he noted.

'He was only doing his job,' I said, sardonically.

'I've just had a word with him. There's no reason why you can't leave here right now.'

'With Carnoustie?'

'I'm afraid not, Alan.'

'How long are they going to keep her locked up?'

'All day. Probably overnight.'

'Overnight!' I exploded. 'Where am I supposed to sleep?'

'We'll find you somewhere,' promised Ian.

'If all else fails, you can stay with us,' said Gordon, eagerly. 'We've rented a small house near Dunino. It'll be a bit of a squeeze but you're very welcome.'

'Er . . . no, thanks . . .'

'Helen is a great fan of yours. She'd love it.'

'Kind of you to offer, Gordon, but – not this time.'

'Bear us in mind,' he insisted.

'I will.'

But I knew that I would never spend the night under Gordon Reeman's roof. Apart from anything else, his wife Helen was an invalid and he would have his work cut out looking after her. I would be a definite imposition. Besides, I wanted to see as little of Gordon as possible. Within the confines of a police station, he was reminding me more and more of my father. The thought of bumping into him outside the bathroom next morning or staring at him over the breakfast table was really unsettling.

His big face crumpled into an apology.

'I can't tell you how sorry I am about all this.'

'Sorry?'

'Well, it reflects so badly on me.'

'I don't see it that way,' soothed Ian.

'Security is my pigeon,' argued Gordon. 'Yet what happens within a mere hundred yards of the clubhouse? A competitor's motor caravan is broken into and then involved in a murder case.'

'You're not to blame,' said Ian.

'I feel that I am.'

'But that's ridiculous!'

'It was on my patch, Ian. I must accept responsibility.'

Gordon took it personally. The complacency I had always detested in him had evaporated; he was a dejected man apologising for what he believed was a serious blemish on his professional record. His new attitude did not endear him to me any the more. It smacked too much of a kind of perverse self-importance. He was trying to claim an indirect involvement.

I decided that the new, contrite, punctured Gordon was even more despicable than the old bright and breezy version. At the same time, I saw that he might actually be of some use to me. He could be an interlocutor between me and the police. Things that I needed to know – and which they would never tell me – he might somehow be able to find out from them. It was certainly worth a try.

'How well do you know Ginger Tom?' I asked.

'Very well.'

'Did he say anything about the case?'

'Only that it was damn inconvenient.'

Ian Calloway sighed. 'I'll second that.'

'What I really meant was—'

'Relax, Alan. You're not a suspect. They're convinced that you didn't murder that girl.' Gordon gave his grim chuckle. 'They feel you can tell them more than you have, mark you, but . . . there's no question of any charges against you.'

'For this relief, much thanks,' breathed Ian.

'I'll want some stuff from Carnoustie. Clubs, clothes and so on.'

'Leave it to me,' assured Gordon. 'I'll have another word.'

He went out smartly and Ian produced a wan smile.

'Gordon's quite a sensitive soul underneath all that military bluster. This has really upset him.

'It hasn't exactly cheered *me* up,' I reminded him.

'Of course not, Alan,' he agreed, solicitously, 'and our first task is to get you away from here. You must be absolutely exhausted.'

'I am.'

'Then let's find you a place where you can flop down and catch up on some sleep. I'm wondering if we might not try—'

'It's all right,' I interrupted. 'Just thought of somewhere. And when I get into that bed, I'm going to stay there for twenty-four hours.'

It was Ian's turn to sound hurt. 'You're not going to miss the dinner this evening, surely?'

In the excitement of events, I had completely forgotten it.

'No, Ian. I won't miss the dinner. I'll be there.'

He relaxed for the first time since he had arrived.

Clive Phelps didn't turn a hair when I rang him and asked if I could use his hotel room during the day. Apart from his urge to help an old friend, I could sense his journalist's instinct at work. Alan Saxon was going to be front-page news in all the nationals. To have exclusive access to me for a while was an irresistible bonus for Clive and he would make sure that I was not pestered by anyone else.

'Just to think, old son,' he observed, when I went around to the Scores Hotel, 'while I was getting pickled with my fellow piss-artists, you were down there in the car park getting bonked on the boko. How is your head, by the way?'

'Still threatening to part company with my body.'

'I feel like that *every* morning,' he confessed.

'I don't wish to know that,' I yawned.

He became businesslike. 'How long have I got?'

'A few minutes. At most.'

'Then I won't waste time. Now, for starters . . .'

In the time that it took me to put down my luggage, order him to stop smoking his foul cigar, draw the curtains, get undressed, climb into the spare bed and take the receiver off the telephone, Clive quizzed me expertly about what had happened. When I gave him a final, valedictory yawn, he blew me a kiss and tiptoed out of the room.

I fell asleep almost at once.

Hour after peaceful hour of my life ebbed away and then I was awake as abruptly as I had gone off. It took me time to get my bearings. I was in a hotel bedroom with the afternoon sun trying to burst in on me around the edges of the curtains. The sound of voices and traffic rose up from outside. There was a faint odour of cigar smoke. A lift was in motion not far from the door. Someone played a distant transistor.

Among the favours I had asked of Clive was that he should contact Nairn for me and postpone the practice round I had fixed for that morning. Body Beautiful would have no problem in finding another playing partner and I would be spared his beaming curiosity. I thought it was vital for me to get in some practice,

62

however, and I was delighted to see that Clive had been able to fit me in elsewhere. On the scrap of paper which he had put under the door was a coded message: J.P.5.9.

I looked at my watch. Almost an hour to spare.

After a lingering soak in the bath, I had the strength and the courage to go out past the widening eyes of the hotel staff and into the road of pointing fingers. Evidently, the word had got around. Nairn, waiting for me on the corner of the Scores, was all agape. He could not have looked more terror-stricken had he been asked to caddy for Jack the Ripper. When I handed him my golf bag, he looked nervously into it as if he was expecting to see an array of murder weapons.

The short journey to the locker room gained us a large audience and the clubhouse terrace rapidly filled as we walked to the first tee. I was ready to brave the ordeal because escape was at hand. Though it would subject me to the public gaze, golf, my game, my talisman, my way of life, would also come to my rescue. No matter how many people stood and stared, I would be impervious to them out on the course. I would lose myself in the mysteries of golf. It was my emergency exit. The one place where I would be free from the nagging guilt about Janie.

My playing partner and his caddie were already on the tee. J.P.5.9. Jeff Piker at 5 p.m. for nine holes. We shook hands and were away.

Luck favoured me. I could not have chosen a better companion that day than the Australian player. A tallish, well-built man with long, flowing brown hair and a full beard, Jeff Piker was a shrewd, tough, self-critical golfer who set himself high standards. He had little time for conversation during a game and would only speak if his partner played an exceptionally good shot or he himself played an exceptionally bad one.

As we walked side by side down the first fairway, I recalled the prediction that Clive Phelps had made. Saxon. Kincaid. Piker. Of the three names, Jeff's was the most likely to reach the prescribed target. My own challenge had now been set back and Horton Kincaid, the defending Open Champion, had been through a bleak phase recently. Jeff Piker, on the other hand, was consistency itself. Though he had yet to win one of the four major titles, he was always in with a shout.

Because of the mood I was in, there was an edge of desperation to my game and I took chances that I would never have considered had it been a tournament. It paid off. My boldness earned me three successive birdies and when my ball went astray at the next hole, I redeemed myself with an amazing recovery shot. Even Nairn was impressed. From that point on, he stopped treating me like Britain's Most Wanted Man.

Instead of being cowed or distracted by my run of success, Jeff strove harder to match it. His raw power sent the ball screaming from the tee and its low trajectory gave it less trouble than most from the swirling wind. His short game, too, was almost flawless. Our practice developed into a real tussle.

The Heathery Hole was the only one to sneak a stroke off me and it put Jeff into a slender lead, but he surrendered it at the Short Hole bunker with his only bad mistake of the round. Since we both birdied the End Hole, we finished level with 32 apiece, four strokes below par. Jeff Piker was as pleased as I was.

'Thanks, Al! You set a cracking pace for me.'

'Pity we're not going all the way,' I suggested. 'On that form, we could get within sight of the course record.'

'Too true, matey.'

We started out on the long walk back to the clubhouse. I was afraid that Jeff might now bring up the subject of the murder but he didn't. He kept the talk strictly to golf and told me that he had been in St Andrews since Friday in order to familiarise himself with the Old Course. His preparation was always meticulous. I found myself wondering yet again why a player of his proven calibre had still not won a major tournament. Now in his mid-thirties, he did not have unlimited time left to make up the deficiency.

'Have a good time tonight, anyway,' he urged.

'Tonight?'

'The dinner for the old champions. Should be a rare evening. Ian Calloway tells me he's expecting eighteen of you – a complete round.'

'With Alan Saxon as the Road Hole!'

'You said it, mate!'

He gave me a good-humoured slap on the back and we laughed.

Inwardly, however, I was having some misgivings about the dinner. To join a public gathering was the last thing I wanted, especially when so many famous figures from the world of golf would be there. I felt that I would be the odd man out. The person who had somehow let them down. The spectre at the feast.

I toyed with the idea of not going but knew how much that would disappoint Ian Calloway. For his sake, I had to make the effort.

'There's the bugger to beat this year!'

'Mm?'

'The Aryan bloody dream,' observed Jeff, bitterly. 'He went round in 68 this morning and the wind was twice as strong as this.'

We had almost reached the clubhouse now and Ulrich Heidensohn was standing on the terrace with some officials. Immensely popular with the fans, he was not generally liked by the players themselves and Jeff's attitude was similar to my own. The West German was arrogant and self-centred. Everyone respected his ability on a golf course, but he seemed to go out of his way to needle his opponents.

Heidensohn stood out from the small crowd on the terrace. He had remarkable presence. Though only of medium height and relatively slight build, his trim frame seemed to attract the eye. His blond hair had been bleached to a rich whiteness by constant sun and his features were bronzed and regular.

Much as I disliked the man, I still owed him an apology.

As I walked towards him, however, he swung round to face me and I was stopped dead. Pinned on to the chest of his sweater was a silvered figure. It was my miniature golfer.

Chapter Four

'Finally, in honour of this year's defending champion, let me tell you a true story. Jesus Christ decided to take up golf.' Ian Calloway paused until the laughter had subsided. 'He went down to a course deep in the heart of Texas to play a round with his old friend, Doubting Thomas. Everything went well until they reached the fifteenth hole. About 150 yards from the tee was a lake and the green was on a small island a further 100 yards or more on. Jesus announced that he would go for the flag with his tee shot. Doubting Thomas, who did not believe in miracles, advised him to play his first shot to the edge of the lake and then carry the water with his second. Jesus was scornful. "It's only 250 yards," he said. "Horton Kincaid would aim for the pin." Another burst of laughter gave Ian the chance to sip his wine. 'Now, although Jesus knew a thing or two about raising the dead, he was still very much a rookie golfer. His tee shot rose up to heaven, then plopped down into the water. He was furious and went racing off down the fairway. When he got to the lake, he began to walk on the water in search of his ball. An onlooker, who did not recognise him, was astonished. "Who does he think he is – Jesus Christ?" "Oh, no," explained Doubting Thomas, "he thinks he's Horton Kincaid."'

The whole room bubbled with mirth and tables were pounded by way of applause. Ian Calloway had reached the end of a long and highly entertaining speech that had delighted his audience. Long after the acclamation had died down, Horton Kincaid was still enjoying the affectionate joke. The giant Texan was one huge smile as he raised his glass in thanks to Ian.

Waiters brought fresh bottles and another speech began.

'Before Jesus Kincaid goes off to turn wine into water . . .'

The Royal and Ancient Golf Club of St Andrews had done

us proud. They had given us an excellent dinner within the hallowed walls of the clubhouse and made it possible for us all to relive our triumphs among the only people who really understood them. Our fellow champions. Winners of the oldest, most prestigious and most loved tournament in the game. An exclusive brotherhood. A race apart. An élite.

Eighteen of us had been able to attend and we had accounted for well over thirty Open Championships between us. The oldest man present was the spritely Claud Morby, now in his eighties, winner at Prestwick's last Open in 1925; and the youngest was Orvill Hume, still in his twenties, winner at Sandwich in 1981. I was saddened to note that only three of us were British and that I alone of the trio was competing in the current Open. For the rest, there were two Australians, two South Africans, a Spaniard and ten Americans.

Half of those Americans were still playing tournaments. I was sitting next to the most famous of them.

'That was one helluva meal.'

'I won't need to eat for the rest of the week,' I said.

'Me neither, Alan. I'm full as a Thanksgiving turkey.'

Horton Kincaid was a living legend. In a room full of big names, his was without question the biggest. Four times winner of the Open, he had earned three green blazers at Augusta as a triple winner of the US Masters, collected the US Open title twice in succession and won the coveted USPGA Championship a record six times.

Fifteen major titles against my one. Yet we were equals that night. Members of a sacred band united by mutual respect. Off-duty heroes. Pages from the history of golf. Friends.

'The course looks in great shape,' drawled Horton.

'It's giving no favours away,' I warned.

'Well, that's nothing new.'

'No.'

'How long you been around, Alan?'

'Sunday.'

'We hit town today.' He sampled the coffee that had just

been poured for him. 'Say, where's all the early dough going this year?'

'On the favourite. Someone called Horton Kincaid.'

'Me! I haven't won a goddam tournament all year.'

'That's when you're at your most lethal,' I grinned.

His laugh rumbled. 'Now, I sure would love to oblige all those good folk but – hell! – I been having swing problems this season. At my age! When you make forty, you don't expect that kind of shit.' He drank some more coffee. 'Know what Ed reckons?'

'What?'

'The smart dough should be on three other guys. Heidensohn, Tanizaki and a bum named Saxon. That's the way Ed sees it.'

Ed Maserewa was Horton's manager. He was a rough, tough, totally unscrupulous operator but he was also a shrewd judge of golf. I was flattered. Ed was yet another person who thought I was a possible champion. There had also been Clive Phelps. Detective-Inspector Lucas Robbie. And the man who had killed Janie.

'You listen to Ed,' he counselled with a smile.

I accepted the compliment with a nod.

Not for the first time, I wondered how such a profoundly nice man as Horton Kincaid had become associated with such a profoundly nasty one as Ed Maserewa. As a team, they certainly worked. Under Ed's patronage and guidance, Horton had gone from Texas farm boy to golfing superstar in five years. He was now a multi-millionaire and did not need to play golf for money any more. Unlike me.

We were at either end of the golfing spectrum. Horton's ranch was set in two thousand acres of prime Texas farmland; my home had four wheels and a dent in the wing. His income flooded in from tournaments, personal appearances, books, instructional golf videos, a syndicated newspaper column, multiple sponsorship deals and a whole range of business investments; my money trickled in via my golf clubs. Horton's name could be found the length and breadth of America on motels, restaurants, golf shops, insurance companies, travel agencies, soft drinks and leisure wear; my name, like cheap socks, had shrunk badly over the years.

He had flown into the RAF station in Leuchars in his private jet and had been driven with his family to the small mansion they had rented in Crail; I was spending the night in the spare bed of a friend's hotel room. Horton had enough money to retire; I found it a struggle to pay my daughter's school fees.

Everything about him should have made me resent him and yet I loved him dearly. And so did everyone else. He was a symbol.

'Ah, I was hoping for a moment, Alan . . .'

Ian Calloway took me aside as the dinner party was breaking up.

'What did you think of the evening?'

'I'm coming back tomorrow night for more,' I promised.

'Would that we all could,' he said, then his expression changed. 'I know you weren't over-keen to come. Things being what they are. But I hope your worst fears were groundless?'

'They were, Ian.'

I knew that I had him to thank. Instead of being interrogated time and again about the murder investigation, I had been talked to solely as a golfer. My problems had been left outside the competitors' car park: inside the clubhouse, it was as if they never existed. Ian had obviously prepared the way for all this with a word to the others.

'Never got the chance to ask about Dubby Gill,' continued Ian. 'Did you call round there on Sunday evening?'

'Yes.'

'And?'

'As you feared. Bad news.'

'Oh dear!' he sighed. 'How is his wife coping?'

'Dubby won't win any awards as a model patient.' I recalled the angry scene in the cottage. 'Ian . . . do they get on? I mean, has it been a happy marriage?'

'As far as I know. Dubby never talked much about his wife but that doesn't mean he beats her. No, from what I saw, they were well-matched.' A memory surfaced. 'Except . . .'

'Go on.'

'Well, there was *one* occasion when he lost his temper with her. And quite violently. Last summer, it would be. Mrs Gill came and asked if she could have access to our archives.'

'Why?'

'She was interested in some pictorial material we have. Wartime and immediately after. Photographs of the Old Course looking sorry for itself. Then being spruced up for the 1946 Open . . . The thing was that she didn't want her husband to know she'd been to us.'

'And Dubby found out?' I guessed.

'He did. He descended on her like an avenging angel. Really bawled her out. It was most unlike him.' He shrugged in puzzlement. 'Mrs Gill hasn't been near us since. I still haven't an idea what that row was about.'

I suspected that I did. A dog.

Ian was caught up in a cluster of departing guests and we were separated. It was time for me to go. I did a last handshake tour, had a final word with Horton Kincaid, then stole one more look at the object that had brought us all together. There are bigger, shinier, more ornate, more costly trophies in golf but none is so revered and sought after as the elegant silver claret jug awarded each year to the Open Champion. It was standing on a plinth whose triple tiers had been banded in silver so that the names of the winners could be inscribed in the roll of honour. I could not resist a glance at my own name, put there all those years ago on a wild and windy day up in Carnoustie. Then I saw the tiny panel waiting to receive the name of this year's champion.

Ambition stirred me. I left in a trance.

Instead of taking me back to the hotel, my legs carried me in the opposite direction and I blinked in surprise when I found myself in the competitors' car park. Dinner guests were still leaving and more than one vehicle gave me a friendly toot on the horn. I walked across to the corner where Carnoustie had been parked on Monday night. The full horror of what had happened seeped back into my mind like a poisonous liquid and I stood there transfixed.

Then a sudden fear seized me. I was being watched. Not in the curious and almost ghoulish way that I had been stared at earlier when I ventured out for my practice round. This was different.

I was under surveillance. I was in danger.

The fact that I could not see the person only served to increase my unease. Taking care not to show my alarm, I swung on my heel and strolled back towards the hotel. Only when I got back inside did I begin to feel secure again. I ignored the lift and took the stairs in threes.

Clive Phelps looked up as I went into the room.

'The food wasn't *that* bad, surely?'

'What? Oh, no . . . It was fine. Splendid meal . . .'

'Who did you sit next to?' he enquired, wryly. 'Banquo's ghost? Your face is as white as the proverbial sheet. Everything okay?'

'Yes, I think so.'

'How was it? An evening of mirth, merriment and joy unconfined?'

'It was great,' I said, recovering. 'Glad I went.'

'You had a phone call. Several, in fact, but this is the important one. Detective-Superintendent Ings.'

'What did he want?'

'To see you, old son. He's sending two armed coppers around in the morning with a set of handcuffs. I'd advise you to go quietly.' He gave me a wicked smirk. 'He'd like you to report to the cop shop at 9 a.m. on the dot. For a cosy little chat.'

'Did he say anything else?' I asked morosely.

'Not a dicky bird.'

'And what about the other phone calls?'

'*I* dealt with them,' he said complacently. 'Gentlemen of the press in search of a quoteable quote from the man of

72

the moment. I told them you'd fled the country.' His eyebrows arched in mock seriousness. 'I hope you realise what this is costing me, Alan. My colleagues in the press tent won't even speak to me now. They think I've got you hidden away so that only our paper can get at you. I, my friend, have been ostracised.'

I sat on the edge of the bed and yawned. 'I'm very grateful for the hospitality, Clive, but it's only for tonight. I expect to be back in Carnoustie by tomorrow.'

'Let's hope so. I'm making real headway with the barmaid here. I can't have you snoring away in one bed while I'm trying to broaden her mind in the other.'

'I can take a hint,' I smiled. 'What about that favour I asked?'

'Which one? I've done so many for you.'

'Heidensohn.'

'Ah!'

'Any luck?'

'Alan, if you want to know where he got that stupid little badge from, why on earth didn't you ask him yourself?'

The stupid little badge was the miniature golfer. When I spoke to the West German on the terrace and gabbled my apology, I did not dare mention the badge. I was too shocked. And excited.

It was my first clue.

'So you didn't manage to find out, Clive?'

'Of course I did. We intrepid newshounds always get what we're after. Mind you, it took some working into the conversation. I mean, there must have been ten or fifteen of us trying to interview him at the same time. And he was there to talk about how he played golf, not what he was wearing.'

'Well?'

'It was a present from an admirer.'

'Name?'

'He couldn't remember. Somehow, I don't think it's their names he's really interested in. Ully's a man of action.'

73

'So that was that,' I said, resignedly.

'Not quite. I had a natter with the porter at his hotel. There's not much gets past a hotel porter. Especially the beady-eyed Scots type. When I asked if any young ladies had been invited up to Ully's room to see his 9-iron, the porter gave a hollow laugh. Ully's had dozens up there. He must be playing some kind of Noah's Ark game because the animals have been going in two by two.'

'So the porter didn't recall any girl in particular?'

'Afraid not. Sorry.'

'Thanks for trying, anyway.'

'Your wish is my command,' he said, bowing. 'I suppose there's no point in asking you *why* you wanted to know about that badge?'

There was no point in telling him. Clive had guessed.

Tiredness brought the biggest yawn yet. 'I'm for a quick bath and then straight to bed,' I decided.

'In that case, I'll slope off to the bar and see if any of my colleagues will talk to me now. Maybe I can trade a few titbits about you for a free drink.' He got up from his chair and crossed to the door. He chuckled admiringly. 'You've got to hand it to Ully. Two at a time. A true golfer's instinct. One to screw and one to act as his caddie. Sleep tight.'

Ten minutes later, I dozed off in the bath.

When I arrived next morning at the police station in North Street, I was conducted to the same featureless interview room. They threatened me with a mug of their tea but I pleaded for mercy and was let off. Ginger Tom stalked into the room with Inspector Robbie at his heels. Both had opted for a change of outfit. The tweed suit had given way to a charcoal grey one that emphasised Ginger Tom's skeletal frame. When he paced around the room with a clipboard under his arm, he looked like a flamingo in mourning. Robbie was wearing a nondescript sports jacket and brown trousers. He had cut himself shaving.

'First, the good news,' said Ginger Tom breezily. 'You can have your motor caravan back today.'

'Now, the bad news,' I quipped. 'You've taken the wheels off.'

'Not exactly, Mr Saxon. But we are holding on to certain items.'

'Eh?'

'For lab tests. You'll get them back in time.'

'What sort of items?' I exclaimed.

His tone was peremptory. 'Those we feel may be of assistance to us in our enquiries. You'll be given a detailed list.'

'Thanks a lot.'

'Now,' he resumed, glancing at his clipboard, 'a few facts. As we suspected, the deceased was not a student at Bristol University.'

'Then who was she?'

'We still don't know that for sure, Mr Saxon. What we do now have, however, is a clearer picture of her movements after she left you on the Edinburgh ring road.' He looked at me with mild humour. 'Incidentally, we also traced the van driver involved in the accident with you on Sunday. He remembers you well. If not fondly.'

'So what happened to Janie after she vanished?'

'She got herself another lift. Young couple in a Renault 5. They took her as far as Cupar. According to them, she said that her name was Lynette.'

'Lynette!' I was shaken. 'But that's my daughter's name.'

'Did you mention that fact to her at all?'

'Yes. Yes, I think I did. When we talked about—' I checked myself from telling them about the miniature golfer. That was *my* lead. 'When we talked about education. She asked me what school my daughter was at.'

'Benenden, I believe, sir,' said Robbie with faint resentment.

'Inspector Robbie is not in favour of fee-paying schools,' said Ginger Tom. 'He thinks they breed the wrong attitudes.'

75

'I couldn't agree more,' I replied, letting my own prejudices hang out. 'If it was left to me, Lynette would have gone to a good Comp.'

'But your wife went to Benenden,' noted Robbie.

'Yes. She did.'

'Your ex-wife, that is,' corrected Ginger Tom. 'Rosemary. Now residing with her parents at Little Aston in Staffordshire.'

In the twenty-four hours since I had seen them, they had obviously found out a lot about me. It did nothing to ease my discomfort or to increase my liking for police procedure. I was at a disadvantage. They knew it. And they were keeping me there.

Ginger Tom consulted his clipboard.

'As to the time and cause of death . . .'

'Wait a minute. You haven't told me about Janie's – about the girl's movements after this lift she was given.'

'That information is not relevant at this point.'

'But I want to know.'

'We shall tell you what we see fit,' he returned, sharply.

'Where did she go?' I demanded.

'Your father warned us you'd be awkward.'

With one sentence, Ginger Tom cut the ground under my feet. He had been in touch with my father. They were accomplices. Old wounds began to smart as I thought about my father and how pleased he would be that I was at last back where he wanted me. Within his sphere of influence. After twenty years.

Ginger Tom could now go on uninterrupted.

'The time of death has been fixed somewhere around 1 a.m. Only three-quarters of an hour or so before the patrol car found you. In other words, the girl was still alive when the alleged attack on you took place in the competitors' car park. Because the body was found so soon after death, it is possible to give a more accurate time of demise. Body temperature is a crucial factor in determining the time. Since the murder took place inside your motor caravan when all its windows and doors were closed, temperature remained constant.'

76

He studied me to see how I was reacting to the news. Time of death. Alleged attack. Killed in Carnoustie.

I was in a complete daze.

'Death was caused by strangulation, probably with bare hands. There is evidence that the deceased put up a struggle during which she sustained bruises and minor abrasions. Sexual intercourse took place not long before death but this may have been with her compliance. The marks on her body are not consistent with rape and there is no internal evidence of sexual violence. A considerable level of alcohol was found in her bloodstream and traces of cannabis were found in her lungs. There was a cigarette burn on her left shoulder. Her stomach contained almost no food . . .' He came to sit opposite me. 'I'm paraphrasing the main points of the report. Much of the detail is unimportant at this stage. As far as you're concerned, anyway.'

The girl had no chance. Heavy drinking on an empty stomach. Smoking pot. Willing intercourse with the man who would afterwards strangle her to death. A cigarette burn on her shoulder.

Had it all taken place in Carnoustie with me there?

'Have you any comment to make, Mr Saxon?'

'No, Superintendent. None at all.'

'It does cast a different light on your statement, doesn't it?'

'If you say so.'

Ginger Tom tensed. 'I want this man,' he hissed. 'And soon.'

'I want him as well.'

I held his gaze and did not flinch at his rising anger.

'Leave this to us, Mr Saxon. Don't get in our way.'

Robbie had more tact. 'We need your co-operation, sir.'

'Isn't that what you've had, Inspector?'

'Up to a point,' he conceded. 'But we feel there's more that you have to tell us. Certain things you've been holding back.'

'Such as why you picked her up in the first place,' specified Ginger Tom. 'And what really happened between you when you stopped for lunch. And why you broke off from a practice round to chase her out of the Old Course and molest her in the street.'

'I'll send you the answers on a postcard.'

'We want them today, Mr Saxon,' he said, levelly.

A look passed between them. Ginger Tom got up and withdrew to a corner of the room where he took out his cigarettes. His colleague chose a different tack.

'What distance would you expect from a 3-wood?'

'Is this another of your trick questions?' I asked, sceptically.

He was hurt. 'No, sir. I'm interested.'

'With a 3-wood, on a good day – 230 yards or more.'

'How is it that I can't get within eighty yards of that?' he sighed. 'My problem is keeping the clubface square to the ball at the moment of impact. I generate plenty of power but I waste it.'

'Common fault, Inspector.'

'My club pro says the shape of my swing is all wrong. I've tried everything but I still keep hooking too often. My club pro says I must draw the ball from right to left. He's advised me to watch certain tournament players to see how they do it.'

'You can always learn from studying the top boys,' I agreed.

'One of the people he mentioned was you, sir.'

I tensed. 'Look, where is all this leading?'

'He thinks you have the perfect swing. Almost poetic, he says.' Robbie scratched his bald head and smiled. 'He also says that you're a good outside bet for the Open.'

'So?'

'You're a golfer's golfer, sir. All the pros rate you highly.'

'So?'

'Do you remember that theory of mine?'

'Yesterday it was a gut reaction.'

'It's firmed up a lot since then.'

Ginger Tom came back into the conversation. 'We have reason to believe that the murder is directly linked with your chances of winning the Open. Somebody wants to nobble you, Mr Saxon.'

'They're going the right way about it,' I conceded. 'But why *me*? I'm no certainty. I'm not even the favourite. There must be fifteen or more players with as good a chance of taking the title.'

'Fifteen or more if the weather stayed calm throughout the championship.' observed Robbie sagely. 'But it won't, sir. There'll be high winds. I don't need to tell you about the north-westerly that howls in from Guardbridge. It can be sadistic. Given those conditions, the Old Course will separate the men from the boys. In my view, only a handful of players will have a realistic hope of winning.'

Ginger Tom read the names off the clipboard. 'Horton Kincaid, Alan Saxon, Yokuri Tanizaki, Jeff Piker, Orville Hume and Ulrich Heidensohn.'

'Stick Brad Devereaux down as well,' I suggested.

'At his age?' queried Robbie.

'Do you know how much he's made on the US Seniors Tour this year? Never write off Brad. Besides, veterans have led the way home before. Old Tom Morris was forty-six when he won his last title. Harry Vardon was forty-four when he became Open Champion for the sixth time.'

I noticed Ginger Tom adding another name to his list.

'How do you get along with each of those players?' asked Robbie.

'As well as I can, I suppose.'

'No bad blood between you and any of them?'

'Duels at dawn, you mean?'

'I think you understand me, sir,' he replied patiently. 'You do seem to have a talent for making enemies in the game.'

'And the odd friend or two,' I said defensively. 'Horton and Jeff, for instance. They're old mates. Brad is Brad, of course. A real loner. Nobody gets close to him. Orvill? Well, I can take him in small doses but that American college boy manner of his gets right up my nose after a while. Tanizaki doesn't speak a word of English and since my Japanese is a bit limited we don't exactly have long chats.'

'Heidensohn?'

'Let's just say that I wouldn't want him to marry my daughter.'

They had a silent conference. Ginger Tom took over.

'What did you do after you left here yesterday?'

'Went round to the Scores Hotel and slept like a log. When I woke up, I played nine holes with Jeff Piker. In the evening I went to the old champions dinner and then back to the hotel for an early night.'

'Did anything happen to you?'

'Happen?'

'Anything unpleasant.'

'Yes. I had half of Fleet Street after me and crowds staring as if I was some kind of sex beast let out on parole.'

'That wasn't quite what I meant, Mr Saxon.'

'Things don't come more unpleasant than that, I can tell you.'

I then recalled the incident in the competitors' car park. That had been chilling.

'Well?' pressed Ginger Tom, sensing something.

'No, Superintendent. Why do you ask?'

'Because you played rather well yesterday, I gather.'

'Four strokes below par for the nine holes,' I said, happily. 'Could have been five but for a spot of bother at the Heathery Hole.'

Robbie smiled admiringly. 'Could even have been six.'

'Eh?'

'You were robbed of another birdie by that spine running through the seventh green.'

'How do you know?'

'That's immaterial,' rejoined Ginger Tom, puffing out smoke. 'The point is that you were in excellent form. In spite of everything.'

'I don't follow.'

'Whoever tried to scupper your challenge in the Open has failed. You've proved that you're still in there fighting.'

Realisation dawned on me and my mouth slowly opened.

'Yes, Mr Saxon,' he confirmed. 'You're still a target.'

My mind was racing. 'Hang on, Superintendent! Jeff Piker had the same score as me. Heidensohn shot a 68 in the morning. Why aren't they in danger as well?'

'Perhaps they are. But we have to operate on facts and what is certain is this: the person, or persons, who had a go at you on Monday night will be back for a second crack. *If* you continue to play well.'

Robbie spoke low. 'And you must, sir.'

I was quicker on the uptake this time. 'You want me as live bait on the hook,' I yelled, jumping to my feet. 'No deal. Find another worm.'

'It has to be you,' explained Ginger Tom. 'There's a reason why you were singled out and we have to learn what it was.'

'Yes! By dangling me in front of this maniac and shouting, "Come and get him!" Forget it, gentlemen. Include me out.'

They waited quietly while I stalked around the room. Ginger Tom finished his cigarette, stubbed it out and lit another. His colleague scratched his bald dome with his index finger. They were giving me time to calm down and assess my position more objectively.

Their ploy worked. My anger cooled. I became rational.

'How am I supposed to play my best golf with a threat like this hanging over me?' I argued.

'You'll manage it,' assured Ginger Tom.

'You're Alan Saxon,' said Robbie, seriously. 'It's in character.'

'To lay my head on the block?'

'No, sir. To keep going. To let nobody and nothing stop you from doing what you want to do. You've got tremendous willpower.'

Ginger Tom smirked behind his cigarette. 'Yes, your father said something like that about you only he put it a different way. He said you were bloody-minded.'

He was right. It came from living with him.

'So what do I have to do, Superintendent? Carry a bodyguard in my golf bag? Fit a walkie-talkie set to my sand wedge?'

'You just have to go your own sweet way, Mr Saxon.'

'With a few of your lads keeping an eye on me.'

'Very discreetly. You won't notice them.'

'I hope not,' I warned. 'Tell them to keep their distance.'

'Don't worry.' He killed another cigarette in the ashtray. 'Right. Let's get on with it, then,' he said, rubbing his hands.

'I can go?'

'When you've given us that second statement, Mr Saxon. The one that fills in all the gaps. After that, you're a free man.'

I liked his macabre sense of humour.

When I had given them the statement, had it read back to me, agreed that it was an accurate record of what I had said, and signed it, I was taken along to Ginger Tom's commandeered office. He showed me a list of the items that had been taken from Carnoustie to be sent off to the forensic laboratory. I quailed. The list covered two whole pages of foolscap. They had confiscated my bedsheets, my pillows, my pyjamas, my curtains, my Kleenex tissues, my television set, my supply of hock, my bottle opener, my address book, some of my crockery, even the little carpet I had fitted around the seats in the cab. I could not bear to read full details of the casualties. It would be much easier to get into Carnoustie and see what, if anything, had *not* been taken.

I was asked to sign at the bottom of each page to show that I approved the loan of the items. Suppressing the urge to refuse, I took out my pen and scrawled my name once more. This time it triggered off a memory.

'That autograph book, Superintendent . . .'

'Yes, we've been in contact with the young man from Liverpool who owned it. He *was* up at Royal Birkdale for the Open last year but has no recollection of the album being stolen. He said he thought he'd lost it.'

'Oh. Well, I daresay he'll be glad to get it back.'

'Afraid not. Reckons he's lost interest in golf now. He's into snooker instead.' Ginger Tom beamed importantly. 'That's my game.'

'I wish it was mine as well!'

When I got to the courtyard, I was in for another shock. Carnoustie was in a terrible state.

She stood there looking hurt, helpless and abused, like a chicken with half of its feathers pulled out. To the bruising she had suffered in the collision in Edinburgh had now been added more severe damage. Her offside panels were badly dented where she had struck a tree as she keeled over in the ditch. The front coachwork had been dented as well, just below the roof line.

Damage to the paintwork was extensive and the offside wing mirror had been twisted out of shape. The wheels were clogged with mud and they had churned it up to spatter the lower half of the bodywork. Along her rear, for a couple of feet on both sides, was deep scoring immediately below the window levels. It was as if she had reversed by mistake into a cavernous mouth and had been bitten by giant teeth as the jaws closed.

The interior was even more depressing.

Carnoustie had been ruthlessly stripped of all the personal touches I had given her to make her into a home. She looked less like a motor caravan with five years of loyal service behind her than a tentative prototype awaiting modification. A faint smell of chemicals hung in the air to remind me that she had undergone a thorough internal examination by practised fingers. Just like Janie – or whatever the girl's real name was. Carnoustie and she were two of a pair. They had both been defiled. Professionally.

To set against the losses were some hideous gains.

Though my vomit had been cleaned up, I could still detect its stink as it mingled with the odour of chemicals. What was much more overwhelming, however, was the sense of unnatural death that pervaded the place. On the double bed which had now been folded neatly away, a young life had been taken with calculated violence. The outrage seemed fresh and pungent and unpleasant to touch. Like wet paint that does not know how to dry. I could hear the girl's voice, I could see her naked body on the green grass, I could feel her hair as it brushed my shoulder. I could share her panic as her breath was strangled out of her. I had picked her up at a motorway service area and I would be giving her a lift for ever.

I wondered if I would ever be able to sleep in there again.

With an effort of will, I drove away.

As soon as I pulled up outside the hotel, I knew that it had been a mistake to go back to collect my things. I was spotted at once and had to push my way past dozens of bodies and questions to get to the hotel steps. By the time I reappeared with Clive in tow, the crowd had swelled appreciably and been infiltrated by news reporters and photographers. Cameras clicked away at random as I put my luggage into Carnoustie and a young woman with a portable cassette recorder and a lot of nerve forced her way through to me, thrust a small microphone under my nose and asked me for a comment. I made none.

Even when I got back in my vehicle, I was not safe. The cameras assaulted me through the windscreen and the young woman tried to open the door to strike up a conversation. Clive was doing his best to clear a path so that I could drive away but he was hopelessly out-numbered. I revved the engine, beeped the horn and inched forward. The crowd came with me. Just as I was about to lose my temper, I was rescued. Gordon Reeman materialised from nowhere with some security guards. They were sturdy men in the company uniform and they made short work of the obstruction. Gordon controlled them like a master shepherd and had a path cleared for me.

I gave him a thumbs-up sign and moved off.

Media coverage of the murder had been comprehensive. We had made the front pages of most nationals and eaten up even more space in the local Scottish newspapers. Television and radio showed similar interest and made the details of the crime into common knowledge. A beautiful medieval city, already under siege by armies of golf fans, had had to withstand a supporting force of newsmen and their equipment.

I found myself wishing for another Falklands crisis or embassy siege or royal wedding. I would even settle for an IRA attack on the House of Commons. Anything to divert attention from me.

When I left St Andrews and headed south-east, I was haunted by the notion that I was being followed but my driving mirror remained clear. To reassure myself, I twice made sharp turns into side-roads where I lurked in wait for my pursuers. Nothing. No sign of Ginger Tom's men or news reporters or prying cameras. Most important of all, there was no sign of any would-be assailant coming back for seconds.

I continued on my journey, amusing myself with the thought of how close the radio reporter at the hotel had come to losing both her microphone and her respectability in one eloquent gesture from an embattled golfer.

Bra-a-a-ark! Bra-a-a-ark!

I had forgotten how pugnacious the sound was.

Bra-a-a-ark! Bra-a-a-ark! Bra-a-a-ark! Bra-a-a-ark!

It used my eardrum as a punchball and would not be denied.

'Hello?'

'Alan? Can you hear me, you bastard!'

'Fiona.'

'I've been trying to ring you since yesterday morning when I heard your sodding name on the car radio. Where've you been?'

'Trying to—'

'Who cares, anyway. Look, I'll make this short and sweet. Goodbye.'

'But Fiona . . .'

'Naked girls in the back of Carnoustie! And you swore to me that you needed to be on your own up there.'

85

'It wasn't like that. When I—'

'So much for all that mental preparation you were going to do. When you left me, you picked up the first pair of tits you found. I hate you, Alan Saxon. I hate you.'

'Don't say that,' I pleaded. 'I could use a lot of love right now.'

'Bullshit.'

'My darling . . .'

'You're full of bullshit.'

'Listen, there is an explanation for—'

'Tell it to the next bloody hitch-hiker you meet.'

'Fiona . . .'

'And don't bother to come back to the flat for your things. I've thrown them out through the window.'

I was alarmed. 'Including my clothes?'

'They were the first to go.'

'But you can't just—'

'Goodbye and good riddance, Mr Saxon.'

The receiver was put down with a vengeance at her end.

It had not been one of her fonder farewells.

As I turned into the road that led to the farm, I reflected how typical it had been of Fiona not even to refer to the murder which had put me on her car radio in the first place. In her codex, murder was a forgiveable crime. She would have condoned arson, blackmail, bank robbery, kidnap or high treason in a lover and she would have rushed to assist him in embezzlement or tax evasion. But infidelity was to her a capital offence. Summary justice had occurred in Northampton.

I had been hanged, drawn and quartered, then evicted through the window of her flat. She lived on the fourth floor.

In less than a minute, a relationship which had lasted for over six long, savoured, sensual months had bitten the dust. I was pained.

The farm came into view and I slowed down.

'Good morning.'

'Aye.'

'Nice day.'

'Aye. Aye, it is.'

'I wondered if I could borrow your hose, please?'

'Ma hose? Aye.'

The farmer ambled off about his chores. He was a big, solid, slow-moving old man in working shirt, jeans and gumboots. Though he and his wife had given me a warm welcome on Sunday evening, I had been worried in case I had worn that welcome out. Some landlords would not take kindly to the idea that their tenants are caught up in a gruesome murder that has been splashed across the nation's newspapers and television screens. My anxiety had been unfounded. The farmer had given me a long, bovine stare and then accepted me back without comment.

Country people are not easy to shock. They live closer to the realities of birth and death. They take them in their stride.

I drove to the farmyard and parked beside the power hose that was coiled up on the wall of the milking parlour. After making sure that the windows were up, I gave Carnoustie a high-pressure shower and tried to restore some shreds of dignity. The jet of water made a loud drumming sound as it played over her bodywork and the noise brought the farm dogs yelping around the corner of the barn. They watched me excitedly until the job was done and then scampered in the small lake I had created.

Carnoustie looked both better and worse. While the shower had brightened and freshened her up, it had also exposed an array of minor scratches and dents that had been hidden by the dirt.

I took her to the privacy of her field and started on the second stage of restoration. Leaving windows and doors open so that the breeze could blow right through, I washed and scrubbed every inch of her interior with disinfectant. She seemed to appreciate it. When everything had dried, I put a shine on her surfaces with some Pledge.

After all this, I could still smell the vomit.

Relieved to find that my motor atlas had been spared by the police, I took it into the sunshine, sat on the grass and searched for the map I wanted. The East Neuk of Fife. A

87

great wedge of land to the north-east of the county that thrusts out into the sea like the head of some gigantic fish. The names in this region sing sweetly in the ear – Largo, Dunino, Earlsferry, St Monans, Newton of Balcormo, Ardross, Kilrenny, Cambo, Stravithie, Drumeldrie, Backmuir of New Gilston, Lochty, Lundin Links and Kellie Castle.

I had to force myself to concentrate.

When I had planned my route, I drove Carnoustie back through the farmyard and on towards the main gate. The farmer approached in his tractor and shouted above the rattle of its engine.

'Ye were not in last night, Mr Saxon.' He made it sound as if I had rented a room, not a two-acre field. 'Ma wife missed ye.'

'I stayed in St Andrews.'

'Aye.'

'Cheerio.'

He raised a finger in farewell and went on past me. I headed north-west in order to avoid the bottleneck of St Andrews again and found myself in pleasant country roads that twisted and criss-crossed at will. I left the East Neuk and drove on to Leuchars, pausing near the fine old Norman church to check my bearings. I located the road I wanted and eventually came to the quiet lane that branched off it.

I reached the spot where we had been on Monday evening.

The ditch was narrow but deep and ran alongside a mixed hedge that was reinforced from time to time with wooden stakes and broken by the occasional tree. It was against one of these trees that Carnoustie had leaned when she went into the ditch. She had left her mark on her accommodation. Some branches had been snapped off and the hedge had been bent inwards towards the field behind it. Lumps of earth had been gouged from the side of the ditch.

I searched carefully but saw no skid marks and no trace of any obstacle that would have taken her impact head-on and stopped her in her tracks. Evidently, she had been rolled into position, using the tree as a pillow on which to rest her head. It had been a rigged accident. Most of her wounds could be accounted for by her position in the ditch, but the scoring along her rear on both sides defied explanation. She must have been backed into a space that was not quite big enough to take her and which had spikes or barbed wire.

The place was totally secluded and no passing motorist could possibly have seen the accident from the main road. I was even more convinced that the anonymous caller was the murderer himself. I trembled as I realised that he might even have used my own telephone.

Still puzzling about the scored bodywork, I walked on down the lane to see if there was a small entry into which Carnoustie might have been reversed. I soon came to a turning and followed the new lane until it gave out on a clearing. In the distance, across the fields, was the dark forest of Tentsmuir. A sign told me that it housed a nature reserve and bird sanctuary.

I was about to walk on further when I felt the same sudden fear that had touched me in the car park after the old champions dinner. Somebody was watching me. It could be one of Ginger Tom's squad of detectives, I considered, but quickly dismissed the idea. The policeman would be there to protect me, and what I sensed was quiet menace.

Without rushing, I strolled slowly back towards Carnoustie. I looked casually all around but saw nobody. The area offered a thousand hiding places. I had no hope of seeing him. My feeling of dread eased as I got closer to Carnoustie and I began to wonder if the whole thing was not some trick of my imagination. The azure sky was fringed in white cloud, the sun was warm, the trees and grass were swaying in the breeze and the birds were twittering happily all around. I was gradually reassured. Whatever danger I had been in was now past. I was completely alone.

I was safe.

After running my finger along the scoring on Carnoustie's side, I took out my keys and unlocked the door. I was just about to climb in when the shot rang out, cutting through the tranquillity of the countryside with brutal unconcern.

The bullet missed me by a foot and thudded into a front tyre, making Carnoustie sag in pain. I dashed around behind her for cover and waited for the next shot. It did not come. After a few minutes, I heard a distant car start up and pull away.

I examined the flat tyre and decided that it had been the target. The marksman had missed me on purpose. This time. It was a warning.

Chapter Five

Wednesday afternoon brought the crowds out in their thousands and they swarmed over the Old Course to watch their favourite players in action, to test vantage points for the morrow, or simply to wallow in the unique atmosphere that builds up on the eve of an Open Championship. They behaved with that strange mixture of reverence and enthusiasm that characterises British spectators and sets them apart from more raucous and demonstrative galleries in other parts of the world. Relaxed and spontaneous, they were nevertheless taking the occasion very seriously. Like the competitors themselves, they were at a dress rehearsal. Postcards and prints of the Old Course tend towards a standard view. The photographer and the artist stand side by side on the first green, feature the ancient stone bridge that spans Swilcan Burn, then look down the double fairway to the clubhouse itself, showing that noble building in isolation, monarch of all it surveys.

The prospect had vanished completely.

Huge grandstands hemmed in the clubhouse and the R. & A. tent loomed up to the left. Beyond it was the press tent, a vast, billowing place in which serried ranks of golf correspondents would man their telephones as they stared up at the giant television screens and scoreboards. The buildings to the right of the fairway as viewed from the first green were transformed into impromptu grandstands with faces at every window and bodies on several roofs. A catering tent could be glimpsed, even some portable toilets. Scaffolding towers to hold the television cameras further altered the prospect. The generous expanse of double fairway was now an apron stage on which melodrama and minor tragedy could be played out.

I prefer the postcards and the prints.

Over a hundred and fifty golfers were due to compete in the Open and almost all of them had now arrived in St Andrews. Pressure for practice rounds was now much greater and the luxury of a twosome was out of the question. When I reached the course in the late afternoon, I learned that I was partnered by Body Beautiful and Jeff Piker. The company of two friends at that point was a welcome solace.

Body Beautiful looked, as usual, like an advertisement for a new line in golf wear. He sported light blue trousers and a dark blue sweater over a medium blue shirt. Even his shoes had a tinge of blue. Jeff Piker had gone for a red sweater and eye-catching check trousers. Beside the two of them, I felt under-dressed in my fawn sweater and matching slacks.

I was grateful for the crowds. Although they still stared at me as a murder suspect rather than as a golfer, I found their presence heartening. They were my security. On my own in a quiet lane I might be at risk; here I was protected. I still had to contend with the problem that had been set by the bullet in Carnoustie's tyre. Did I accept the warning or did I defy it?

I had to play badly if I wanted to stay alive.

Jeff Piker was first away with a zooming drive.

'Good shot,' nodded Body Beautiful.

My own tee shot was well short of Jeff's but I still collected the polite compliment from our partner. Over the first few holes, however, I quickly lagged behind. Jeff got seven 'good shot' awards to my two and a 'well played' at each green. I began to fight back. Nothing was going to make me play badly on a golf course if I had the power to play well. By the turn, I was putting my game together much more effectively and had managed two birdies. Jeff had contrived three and led at the halfway mark.

The homeward trek was a revelation.

While Jeff and I maintained our standard of golf, Body Beautiful seemed to change gear. He raised his game to a level that I had never seen him achieve before. His tee shots found extra yardage, his approach shots greater accuracy, his short game more control. But it was his attitude that really impressed. He tempered his bounding enthusiasm with ice-cool deliberation and showed a new maturity and bite. By the time we reached the Long Hole, he had snatched the lead and was forging ahead.

Body Beautiful was fulfilling his promise at last.

A practice round is very different from a tournament. Most golfers use it as a chance to get on intimate terms with a course and to work on certain shots. If they have difficulty with a certain hole, they may stay there to iron out the fault, waving through any players who catch them up. In a practice round, in short, you play yourself.

Body Beautiful had altered that. His game had taken such flight that it brought out the competitive streak in both of us. Instead of playing ourselves, we tried to catch him. Our pursuit was in vain. He arrived at the Road Hole with a cushion of four strokes and had improved it to five as we moved across the eighteenth tee.

I felt humbled. Here was a man without a single tournament win of any consequence in his professional career beating two experienced golfers with apparent ease. Body Beautiful's last success, in fact, had been as an amateur when he won the President's Putter, the Oxford and Cambridge Golfing Society's annual match-play competition at Rye. Yet now he was asserting his superiority over a former Open Champion and the best golfer in Australia. He had come of age.

The Tom Morris Hole underlined this fact.

His tee shot was exemplary. Following the traditional advice, he aimed at the clock on the clubhouse wall and had the satisfaction of seeing his ball land just beyond Granny Clark's Wynd and to the left of the fairway. His second shot was bungled. In attempting a full pitch to the green, he mishit badly and sent his ball right into the middle of the Valley of Sin, the wide and treacherous hollow just in front of the left half of the green. Both Jeff and I found the green with our second shots and so it fell to our opponent to play first.

Body Beautiful produced the shot of the day. After

carefully pacing the distance to the flag and noting the impish burrows on the way, he played a firm stroke and ran his ball at speed along the ground. Spectators behind the ropes and on the terrace broke into applause as it dropped into the cup. We needed two putts apiece to finish.

He had shot a round of 67. We were nowhere.

Nairn MacNicol summed up our feelings with a muttered aside.

'If he plays like *that*, he'll be Open Champion.'

Success had an odd effect on Body Beautiful. It put more than a touch of condescension into his remarks to us and his beaming friendliness had gone. He had a self-congratulatory air about him as if he had sprung a well-kept surprise on us and caught us out.

Jeff was sceptical. 'How many flukes did you count, Alan?'

'None.' I was being honest.

'He can never turn it on again like that.'

I looked across at Body Beautiful who was preening himself on the terrace as members told him how magnificent his final putt had been. Somehow I did not see his victory as a flash in the pan. When the real tournament began, he would be a serious contender for the title. I thought of our earlier round together. Had he been holding out on me?

I knew one thing: I liked him better when he lost.

The journey back to Carnoustie promised to be another ordeal and I decided on a sprint from the exit. It proved unnecessary. A detail of stewards had been assigned to escort me across the road and make sure nobody followed me into the car park. They even waited until I drove out in case I met trouble.

Traffic was thick at the top of Golf Place and I had to take my turn in the queue. Up ahead of me on the right-hand pavement was a gaggle of people making a lot of noise and jostling each other. It was only when I got closer that I saw what was happening. Ulrich Heidensohn had come out of Tom Auchterlonie's golf shop on the

corner to be engulfed by his fans. Most of them were
teenage girls and several had autograph albums or
programmes to sign.

Heidensohn was in his element. He joked with his
admirers, signed everything that was put into his hands,
and waved away the help of the policeman who strolled
towards him. With the West German, however, was
someone who was patently not enjoying the scene. He was
a tall, pale, hard-faced man in his sixties with iron-grey
hair cut short and combed straight back over his head.
The cast of feature suggested that he too was German, but
he did not share his fellow-countryman's love of female
adulation. He kept pushing the girls away from
Heidensohn and when one of them jumped forward to
plant a kiss on the player's face, the old man grabbed at
her. Heidensohn moved on and the rest followed.

As I was still mulling over what I had seen, I noticed
something that made me sit up so smartly I stalled the
engine. Leaning against the window of the golf shop and
pointing a walking stick in anger after the departing crowd
was Dubby Gill. I could not believe it.

Before I could make certain that it was him, traffic
coming into Golf Place blocked him from my view and I
was beckoned forward by the policeman on point duty. I
had to turn the corner and drive on.

My mind was a jumble of images. I thought of Body
Beautiful basking in his victory, Jeff Piker as baffled as I
had been. The helpful stewards. Heidensohn showing off
in front of his fans. His scowling companion. The girls.

Janie's face intruded. When I last saw her alive, *she* had
been one of Heidensohn's girls. I remembered the
miniature golfer on his sweater. A present from an
admirer. Janie? Or had she told him her name was
Lynette?

One image finally dominated. That of a frail figure
propping himself up against a shop window and venting
his spleen with what little strength he had left. Dubby Gill
had been dying in an armchair on Sunday evening. Could
it really have been him?

The question nagged at me so much I doubled back and drove to the old stone cottage. Beth Gill flung open the door when I knocked and stepped back in surprise.

'Oh, Mr Saxon!' My notoriety had struck again.

'Hello, Mrs Gill. I've come to see Dubby.'

Any qualms about me were lost in a rush of emotion as she burst into tears, clutched at my arms and pulled me into the passage. 'He's gone, Mr Saxon. Desmond has gone!' A note of pleading came into her voice as she tried to exonerate herself from blame. 'I slipped out shopping for an hour. We have to buy food, Mr Saxon. I can't watch him every minute of the day. While I was out, Desmond must have left.'

'I think I saw him, Mrs Gill.'

'Where? Where?' She clutched at me again.

'Near the Old Course.'

'I knew it!' she wept, bitterly. 'He said he would.'

'Said what?'

'I must go to him, Mr Saxon. I must find him.'

'Just tell me what he said,' I insisted gently. 'Then we'll both go and find him.'

She looked up at me. 'That German player . . .'

'Heidensohn?'

'Desmond read about him in the paper. He hates Germans. He said a German should never be allowed on the Old Course again. He said . . .' She used a handkerchief to stem fresh tears. 'He said he'd kill him.'

Dubby was much more likely to kill himself.

'Come on, Mrs Gill. Let's bring him home.'

I took her out to Carnoustie and helped her in but our journey was a very short one. Before we got to the end of the road, a Vauxhall Carlton appeared with Gordon Reeman at the wheel. He saw Carnoustie, flashed his headlights in recognition, then drove past us to the cottage. Dubby was in the back seat of the car between two stewards. I reversed quickly and parked behind the Vauxhall.

'He collapsed in Golf Place,' explained Gordon.

'Why did you leave the house?' blubbered his wife,

taking an arm to help him into the house with the stewards. 'The doctor warned you.'

'Thanks,' I said to Gordon.

'He shouldn't be out in that condition, Alan.'

'I know.'

'Just as well some of my lads spotted him.'

'They've been on the ball today. Twice got *me* out of an awkward corner. Pass on my thanks.'

'All part of the service.'

We went inside to see Dubby being lowered into his armchair by Beth Gill and the two men. She was alternately chiding and soothing her husband but he heard nothing. He looked desperately tired and his eyes kept filming over. She put a cushion behind his head, tucked his blanket around his legs and fussed over him until he dozed off.

Gordon sent the stewards out with a nod. When he made to follow them, Beth crossed to him and touched his shoulder in gratitude. His clipped delivery for once had some affection in it.

'Keep him at home until he's fit and well again, Mrs Gill. They think a lot of Dubby at the R. & A. Marvellous servant to the place for all those years. Part of the scenery there. We don't want anything to happen to him.'

'I'll take care of him, Mr Reeman,' she promised.

But she was too late. Dubby tensed for a second, made a curious wheezing noise, then went completely limp. The effort of struggling out of the house in order to express a hatred had been too much for him.

He was dead.

Clive Phelps was understandably annoyed when I arrived late for our rendezvous. He had had well over an hour to rehearse his complaints and they came out in a long, reproachful stream.

'Where the hell have you been, Alan. I've got better things to do with my life than sit on my arse in a side-road waiting for you. Jesus H. Christ! I give you bed, board, advice, protection, the pleasure of my company and the supreme bloody compliment of my fiver. I even neglect my gainful employ to run your frigging errands for you! I mean, what more could I give you except my right arm and my left ball? And are you grateful? Like hell you are. Here am I, bending over backwards to help you, and you can't even do me the courtesy of rolling up on time for a sodding meeting. Well, just you wait, old son. Vengeance is mine, saith the golf correspondent. Open my paper tomorrow and read all about it. Extra! Extra! Alan Saxon an Ungrateful Turd. Gory Details.'

He paused to get his breath back and light up his cigar.

'Dubby Gill has just died,' I explained.

'I don't care if an entire regiment of the Queen's Highlanders has kicked the bucket. Where in the sacred name of Bobby Jones have you been, you inconsiderate swine?'

'Consoling his widow.'

'That is no excuse.' He pulled hard on his cigar until it glowed angrily. Then he reflected on what I had said. 'When? Where?'

'About an hour ago. At his home.'

'You were supposed to be *here*, not keeping a deathbed vigil.'

'Sorry, Clive, but Mrs Gill's need was greater than yours.'

He sighed in agreement. 'Poor old Dub. What happened?'

We were sitting in his car in a side-road a few miles out of St Andrews. I gave him a shortened version of events and he was as mystified as I had been when he heard about Dubby's peculiar behaviour outside the golf shop. It did not square with his memory of the man.

'He hated Germans? Since when? I've covered dozens of events at the Old Course when there have been fiendish Huns among the competitors and I didn't notice the head greenkeeper trying to attack them.' He tugged thoughtfully at his Victorian poisoner's moustache. 'Maybe he has a particular dislike of Ully?'

'Don't we all?' I murmured. 'His wife said that he read something in the paper about Heidensohn and that set him off. What beats me is how a crazy old man dragging himself along on a walking stick could even hope to get near Heidensohn in the sort of crowds we've had.'

'Try reading the papers, Alan.'

'I gave up that nasty habit when I made the front pages this week.'

'Pity. You'd have seen the advert.'

'For what?'

'Some promotional gimmick they dreamed up for Ully. It was in all the local rags. On the front page of the *Dundee Evening Telegraph*. Yes, beneath a rather unflattering photo of you, old son.' He flicked cigar ash nonchalantly through the open window. 'Ully was due to make a personal appearance at the shop to push a range of golf accessories that some Kraut firm has put his name on. In other words—'

'Dubby knew the time and place where he'd be.'

'All he had to do was hack his way past a hundred screaming females and batter Ully's brains out with his walking stick.' He became restive. 'I must make tracks.'

'But you haven't told me what I want to hear.'

'It'll keep.'

'Clive!'

'Teach you to be punctual next time. Oh, and while we're on the subject of next time, could we miss out on all the cloak and dagger stuff? I appreciate that you want to avoid public places but there's a much easier way for me to tell you things. Why don't I vamoose now and speak later on the telephone?'

'Because I want the bullet back.'

'If you'd been any later, you'd have got it. Between the eyes.'

I could see that he was only teasing me, getting his own back for being kept hanging around. Clive eventually tired of the game and decided that he might have some information for me after all.

'You do give me the bum jobs, Alan. First, I ask Ully

which of his lovely ladies gave him some potty little badge. Then you give me a bullet and ask me to find the gun that fired it.'

'Did you?'

'Why couldn't you do your own dirty work?' He stifled my protest with a raised palm. 'Oh, I forgot. You're travelling incognito.'

'Get on with it, Clive,' I urged.

'Don't rush me. I've gone to a lot of trouble on your behalf, old son, and you're going to hear a full, blow-by-blow account. Ready?'

'Ready.'

'Call number one was to the friendly neighbourhood gunsmith in St Andrews. A Mr Peppard. I asked him if he recognised the bullet. He immediately asked where it came from, so I told him I stumbled across it in the thick-pile carpet while walking through the restaurant at the Scores Hotel. Somehow I don't think he believed me.'

'Was he able to identify the bullet?'

'Oh, yes. It was from an automatic rifle. Unfortunately, he couldn't tell me which one. He specialises in sporting rifles, you see. However, he did know someone.'

'Call number two.'

'All the way to Cupar to meet a Jamie Vout who is something to do with the Fife and Kinross Small Bore League. Actually, he'd make his mark in the large bore league as well because he can talk the hind leg off a donkey. Mr Vout *thought* he knew which rifle had fired the bullet but he wasn't sure. So while he was trying to work it out, he gave me a potted history of firearms and introduced me to the joys of bolt action, delayed blowback, cannelure, rimfire and smokeless powder. In the end, he hazarded a guess about the bullet and then suggested I try a friend of his in Tayport.'

'Call number three.'

'After a not too pleasant drive in a stuffy car.'

'I'll pay for your petrol, Clive. Now, you got to Tayport . . .'

'And discovered that Mr Matthewson lives there but

works in Dundee. So, it's on to his office there, near the city centre.'

'What does he do?'

'By day, he's an accountant with a firm called Hill, Matthewson and Ruddock; but by night he's an expert on military firearms.'

I was taken aback. 'Military?'

'It's no ordinary bullet, Alan. Matthewson was tickled pink when he saw it. He knocked off work an hour early and I followed him back to his house in Tayport. House? It's a bloody arsenal. Singlehanded, that man could back the PLO. As for the books he's got . . .'

'So what's the name of the rifle?'

'I told you not to rush me,' said Clive, taking a ring-top pad from his pocket. 'I've written it all down. The bullet is from a Heckler and Koch automatic rifle. Pause for background details. After the last war, the Mauser factory at Oberndorf was emptied by the French who carted everything off as war reparations. The buildings stood idle until the 1950s when arms manufacture got going again in West Germany. This new firm of Heckler and Koch took over the premises. At the time, the Bundeswehr were looking at a rifle that had been offered to them by a Dutch company but they were naturally keen to grant the licence to a home-based firm. Heckler and Koch got that licence by dint of a weapon called the Gewehr 3 and this G3 entered service in 1959. Are you still with me, Alan?'

'Every inch of the way.'

'There have been many variants of the G3 and Matthewson knew them all. The basic model has plastic butt and fore-end, is in 7.62 mm NATO calibre, and holds a 20-round magazine. Some versions have sighting telescopes and some have lightweight tripods as well. Matthewson reckons your bullet is from a sniper version and dated it in the mid-1960s. The model number is here.' He tore off a page and handed it to me. 'So there you are, Alan.'

'Where?'

'You were shot at by a German Army rifle.'

I hunched my shoulders in a question. 'Who says I was shot at?'

'Okay, have it your way. When you cracked open your boiled egg this morning, you found the bullet inside. And *that's* why you had me running around like a blue-arsed fly and why there's a new tyre on Carnoustie.'

'Thanks for all you've done, Clive. You're a real pal.'

'Then let a real pal give you some advice. Go to the police.'

'No way.'

'Alan,' he rejoined with concern. 'You're not playing with an amateur here. He gets into your motor caravan, knocks you out, commits a murder, then takes a pot shot at you with an automatic rifle. What do you suppose he does for a finale?'

'I won't give him the chance to show me,' I vowed.

'You're a marked man, old son. So why not take the bullet along to the cop shop and tell them everything?' When I shook my head, his voice became impatient. 'There's such a thing as withholding evidence.'

'I know. I've been doing it for years.'

'For God's sake, Alan, the coppers are there to protect you,' he argued through a haze of cigar smoke. 'Why don't you trust them?'

'You must meet my father some time.'

'I've got a feeling I will. At your funeral.' His eyebrows met in an arch of consternation. 'We go back a long way together. I'd like to think we could go a long way forward as well.'

'We will,' I assured him, squeezing his arm.

'Then use your loaf. Don't take risks.'

'You know me, Clive. I always play my natural game. And that involves taking chances. In my experience, boldness pays off.'

'On the golf course, maybe. But this is different.'

'Not in my book.'

'I hope you live to write it, old son.'

'Oh, I intend to, don't worry. I'm a survivor.'

Clive took the bullet from his pocket and held it

between his thumb and index finger. 'Not many people survive these.'

I put the bullet on the palm of my hand, studied it for a few moments, then clenched my fist and punched him playfully. He followed me as I got out of the car and walked over to Carnoustie.

'If you need me for any more chores,' he said plaintively, 'try to remember that I have a job to do as well.'

'I will,' I promised. 'And by the way, Clive . . . This may be small return for all you've done for me, but a gambling man can always use a hot tip. If you've got another five to spare, stick it on Tim Quentin.'

He was astonished. 'Body Beautiful?'

'That's what I said.'

'Alan, this is an Open Championship not a Mr Universe competition. Body Beautiful will go out on that course looking fantastic and miss the cut after thirty-six holes. As he usually does.'

'We'll see.'

I got into the cab and switched on the engine. Clive came up to the open window and gave me that sinister grin I know so well. It is the smug look on the face of a Victorian poisoner as he gazes down at another victim. Clive had more to tell me. He had saved the best bit right to the end.

'This may or may not be relevant . . .'

'Spit it out, Clive.'

'Mr Peppard let it slip. Remember him?'

'Call number one. The friendly neighbourhood gunsmith.'

'He knew at once why I'd come to St Andrews.'

I gave a derisive laugh. 'Hardly an inspired guess. Everyone's here for the same reason this week.'

'But not everyone is wearing this,' he boasted, fingering his tie. Clive was very proud to be a member of the Royal and Ancient Golf Club and always wore its tie when he was in Scotland. 'Peppard asked me if I knew any of the top brass down at the R. & A. When I said I did, he told me that one of them was a regular customer of his.'

'Who?' I switched off the engine at once.

'Ian Calloway.'

'Ian!' It seemed so unlikely.

'Yes. Last man I could envisage with a gun in his hand but it shows you how wrong you can be. Never judge a sausage by the skin, Alan. Shooting is Ian's hobby. When he's not organising a tournament, or sitting on one of his committees, or flying off around the world on behalf of the R. & A., he likes to relax with a sporting rifle. He's good, too. Peppard reckons that Ian is a crack shot.'

I gave an involuntary shiver.

After stopping for petrol at a garage and for food at a village shop, I went straight back to the farm. It was beginning to feel like the only secure place I could be. I drove right to the middle of my two acres and looked through the windows on all four sides of my home. Comfortingly large areas of rough field grass were all around me like a green moat. I was content.

As I made myself a light tea, I assessed the day's takings. An unsettling interview with Ginger Tom and the golfing Inspector. A sad reunion with Carnoustie. A fiery parting of the ways with Fiona. A return to the farm for a thorough wash, clean and brush-up. A visit to what I assumed to be the scene of the crime. The feeling of being watched again. A warning bullet. The practice round with Jeff Piker and the New Body Beautiful. Ulrich Heidensohn outside the golf shop. Delirious female fans. The hard-faced old man. Dubby Gill enraged. His death at the cottage. My rendezvous with Clive. The shock news about Ian Calloway.

I had had less eventful days.

In every way it had been a time of shifting relationships. My instinctive rapport with Carnoustie had gone. The lovely Fiona had hurled me out of her life. Body Beautiful had changed from being an amiable companion into a gloating rival. Dubby Gill's death had robbed me of a long-standing friendship and turned me into a chief support of a grieving widow. And Ian Calloway looked different.

My relationship with the general public, of course, had been quite transformed by Monday night's adventures. When you wake up in a motor caravan next to the dead body of a young girl, nobody is going to believe you were an innocent bystander. The facts were simple. I gave her a lift. She ended up on my double bed, naked, abused, murdered. Every picture tells a story.

I had been framed like a golfing print.

What perplexed me was the way the girl herself had vanished into thin air. After climbing into Carnoustie and setting in motion a whole train of disasters, she had disappeared. Janie, the student of psychology from Bristol University, had become Lynette, the hitch-hiker in the young couple's Renault 5. I felt certain that she would become somebody else very soon.

Changes of identity all around me. The awful sense of the ground trembling beneath my feet. The conviction that there would be many more changes to come. I wondered who would be next.

Horton Kincaid? Nairn MacNicol? Ginger Tom? Clive even?

Only my father would remain immovably the same.

When I finished my meal, I did the washing up and put the crockery away. I caught sight of my face in the shaving mirror above the sink and stared at it with growing disquiet. I, too, had changed. For the worse. My teeth were clenched, my jaw tight, my skin pale and dry, my forehead puckered and my eyes shadowed with dark pouches. I had the tired, hunted and unloved look of a man on the run.

The change had been total. I had left Northampton in the perfect frame of mind and I was now a bundle of fears and neuroses. For the first time in years, I had been quietly confident that I could mount a serious challenge for the Open title and other people had been of the same opinion. What price my chances now?

In a world of shifting relationships, the most basic one of all had been altered. That with myself.

As I felt the seductive pull of morbid introspection, I

shook myself hard and went outside into the fresh air. The only way that I could make amends to Janie was to find her killer; the only way I could make amends to myself was to win the Open Championship.

On a sudden impulse, I got the tartan blanket out of Carnoustie and laid it out on the ground near the corner of the field. I took three-dozen golf balls to a point some sixty yards away and began to aim at the target with a sand wedge. My first few attempts were well short, so I lengthened both the backswing and the follow-through. I was soon hitting the blanket regularly. When I had worked my way through the balls, I went off to collect them up, found a new angle and distance from which to aim, and went through the process again.

It was a simple exercise but enormously cleansing.

I kept myself at it for well over an hour before gathering the balls into the blanket. Only then did I realise that the farmer was watching over a hedge with the neutral curiosity of a dairy cow. I strolled over to him and smiled.

'Practice makes perfect,' I explained.

'Aye.'

'After that little session, I'll have no qualms about my wedge shots on the Old Course tomorrow.'

'Tomorrow?' he said in surprise.

'First round of the Open.'

'Aye, but . . . the pepper . . .'

I could see his point. Many players in my position might feel that they would be better off withdrawing from the championship. Being mixed up in a sensational murder case is not a recommended way to improve your golf. But I was obeying certain imperatives and could not just turn my back on the event.

'Which paper was that?' I asked.

'The pepper,' he replied, as if there was only one. 'Tel'gruff.'

I deciphered it as the *Dundee Evening Telegraph* and recalled what Clive had told me. I asked the farmer if he had last night's edition and if I could possibly borrow it.

'Aye.'

'Shall I come up to the farmhouse for it?'

'Ma wife'll bring it to ye. Nae bother.'

He sauntered off and I went back to Carnoustie. In no time at all, his wife came out with the paper, handed it to me in silence and went away. She met her husband at the gate and they exchanged a few words as they looked back at me. I waved the paper.

'I shall be in tonight,' I called.

They nodded in unison and headed for the farmhouse.

I sat in Carnoustie and studied the newspaper. It was the first time I had really dared to see how the story was being handled in the press and I was soon wishing I hadn't bothered. Beneath the banner headline *Death Riddle at Open* was a brief summary of the facts and a few quoted remarks from Ginger Tom. My name seemed to crop up in every other sentence and the picture of me they had printed did nothing to allay suspicion.

Captioned 'Golf Ace Saxon', it had been taken out of a group photograph of former champions at the 1978 Open at St Andrews. I was one of six kneeling in the front row and the camera had caught me when I blinked. What the readership of the newspaper got, therefore, was an image of a man with a strained smile closing his eyes in embarrassment. Because I was in mid-shot, the arms of the players either side of me were seen and it looked as if they were detectives escorting me away.

The camera never lies.

At the bottom of the page was a boxed advertisement for the personal appearance of Ulrich Heidensohn to promote a range of golf accessories. A head-and-shoulders shot of him gave us a grinning, carefree face with the arrogance completely gone. No doubt about it. He was certainly more photogenic than me. And while I was only an ace, he was 'Ully, Golfing Megastar'.

I flipped through the rest of the paper and was halted by yet another photograph of Heidensohn. This time he was on the tee, driving a ball with vicious power, his blond hair blowing in the wind. The article about him spoke of his startling progress on the US Tour and tipped him as the man most likely to beat Horton Kincaid in the Open. But the real interest of the piece was in the last paragraph. It told how a coach party of fans from his home town of Braunschweig had come to St Andrews to support their local hero. The trip had been organised by Heidensohn's uncle – 'a retired officer from the German Army'.

Bra-a-a-ark! Bra-a-a-ark!

How good was Uncle with an automatic rifle?

Bra-a-a-ark! Bra-a-a-ark!

Was he the grim-faced man I saw outside the golf shop?

Bra-a-a-ark! Bra-a-a-ark! Bra-a-a-ark! Bra-a-a-ark!

'Yes?' I said, snatching up the receiver. 'Who is it?'

'Rosemary. How are you, Alan?'

I knew that she would ring sooner or later but the call still made me recoil. As soon as I heard the calm, well-modulated voice of my ex-wife, I felt despair creeping up on me.

'I asked how you were.'

'Having a ball.'

'There's no need to be facetious, Alan. Are you alone?'

'No, I'm being held down by four policemen.'

'You are alone, then,' she said smoothly. 'Good. We can talk. I've been rather anxious about you. As you might expect.'

Rosemary only ever contacts me for one of three reasons. To check that I've paid the school fees. To see if I've remembered the date of Lynette's birthday. And to express anxiety. On balance, I prefer the school fees call. It never lasts more than thirty seconds.

'Are you listening to me, Alan?'

'I'm afraid so,' I sighed.

'Now don't start all that again. I'm trying to offer sympathy.'

Rosemary's sympathy can be very lowering. 'Thank you,' I croaked.

'You must be going through a dreadful time.'

It had begun the moment I answered the telephone.

'We were shocked at first, naturally,' she continued. 'I mean, none of us realised that you were in the habit of picking up stray girls on motorways.'

'Rosemary, it is not a *habit*,' I corrected.

I should hope not. You see now where it can lead . . . Anyway, we began to feel desperately sorry for you and to imagine the kind of ordeal you must be enduring. So I decided to ring.'

'Thank you.'

'I must say, we were staggered to read in *The Times* today that you still intend to compete in the Open. Is that altogether wise?'

'No,' I conceded.

'Then why not withdraw?'

'Because I can't.'

'I believe that you can and should. So does Daddy. He sends his regards, by the way. Oh, and a message. If you need a good lawyer, he can fix all that for you.'

'I'm sure,' I said under my breath.

'So will you now pull out of the Championship?'

'No, Rosemary.'

'Now don't be stubborn about this. I'm certain that it would be the best thing all round. Apart from anything else, you have to think of the reputation of the Open itself . . .'

That was her father's phrase. Rosemary didn't care two hoots about the Open. Or about any other golf tournament. Daddy, as usual, was putting words into her mouth.

'Have you thought it over properly, Alan?'

'I'm playing tomorrow,' I affirmed. 'It's my job.'

'You don't need to remind *me* of that,' she rejoined. There was a pause, then her tone softened. 'Is there anyone at the moment?'

'No, Rosemary.'

'That poor creature you picked up on the motorway . . .'

'*No*, Rosemary.'

'Oh well, that's a relief,' she said, easily. 'Of course, you have only yourself to blame. This situation would never have arisen if you didn't insist on driving around in that caravan like a gipsy. I hope this has taught you a lesson. Stay at a good hotel in future.'

'I can't afford a good hotel.'

'There are medium-priced establishments.'

'I like it *here*.'

'After all that's happened?'

I controlled myself before answering. 'Goodbye, Rosemary.'

'This is going to come as a blow to Lynette. She's always rather looked up to her father.'

I could feel the knife being turned in the wound.

'The only consolation is that she's missed the worst of it by being abroad. But she'll have to know everything when she gets back.'

'I'll explain to her,' I mumbled. 'Where is she now?'

'Still in Italy. Switzerland next, then on to Germany. She's going to be disappointed in you, Alan. It's inevitable.'

'I know. Goodbye now.'

I put the receiver down and took several deep breaths. Rosemary always had this effect on me. It made me wonder again why I ever married her. Yet I did. We were both still paying for the mistake.

Golf had brought us together and golf had torn us apart.

We first met one Saturday afternoon in leafy Staffordshire. I was playing in a tournament at Little Aston, one of the finest parkland courses in the Midlands. The clubhouse is approached via Roman Road, a private way that runs through an estate of large, lovely, luxurious houses that stand in their own grounds and invite the local nickname of Millionaire's Row. Late for my tournament, I came racing around the edge of Sutton Park in my old Morris Minor and swung in through the gate at the end of Roman Road.

Nobody had warned me about the speed bumps.

When I hit the first one, I thought the car was going to fall to pieces. The impact was sickening; it sent two hub caps bursting off their wheels and caused a loud rattle under the bonnet. I screeched to a halt just in time to miss the second lethal speed bump. Out of a driveway up ahead came a stately figure on a grey horse. She was in full riding kit and the sun, slanting down through the avenue of trees, shone on the gloss of her boots and the horse's flanks. Full of concern when she cantered up, she relaxed when she saw I wasn't injured and then she noticed the hub caps.

We laughed. Not a polite laugh of relief but a long, hysterical, almost uncontrollable giggle that made the horse shy. It was a shared laugh that saved all the bother of introductions.

The girl was Rosemary. I remember noticing that the mane of the horse was the same colour as my own hair. I went on to the clubhouse and was just in time. Rosemary vanished.

Little Aston Golf Course starts in parkland, then strikes out into heathery country before returning to the parkland. It is always superbly groomed and a delight to play on. I was in form that day. When I reached the seventeenth hole with its lake on one side and its green plateau beset with bunkers, I saw someone watching me from the distance. She was still in jodhpurs and hacking jacket but had removed her riding hat to let her fair hair hang free. I won the tournament.

It became my favourite course for a while.

We were married in the little church nearby.

That same tall girl who had ridden up to help me could now jangle my nerves without even trying. I had become the old Morris Minor and Rosemary was the speed bump. When we met in any conversation, I always lost a hub cap or two. And there was no longer shared laughter to ease my pain.

I took the receiver off its hook. I was out of reach.

In her usual poised, well-bred way, Rosemary had stirred up my guilt with a vengeance. The thought of having to admit to Lynette that I had lost the miniature golfer had been daunting enough. How could I tell her that her present to me was a key element in a murder inquiry? Lynette had given it to me as a good luck charm and it had worked. With it, I had had a run of success; without it, I had found misfortune.

I sat there wondering how Lynette would first learn about the mess in which her father had landed himself. It would hurt her deeply and I wouldn't be there to soothe that hurt. I could count on Rosemary to use it as a means of drawing our daughter closer to her and further away from me. All I could hope was that the matter would be cleared up before she came back to England.

'Still in Italy. Switzerland next, then on to Germany . . .'

I heard Rosemary's voice again and the words bit harder.

'Then on to Germany . . .'

I wished it could have been anywhere else in the world.

Night brought its own problems. No sooner had I set up the double bed than I saw the naked body stretched out on it. I wrestled with my torment for a long while, then put the bed away again. Crawling deep into my old sleeping bag, I spent the night on the floor.

A flapping sound awoke me. I thought at first that it must be a bird, caught up somehow and beating its wings against Carnoustie to escape. I checked my watch. It was 7.25 a.m. Other sounds made themselves known. A stiff breeze whistled. Birds were chattering over a late breakfast. Cows were being milked in the parlour. A lorry was going past on the main road.

I got up and took down the makeshift curtains from the rear window. The day was bright and fresh and I was all alone in my two acres. Yet the flapping continued. I pulled on clothes and went outside. Trapped under my windscreen wiper and teased by the strong breeze was a newspaper. I took it inside and smoothed out its wrinkles, assuming that the farmer must have left it there for his guest. When I saw that it was the newspaper for which Clive Phelps wrote, I turned at once to the sports pages. He had promised me a mention in his preview of the Open but I was not prepared for the feature article and large photograph.

SAXON ANGLES

Who *is* Alan Saxon? Take your pick. He has been the Great White Hope of British Golf and the spectacular flop. He has been the scouge of the US Tour, the media personality, the voice in the wilderness. He has been winner, loser, saint, sinner, favourite, outcast, champion and chump.

So who *is* Alan Saxon?

Let me nail my colours to the mast. I believe he is the one man who can beat off the awesome challenge of American might in this year's Open Championship at St Andrews. I believe that he has the skill and guile and sheer guts to put a British name on the trophy again. I believe that Alan Saxon, the original has-been, can make a triumphant comeback.

Who is Alan Saxon?

He is the man who has been there before. When he won the Open at Carnoustie on the toughest course I have ever seen in all my years as a golfing correspondent, he showed the world that he had arrived with a bang. He went on to gain some remarkable victories on the US circuit and looked set to dominate the game for years to come. What went wrong? The reasons are all too familiar and need not be dwelt on here. The salient point is that Alan Saxon is back in form. He is once again the man most likely to trounce the Americans . . .

There was much more in the same vein. Clive was backing me to the hilt. By the time I finished the article, he had almost convinced me that I *could* go out and win the Open again. Under any other circumstances, his piece would have been heart-warming and uplifting. It would have sent me out on to the Old Course with greater zest and determination.

Instead, it aroused a cold panic.

The farmer had not left the newspaper for me. It had been delivered by the hand that had been on the trigger of an automatic rifle. And on the throat of a defenceless girl. I was being given another warning. I was being told to prove that Clive Phelps was wrong.

Who is Alan Saxon? The man who must *not* win.

When Clive had written the article, he had done so as a good friend and as an acute observer of the game. But he did not know the plight I was in. I read through the piece again and imagined what would happen if I did fulfil his hopes for me and stage a major comeback.

I would win the Open and lose my life.

Unwittingly, Clive Phelps had signed my death warrant.

Chapter Six

The first day of an Open is always a very special occasion. Tension is at a peak among the players and nerves are taut as they make their initial bid for what is, in effect, the world championship of the game. Officials are on their mettle and golfing correspondents from every corner of the globe watch with eager anticipation to see if their private hopes and public predictions blossom. There is an infectious air of excitement about and you can feel a great, surging, collective love of the game all around you.

Then there are the spectators.

Crowds steadily grow and are at their largest and most inflammable on the last day, but the true fans are in at the start. They know that an Open Championship is decided over four long days of golf and that the foundations of any later success are laid at the very beginning. They come to watch the whole event, not just the closing stages. They are there for the golf, not simply for the result.

As I waited in a queue to get to the competitors' car park, I could sense the familiar hum of golfing mania as herds of people converged on the entrances to swell the galleries already inside the Old Course. Though I was still the object of many suspicious glances, I also got a number of waves and shouts of encouragement from passing fans. Clive Phelps had obviously had a lot of readers that morning.

I parked Carnoustie and gave Nairn MacNicol a cheery salute as he came towards me. Three days of sobriety had taken years off him and he was looking more boyish than ever. He took possession of my clubs.

'How are the early birds doing, Nairn?'

'Struggling, Mr Saxon.'

'This wind is going to be a real headache,' I sighed.

'Ye'll be lucky to make par.'

I would be lucky to get through the four rounds alive.

Play had started at 7.30 a.m. and several competitors were already out on the course engaged in three-sided battles. Distant cheers and groans spoke of joy and heartbreak on the first green.

Security men arrived to escort us to the locker rooms. Since we had time in hand, I then took the trouble to seek out Gordon Reeman. He was my go-between with the police and there were some things I was keen to know about their activities. I found him on the clubhouse terrace, talking with his wife, a thin, handsome, middle-aged woman in a wheelchair. When he saw that I wanted him, he took me aside.

'Are you being properly looked after, Alan?'

'By your lads, yes.'

'Good.'

'As soon as I get within a hundred yards of this place, a guard of honour comes to my aid. Thanks, Gordon.' I glanced around. 'What I haven't seen any sign of so far is the police. Superintendent Ings said that there would be detectives keeping a friendly eye on me.'

'There are, Alan.'

'How many?'

'I've seen two so far this morning.'

'Can you point them out?'

'I'm not sure if that would be wise,' he said cautiously. 'Isn't it better if you don't know?'

'Where are they?' I insisted.

After a moment's consideration, he gestured towards the course.

'One of them is dressed as a steward and will help with crowd control as he follows you around. The other has a BBC armband and will be carrying a television camera.'

I was at once reassured and unsettled to know that Ginger Tom's men were at hand. The protection was welcome but my game would suffer if I became too aware of my minders. What I wanted to know was where the detectives had been when I really needed them. At the scene of the crime and during the night. I could have done with a steward who saw the man with the automatic rifle. I would have been glad of a television cameraman who nabbed my early morning paper boy.

'They know who she is now,' confided Gordon. 'That girl.'

'Oh?'

'She was called Veronica Willis.'

'Veronica?' It was a long way from Janie or Lynette.

'Lived with her grandmother in Southampton.'

'And?'

'Been unemployed for the last year or so.'

'*And*?'

'That's all they'd tell me, I'm afraid. Ginger Tom does rather like to hold his cards close to his chest.'

'Have they made any other progress?'

'He's being cagey about that as well.' He smiled and changed the subject. 'Splendid piece about you by Clive Phelps this morning. Sings your praises in real style. Got a copy of the paper in my office if you'd like to—'

'I've seen it, Gordon.'

'Good, good. It should put some fizz in your tail.'

'I need it,' I confessed. 'Well, I must go.'

'One last thing, old chap. Dubby Gill. I've taken care of all the funeral arrangements. Didn't know him that well but Mrs Gill has nobody else to help her. So I offered to do the necessary.'

'Very kind of you. When is the funeral?'

'Monday. I hope you'll be able to stay on for it.'

I spoke with genuine feeling. 'So do I.'

I knew that I would be at the funeral. In some capacity.

We paused to watch a young golfer addressing his ball on the first tee. He sent it shooting off down the fairway to modest applause. Gordon shook his head ruefully, glanced over at his wife, then turned back to me.

'I do envy you people, you know.'

'Why?'

'The rich pickings.'

'Wish you'd tell me where they are.'

117

'Four rounds of golf and you can win an absolute fortune.'

'That may be true for the Open Champion,' I corrected, 'but most of the field will have to settle for a hell of a lot less.'

'Even so . . .' He eyed me up and down, then suddenly became briskly jovial. 'Feel nervous?'

'No. I always tremble like this.'

'All the best, anyway.'

'Thanks.'

The transmitter beneath his jacket crackled into life and he took it out to speak into it. I waved a goodbye and slipped off to find Nairn. It was time to collect my thoughts.

Golf is played as much with the mind as with the body. I made an effort to summon up my full concentration and to forget all the things that might distract me. Ian Calloway's hobby. Ulrich Heidensohn's uncle. Rosemary's phone call. Clive Phelps's article. Dubby Gill's funeral. Gordon Reeman's envy. Veronica Willis.

I also had to forget a steward and a television cameraman.

Luck plays a part in all sports but it can often take on a leading role in golf, especially on a links course. Since weather is very much a determining factor, it helps enormously if you play during the mildest part of the day. At St Andrews that usually means in the morning because the wind tends to freshen as the afternoon draws on. The players taking part in the fifty-second and last game of the round at 4.35 p.m. were thus likely to have tougher conditions than we would experience at 9.15 a.m. Such is the nature of this unique game.

Playing partners, too, can make a significant difference. An excitable or garrulous player can be a severe handicap and a slow, deliberate golfer can test your patience to the limit. If you're teamed with someone who is out of form it can be a sore distraction, and if your partner is on song and strokes ahead of you then that, also, can have a dampening effect. In theory, professional golfers should not be

118

influenced in any way by their playing partner; in practice, they almost always are.

Fortune favoured me. For the first two rounds, I had drawn Horton Kincaid and Yokuri Tanizaki. I could not have chosen better myself.

They would be doughty opponents but congenial ones. Horton was the grand master of the game and I learned from him every time we met on a course. Tanizaki, the genial little Japanese player, was a wizard with the putter and the soul of courtesy. Neither man spoke much during a round and this suited me perfectly.

'Game number eleven. On the tee – Yokuri Tanizaki.'

A ripple of applause greeted the announcement and he drove his ball hard and to the left. Then he turned to the largest section of the crowd and gave them a polite bow that earned him another round of clapping. Tanizaki would repeat that bow at each hole. It was his acknowledged trademark.

Mine was pulling down the peak of my hat before each shot.

I began to wish the peak was large enough to hide me completely.

'On the tee – Horton Kincaid.'

The applause was long and loud as the grandstands gave the defending champion a warm ovation to acknowledge his special status in the game. Horton had been faithful to the Open throughout his career and had never failed to make the annual pilgrimage across the Atlantic. Some years he had not even taken enough prize money away to cover his expenses but it did not deter him from coming back for more and thereby setting an example to other American players. The spectators were telling him how much they appreciated his commitment.

After giving them his best John Wayne grin, Horton got down to business. He addressed the ball, shifted his feet until he was happy with their position, drew back his club in a huge arc, then unleashed a shot of devastating power. Even though he was driving into a headwind, his ball rocketed off down the fairway and finished forty yards or more beyond Tanizaki's.

In every way, Horton would be a difficult act to follow.

Butterflies played games in my stomach and my mouth

went dry as I took my driver from Nairn. I braced myself for polite, muted applause but it never came. As the official announced my name, the grandstands showed that they put golf before anything else.

'On the tee – Alan Saxon.'

It was sympathetic rather than ecstatic but there was an affection there that I had not dared to expect. Lifted by the response, I played a good tee shot and made off down the fairway with the others.

Nairn was right. The wind had decided to be a spoilsport. It was being very possessive about each hole, making the course seem much longer than it had been during my practice rounds. We had soon dropped a couple of strokes apiece and were beginning to wonder if there was any hope of reclaiming them.

Even the Loop, between the seventh and eleventh holes and by far the easiest part of the course, was in an ungenerous mood. Because they are flat, open and without blind shots, the eighth, ninth and tenth holes are particularly vulnerable but they had built new fortifications now. With consummate ease, they resisted Horton's power, my cunning and Tanizaki's magic touch on the greens.

It was dispiriting to realise that the more testing half of the round was yet to come. The one consolation was that other players were facing the same, or even worse, traumas. On the various scoreboards near greens and fairways was a sorry tale of disappointment, setback and occasional calamity. It soon became clear that only a tiny minority would finish the round under par.

While the Old Course presented me with a hundred big problems, it solved the giant one for me. I had left the farm in a quandary, not knowing if I should play or not. With all the pressures that were on me, how could I have any chance of doing myself justice in the first round? Besides, why should I continue to offer myself as target practice for a killer with an automatic rifle?

The Old Course answered my questions. As soon as I drove from the first tee, I was caught up in its spell and could think of nothing but producing the golf that it was demanding. Horton and Tanizaki endorsed the decision. By pitting their skills against the Old Course, they helped to carry me along.

Whether it was because we strengthened our attack or because it weakened its defences, I do not know but the journey home was more rewarding. Each of us picked up the strokes we had dropped and Tanizaki got additional birdies to go two under. Horton gave us a flash of true class by wresting a stroke off the Road Hole and then, with the wind at his back, reached the green of the Tom Morris hole with his tee shot. The ball explored the air for almost 300 yards and rolled the rest of the way, leaving him with two putts to end his round and earn another ovation. The Japanese player and I also managed a birdie to complete a gruelling four hours of golf with a flourish.

Tanizaki – 69. Kincaid – 70. Saxon – 71.

There would not be many lower scores in that wind.

We crossed to the terrace to receive a barrage of comment and congratulation. Although I was tired and strained, I felt more relaxed than I had done for days. We had come through a close scrutiny of our skills with some honour and everybody seemed to be going out of their way to be pleasant to me. The Old Course had given me my credentials back. I was accepted in the place where it mattered most.

'Well played, Alan!'

'Thanks.'

'All three of you did magnificently.'

Ian Calloway was wearing a club blazer and tie with smart flannels and gleaming shoes. As he talked lovingly about the course and the havoc it was wreaking on many scorecards, I found it difficult to accept that he could be connected in any way with the shot fired into Carnoustie's tyre.

What could he gain by frightening me out of the Open? Of all the people I had ever met, Ian was the one who was happiest in his work. He had a job he revered. He needed nothing else. I became ashamed that I had suspected him for a moment.

'Turning to other matters,' he said, his frown accentuating,

'I was very distressed to hear about Dubby. It was a blessing that you and Gordon were in the cottage when it happened. To help his wife, I mean.'

'It did rather knock the stuffing out of her.'

'So Gordon says. Which makes it all the more puzzling . . .'

'Puzzling?'

'Yes. I popped round to the cottage myself last night. Could only spare a few minutes but I thought Mrs Gill might appreciate it.'

'And didn't she?'

'Of course, but . . .'

'Well?'

'She must have made a recovery since you and Gordon were there. No tears, no moans. She was enjoying a cup of tea with the woman from next door as if nothing had happened.'

'Was Dubby still there?'

'No. After the doctor had signed the death certificate, the body was taken to the funeral home.' He ran a hand across his chin. 'I know that mourning takes strange forms sometimes and that bereaved people often act in peculiar ways but . . . quite frankly, Alan, I was a little shocked.'

'I think I would have been.'

'She made a bit of an effort as I was leaving – taking out her handkerchief and so on – but she was only going through the motions. I'm not saying that Mrs Gill was *glad* her husband had died. She just wasn't terribly upset about it either.'

The information prompted a question.

'Would it be possible for me to look through your archives?' I heard myself saying. 'That material from the wartime and just after . . .'

'Why?'

'Interest. Could I?'

'If you wish . . .'

'Later on today?' I pressed.

'It's going to be madly busy around here, Alan . . .'

'You could find me a quiet corner for half an hour.'

'I suppose so. What time shall we say?'

'Around seven?'

He was still not happy with the idea. 'Well, all right.'

'Thanks a lot, Ian.'

'I would like to know what this is all about, though. Why search through all those old photographs?'

I gave him a smile. 'To see a man about a dog.'

Detective-Inspector Lucas Robbie was loitering with intent outside the entrance to the car park. I had more time for him than for Ginger Tom but I could cheerfully spare both of them from my social diary. Robbie had the earnest, beetle-browed look of a man whose duty conflicts with his pleasures and he bore down on me as if uncertain whether to arrest or congratulate me.

'I wonder if I might have a word, Mr Saxon?'

'Depends what that word is, Inspector.'

'If it's not inconvenient, I'd like you to accompany me to the station, sir. Er, in your vehicle.'

I bridled. 'It's highly inconvenient.'

'Police work always is. We learn to live with it.' He allowed himself an off-duty smirk. 'You played well this morning, sir.'

'Were you watching me?'

'Tempo. That's what separates you pros from us ordinary mortals. Tempo. With you lot it seems to come so natural. Tempo, sir.' The smirk crumpled into a frown. 'Superintendent Ings would like to see you straight away. We've been making further enquiries.'

I glanced at my watch. 'But it's lunchtime.'

'You're welcome to eat at the station with us, sir.'

'Threats will get you nowhere, Inspector.'

He chuckled. 'Very dry, Mr Saxon.'

'Thank you.'

'Er, shall we go now?'

'Do I have any choice in the matter?' I asked pointedly.

'Of course. We can walk there, if you prefer.'

He did a passable imitation of my father and I saw that

the conversation was over. I led the way to Carnoustie. Robbie walked all around her as if seeing the vehicle for the first time before getting in. Having him as a passenger made a difference. Policemen seemed to know that we were coming and held back crowds for us. We reached the police station in less than a minute.

Carnoustie was not too pleased to be back in the courtyard and ticked in irritation when I switched the engine off. Robbie took me inside and conducted me to his superior's office.

Ginger Tom was standing behind the desk in his shirtsleeves. He was munching noisily and his Adam's apple was on the go. With a long, bony finger he indicated the plate of sandwiches on a side-table.

'Help yourselves, gentlemen.'

'I will,' said Robbie, picking up a plate.

'I won't, Superintendent.'

'Can we offer you some tea, Mr Saxon?'

'You can offer it,' I said, 'but I'll refuse.'

Ginger Tom crossed to the large china teapot and poured tea into three thick mugs. He set one down in front of me on the desk.

'Just in case you change your mind.'

Robbie was peering at the sandwich. 'What's in this, sir?'

'You're the detective.' Ginger Tom spooned sugar into his own tea and sat down behind the desk. 'We know who the girl is.'

'Oh?' I said, feigning surprise.

'Her name, as Mr Reeman will have told you, is Veronica Willis.' He glanced down at his clipboard on the desk. 'She was born in Gloucester in 1963. Her parents split up when she was still a baby and neither was very keen to have custody. She seems to have been shunted to and fro between the pair of them. When she was with the mother, there was always a new "father" about and her own father doesn't appear to have been a monk. When Veronica was ten, she was sent to her grandmother in Southampton for a short holiday. It lasted eight years.'

I was shocked. 'She was just dumped?'

'Yes. In fact, it was probably the best thing that could have happened to her. The grandmother, a Mrs Edbroke, at least gave her three square meals a day and made sure she went to school. Veronica was a bright girl and soon caught up what she'd missed. But she was a bit of a handful for the teachers. Identity problems.'

'It was tongue,' decided Robbie, licking his lips.

'Try the corned beef,' advised Ginger Tom.

His colleague went detecting among the sandwiches again.

'So what happened to the girl then?' I asked.

'Usual pattern. Trouble at school. Referral to the educational psychologist. More trouble. Another referral. More trouble. Another school. And that's where we came into the picture.'

'You, Superintendent?'

'The law. In this case, juvenile court.'

'What had she done?'

'Petty larceny. Couldn't stop pinching things.'

I thought about the miniature golfer and the autograph album. 'Why did she call herself Janie?' I wondered.

'It was one of the symptoms of her condition, Mr Saxon.'

'Symptoms?'

He tried a sip of tea, then added more sugar. 'She'd not long discharged herself from hospital when you met up with her.'

'What was wrong with her?'

'They've got some high-faluting term for it in her case history but what it boils down to is this – she didn't like herself. Hated her life, her parents, her name. She escaped by becoming someone else. On a compulsive basis, I mean. Role-playing.'

I nodded ruefully. 'And I got her performance as Janie, the student of psychology at Bristol University.'

'That was what put us on to her, Mr Saxon. The psychology touch. You mentioned that she'd talked to you about her course in some detail and described how she'd been observing in some hospital. It was true. Except that she was a patient not a student. The person handling her case was a Dr Jane Lorimer.'

'Where was this?'

'At a psychiatric hospital in Birmingham. On the Bristol Road.'

Janie. Student. Psychology. Bristol. It all fitted.

I felt an upsurge of guilt that made my head pound. It quickly converted into cold anger. I wanted more than ever to catch up with the man who had killed her and no amount of warnings would stop me.

Ginger Tom read my mind. 'We want him as well, Mr Saxon.'

'Do you have any other leads?' I demanded.

'We're pursuing various lines of inquiry.'

'Look, don't give me that,' I protested. 'Why do you people always have to hide behind those bloody clichés all the time? If you're on to something, let me know.'

'I was about to say the same thing to you,' he replied.

Still eating, Robbie came into the argument.

'We believe that you're concealing things from us, sir.'

'Now why should I do that?' I asked with heavy sarcasm.

'Your father had one explanation.'

'I don't want to hear it,' I snapped.

'No, sir. He said you wouldn't.'

'So what am I supposed to be concealing?'

'All sorts of things. Let's start with your fellow golfers. You've not exactly been honest about your relationship with them.'

'We're just good friends, Inspector.'

Ginger Tom elaborated. 'If someone is trying to prevent person A from winning the Open, it's because they want person B to succeed instead. The first possibility, of course, is that the man who attacked you in your motor caravan and murdered Veronica Willis may be person B himself. It was certainly someone fit and strong and a professional golfer comes straight into that category. Last time we spoke, I gave you a list of five men with a realistic hope of winning the title. You added a sixth. Think about those names, Mr Saxon. Think about them very hard. Kincaid. Tanizaki. Piker. Hume. Heidensohn. Devereaux. Are any of them capable of murder in order to win?'

'Yes,' I said. 'All of them.'

'Mr Saxon . . .'

'I'm serious. Every golfer wants to win the Open. It's the big one. The Holy Grail. When you get out on that course, the desire to be champion burns inside you like a forest fire. You feel you'd do anything – and I mean *anything* – to win. I'm not saying that those six men *would* kill their way to the title. But in their hearts they'd be capable of it. So would all the other players in the field.'

'Does that include you?'

'Especially me. There's a homicidal impulse in most sportsmen. Only it's usually known as competitive instinct.'

'I've certainly felt like murdering *my* playing partner out on a golf course,' confessed Robbie lugubriously. He asked for another offence to be taken into consideration. 'I once hurled a brand new putter into the middle of a loch because it let me down at a crucial point in a three-ball.'

'Take up snooker,' said Ginger Tom. 'Breeds self-control.' He drank more tea and flipped over a page on his clipboard. 'Who, then, is person B? We can rule out Kincaid and Tanizaki for a start because neither of them was even in this country on Monday night. That introduces the possibility that person B is working on their behalf.'

'No,' I argued. 'Horton Kincaid would never get mixed up in anything like this. He's the straightest man in the game.'

'What about his manager?'

'Ed Maserewa?'

'I'm told he's the sort of man who can swallow nails and shit screws. Is that a fair assessment?'

'No, Superintendent. Much too kind.'

Ed Maserewa was more than capable of committing a

murder but I could not believe that Horton would set him up to it. Once again, Ginger Tom guessed what I was thinking.

'Person B could be working on his behalf. And he might not even know about it. Maserewa has been in Scotland since Sunday.' He gave me a moment to clock the information. 'Now for the happy Jappy . . .'

'I see you're doing your bit for race relations.'

'Tanizaki has the reputation of being a friend to all the world but he's backed by a consortium of Tokyo businessmen. Their speciality is exporting to other countries but I'm sure they'd love to import the Open Championship trophy.'

Robbie selected a final sandwich. 'I don't need to tell you about the golf explosion in Japan. They're mad about the game. If Tanizaki could become the first oriental to win the Open, it would mean a tremendous amount to them.'

'Coming back to those other names,' said Ginger Tom. 'You've been holding out on us. Why didn't you tell us that you and Devereaux have had the gloves on? He's said some very scathing things about you in the American golfing press.'

'That's Brad,' I shrugged. 'I pay no attention.'

'And yet you wrote a long letter of reply to one of the magazines. Vitriolic stuff, too. You certainly didn't give Devereaux a vote of thanks. As for Heidensohn . . .'

'I admitted I didn't like him, Superintendent.'

'But you didn't mention the row you had last year.'

'Don't believe everything you read in the papers.'

'You almost came to blows, I believe. Over what?'

'Cheating.'

'You or him?'

'That bastard, of course. The rules say that you should play the ball as it lies. He was trying to—' I controlled my anger and spoke more calmly. 'Okay, Superintendent. I've fallen out with Brad. I'm not exactly bosom pals with Heidensohn. I soon get cheesed off with Orvill Hume. And I've even had the odd harsh word with Jeff Piker.

128

That doesn't mean that all four of them would want me out of the Open.'

'Then who would, Mr Saxon?'

An answer popped out before I could stop it. 'Tim Quentin.'

'Yes, we have his name under review,' explained Robbie. 'That was quite some practice round he played against you and Piker.'

I could not understand why I had singled out Body Beautiful.

Ginger Tom regarded me through narrowed eyes. 'At the risk of using another of our old clichés, this is an inside job. Person B is somebody within the enclosed world of professional golf. He could be a player, a manager, an agent, a caddie, an official, or even someone involved with the game on the manufacturing side. The point is this, Mr Saxon. You are on the inside; we are not. You are in the best position to get the information we need. All we ask is that you pass it on instead of suppressing it. Right?'

'Right,' I sighed.

'Mix with the players. Talk with their managers, their wives, their mistresses. Listen to the caddies, the officials, everyone. And tell us everything you find out, however trivial it may seem.'

'Run a sort of gossip column, you mean?'

'Person B is down at the Old Course somewhere. Help us to identify him.' He got a signal from his colleague. 'Ah, yes. Inspector Robbie has another theory about person B.'

'Don't tell me,' I quipped. 'It's a woman.'

'We discounted that possibility, sir, for various reasons.'

'So what's your theory?'

'More of a hunch, really . . .'

'It should go well with your gut reaction.'

'Let the Inspector speak,' ordered Ginger Tom.

Robbie crossed over to me. 'There's a person C as well.'

'We're looking for two of them,' confirmed his superior.

They chatted more informally for a while, trying to

probe me for details they sensed I was holding back. But I held on to my own clues tenaciously. They could have person B and person C with pleasure. But only when person A had finished with them.

It was mid-afternoon when the interview finally ended. The mug of tea which had been put before me had gone stone cold and acquired a dark, thick scum on its surface. Tired and hungry myself, I had become conscious of how weary they were from long hours and the punishing tedium of their investigations. All three of us were drawing on nervous energy to keep going.

Ginger Tom answered a telephone call, jotted down a message on a pad, then rang off. He put his coat on and walked me back to Carnoustie.

'New tyre?' he noted.

'I had a puncture.'

He pondered. 'Mr Saxon, you didn't drive down to the beach when you came to St Andrews, did you? Before Monday night, that is.'

'No. I'd have said so in my statement.' He raised a cynical eyebrow. 'Why do you ask?'

'Because we found sand in the treads of your tyres. When your motor caravan left the car park, it must have been driven to some part of the beach. There were traces of the same sand in the girl's hair.'

'I see.'

'Well, I must away. We'll be in touch.' He halted by the door. 'I almost forgot. Veronica Willis was born on July 22nd. She would have been twenty-one this Sunday. Let's give her a birthday present, shall we?'

He was gone.

Refreshed by a meal, a light sleep and the relative calm of the countryside, I felt able to take stock and plan ahead. I now had several clues to follow and theories to explore. What I lacked was the connecting thread to pull them all together into a recognisable pattern. I hoped that it would come if I persisted.

130

We had parked in a wooded area not far from the Pittscottie road and the drive back to St Andrews was not a long one. The city itself, however, made me crawl through heavy traffic before I got to my destination. Beth Gill was surprised to see me.

'Come on in, Mr Saxon.'

'Thanks. I just stopped by to see how you were.'

'I'm fine, really,' she said, leading me into the living room.

'Good. I understand that Ian Calloway called in last night.'

'Yes. And other friends of Desmond have been around. People have been so kind. It's very touching.'

Beth Gill was not the tearful widow of twenty-four hours ago. She was wearing a smart blouse and skirt and had been to the hairdresser. Her manner was now almost girlish.

But the major change had been in the room itself. It seemed bigger and brighter. Fresh air was blowing in through the window and lifting the flap of the clean white tablecloth, and I noticed that the picture over the mantelpiece had been replaced. Several things had been taken out, including Dubbie's armchair and the pipe rack that had been screwed to the wall beside it. Beth Gill had moved out all the memories of her husband and stamped her own character on the room.

'You'll stay for a cup of tea.'

'I don't really have the time . . .'

But she had already bustled into the kitchen and I could hear the kettle being filled. I took another look around and saw something which made me dart across to the little coffee table. It was a copy of Tuesday night's edition of the *Dundee Evening Telegraph*, the newspaper I had borrowed from the farmer and which had contained the news about the coach party from Braunschweig that was coming to the Open to cheer on Ulrich Heidensohn. When I turned to the correct page to check the article, I saw that it had been cut out.

Beth Gill came in from the kitchen.

'Did you want something, Mr Saxon?'

'Er, no . . . There's something missing from this page. I suppose that Dubby . . . that Desmond cut it out.'

'No,' she said firmly. 'I did.'

She motioned me to a chair, made polite remarks about the Open and said that she'd seen some of the day's play on television. Her features saddened whenever she mentioned Dubby but it seemed more of a reflex action than any indication of real grief. She made it sound like a distant death.

Tea came and the pleasantries continued. I asked her what plans she had for the future but she was very evasive. After the funeral, she told me, she would be going to stay with her brother in London. When it was time to leave, I put to her the question that I had really come to ask, doing my best to sound casual. I did not succeed.

'Do you remember that time you went down to the R. & A. last year to look through their archives?'

She stiffened. 'No, Mr Saxon. I don't.'

'Ian Calloway happened to mention it.'

'He must have got it wrong.'

'His memory is usually pretty reliable, Mrs Gill.'

'He's got it wrong,' she affirmed.

'According to him—'

'Why are you bothering me with all this?' she said, starting to get flustered. 'I never went there. Stop pestering me, will you?'

'Of course. Ian obviously made a mistake.'

'He did. Now, please don't say any more.'

'Mrs Gill . . .'

She swept up the tray, put the cups on it and took it out. I followed her into the kitchen and made soothing noises but they soon died in my throat. On the wall beside the kitchen table, and now neatly framed, was the photograph of the German prisoners of war working on the Old Course. The memento she had promised to throw away had pride of place in the room where she spent most time.

*

The long day's play was still in progress when I got to the clubhouse and a keen, forcing wind was continuing to cause difficulties. I felt sorry for the younger players making their first visit to an Open at St Andrews. Veterans like me knew what to expect from the Old Course but newcomers were having a baptism of fire. Several scores had gone up into the 80s and there had been many red faces leaving the eighteenth green. Everybody was praying for milder weather on the morrow.

Ian was still not eager to let me have access to the archives and I had to press my case before he finally took me to his room. On his desk were some leather-bound volumes embossed with gold lettering.

'I . . . looked them out for you just in case you came back.'

'Thanks, Ian. Be as quick as I can.'

'Maybe you'll tell me what you're looking for . . . afterwards.'

'Maybe.'

He left me alone and I got to work. The material was fascinating; I could have sat there all evening sifting through old programmes and press cuttings and photographs. Dubby cropped up from time to time, tending a green or mowing a fairway, and he had that jaunty, devil-may-care look that I remembered most about him in later years.

Eventually, I found what I was after – the material relating to the preparation of the course for the Open Championship in 1946. I came to a sequence of photographs showing people at work under the direction of the greenkeeping team. It was seven years since the previous Open, also at St Andrews, had been held and wartime neglect had left a lot of work to be done to get the Old Course up to its true championship standard. Local help had been augmented by the drafting in of German prisoners of war and it was the latter that interested me.

I soon recognised the four men on the wall of Beth Gill's kitchen. Someone had taken an almost identical picture of them. Gip, the white dog with the black markings, was sitting in the foreground and three of the men were busy at

133

work. The fourth, once again, was facing the camera. This time there was a suggestion of a grimace.

Almost a dozen photographs featured the same group of men and they seemed to have been taken over a period. Clothing was discarded in stages as the weather improved, though rules clearly forbade them from taking off their shirts as local people had done in some of the other photographs. Rough clearance work advanced steadily throughout the sequence. Two other changes were noticeable. Halfway through the collection, the German who was always looking at the camera had his right arm heavily bandaged. And from that point on, the dog, who had got himself into every earlier group, had disappeared.

I went through them again and tried to listen to the story they were telling. Somewhere in the photographs was the explanation of the weird behaviour between Dubby Gill and his wife. There was some link between four men doing rough clearance, a dog, a woman weeping in her kitchen, a retired greenkeeper abusing a German golfer, an article about a coach party from Braunschweig and a new hairstyle.

I thought I knew what it was.

Before I closed the volume, I took a closer look at the picture which matched the one in the cottage. The man who smiled up at Beth Gill's camera was now scowling with resentment as if something very unpleasant had just been said to him. Recalling the scribbled words on the reverse of Beth's photograph, I took this one gently by its edges and detached it from its mounting.

Five names had been written in blue ink.

Max. Gip. Otto. Karl-Jürgen. Franz.

I had made progress. Beth Gill was getting her smile from Max.

'What on earth are you doing here?' The door had opened without a sound and Gordon Reeman was glaring accusingly at me. 'Well?'

'Ian gave me permission.'

'Are you sure?' he asked, crossing to look over my shoulder at the photograph. 'What exactly are you up to?'

'I might ask the same of you,' I snapped.

'Security is my province, Alan.'

'Then go off and do your job,' I suggested, standing up to face him. 'I'm not trying to sneak in without paying. I haven't come here to nick the takings. And I'm not planning to vandalise the greens during the night. Okay? Now please leave me alone.

He walked slowly around the desk. 'Archives. What interest have you got in the archives, then?'

He met my gaze and for once we both let our dislike of the other show. Gordon nodded gently as if making some sort of assessment, then he strolled back towards the door. There was an arrogant, proprietary tone in his voice when he spoke.

'Very well. But hurry up in here and then get out.'

'You've no right to order me about,' I retorted hotly.

He swung round to look at me. 'Just do as I say.'

Before I could reply, he had closed the door behind me.

It had been a brief but jangling exchange. Gordon's mask had finally slipped and I had seen the face behind it. An angry, bitter, watchful, suspicious face that was lined by envy and darkened by malice. What had I done to make him stare at me like that? Where had his surface bonhomie gone? Was this the same man who had been so considerate to Beth Gill?

Why had he come into the room at all?

I put the photograph away and stacked the volume neatly with the others. Still thinking about my unexpected visitor, I walked to the window and went out on the iron balcony. The Secretary's room occupies a prime position at the top of the clubhouse and it offers a superb view of the Old Course. I stood there for some minutes, enjoying the prospect, letting the breeze flap at my clothes, reflecting on what I had found in the archives before I was interrupted.

When I left the office, I went back downstairs to thank Ian for letting me do my research. He was out on the terrace with a group of members but he moved aside with Ulrich Heidensohn as I approached. They did not see me and I stopped in my tracks when I overheard a snatch of their conversation.

Ian Calloway, the most English of English gentlemen, was talking in fluent German.

135

Chapter Seven

I looked up at a murderer but could not find his name. He refused to identify himself. For personal reasons. Perhaps he was too shy.

In the dying light of a blustery July day, I looked up at the leader board by the main entrance to the course and searched for a killer. If police theories were correct and my instinct was sound, then the person we were after, or one of them, was up there somewhere on the massive scoreboard. I had plenty to choose from.

LEADER BOARD

Holes	+Par–	Players	Score
18	–4	HUME	68
18	–3	TANIZAKI	69
18	–2	HEIDENSOHN	70
18	–2	KINCAID	70
18	–1	SAXON	71
18	–1	PIKER	71
18	–1	QUENTIN	71
18	E	DEVEREAUX	72
18	E	BRYMER	72
18	E	NICHOLSON	72

America setting the pace yet again. Japan in second place. West Germany vying for third spot with America. A double issue of Britain held apart by Australia, America, South Africa, New Zealand.

In the geography of success high above, I kept looking for a sign that said You Are Here. But it was invisible. The killer was stateless. I could still not decide on his country.

136

The Old Course had shown an imperious disdain. Only seven of the world's finest golfers had been able to break par and only another three had managed a par round. Off the leader board, scores went high and reputations were lowered. Only the cream had survived.

I ran down the names and weighed them in my mind.

The college boy grin of Orvill Hume. The lethal putter of Yokuri Tanizaki. The cavalier arrogance of Ulrich Heidensohn. A legend called Horton Kincaid. Me. The manic application of Jeff Piker. Body Beautiful, an enthusiastic upstart. Old foxery from Brad Devereaux. Elegance from the veldt with Vance Brymer. Percentage golf from Stu Nicholson.

Who was he?

'Nobody believed me. As usual.'

'I didn't believe you myself, Clive.'

'The proof of the pudding is on the leader board. You're there.'

'With three more rounds to go.'

'You can stay the pace, Alan. That's your secret. You play golf the way I screw – slow at first but with a sensational finish.'

'Is that what the barmaid thinks?'

'No,' he admitted with a sigh. 'She turned me down.'

'Denial is good for the soul.'

'So they tell me.'

Clive Phelps was pleasantly sozzled. He had joined me near the main entrance where I had been watching the identity parade. I still could not tap the right man on the shoulder. I sought his help.

'Who wants to win the Open the most, Clive?'

'Every golfer over the age of five.'

'From that list of names up there.'

He didn't need to look. 'Tim Quentin, the Body B.'

'That was my feeling.' I put an arm round his shoulder and walked him up towards the Scores Hotel. 'I haven't had a chance to thank you for that article. It was terrific.'

'Does that mean you've started reading newspapers again?'

'Only if there's fish and chips in them.'

There were several people about but I was no longer in hiding from them. The all-pervading wonder of the Open had rescued me, and I was being greeted as a golfer again. As Ginger Tom had suggested, I had stayed around that evening to mix and chat and ferret. I had found out a deal of scandal about other players' love lives and business involvements, but no hard facts about the murderer.

'Why have you got your arm around me?' asked Clive.

'Because you need moral support, old son.'

'It could excite rumour about us.'

'With your track record among hotel barmaids?' I laughed.

'Fair point.'

Even in the fresh air, his cigar was a health hazard and had me coughing at every step. When we reached the hotel, I moved a pace or two away. The atmosphere was nicer out there.

'Ask me.'

'Ask you what?'

'Go on, Alan. I can see a favour trembling on your tongue. Ask it. Then I can say no and go back to the bar.'

'It's such a small thing, really . . .'

'As the bishop said to the actress!'

'So I will ask. There's a coach party from Heidensohn's home town. Over here to watch him march in triumph down the eighteenth fairway on Sunday. I want their names, please.'

'Their *names*! Have you taken leave of your senses?'

'It wasn't a very large coach, Clive.'

'If it was a motorbike and sidecar, then it's too large for me. How am I supposed to get the name, rank and serial number of thirty or forty Krauts? This has got to be a joke.'

'Use your initiative, Clive. Tell the tale.'

'What bloody tale?'

'About the article you're hoping to write.'

He was baffled. 'Article?'

'On them,' I explained. 'Shouldn't be difficult to find out which hotel they're at. Make contact, show interest, get their names.'

'Anything else?' he asked, sarcastically. 'Shall I make a note of their shoe sizes and ask how many of them carry a Heckler and Koch automatic rifle?'

'Speak to the party leader. He's Heidensohn's uncle.'

'Badges, bullets, uncles! You do give me the peach assignments.'

I put an arm around him again. 'It's because you handle them so well,' I coaxed. 'Now, when you've finished that . . .'

'I haven't said I'll start it yet,' he wailed.

'Find out the address of every man on that leader board.'

'I can tell you that now. The R. & A. clubhouse.'

'Their private addresses. Where they're shacked up. Oh, don't bother with Horton. I know his pad. And we both know where Heidensohn is staying, don't we?' I slapped him on the back. 'Thanks, Clive.'

'What do I get in reward for all this?'

'The satisfaction of knowing that you helped a friend in need.'

'Bollocks.'

'Sweet dreams.'

He grabbed me as I tried to walk away. 'Don't leave me. Come on in for a nightcap or two.' I shook my head ruefully. 'It'll be okay this time. I'll walk you back to the car park afterwards.'

'I'm off now,' I insisted. 'Want to be in bed before dark.'

'So do I but she won't play ball.'

'Then ring your wife up and tell her you love her. That might take the edge off your ugly lust.'

I gave him a friendly pat on the cheek and left him to his cigar. Clive had protested but he would do the favours for me and do them at speed. I was glad to be able to stroll back to the car park while it was still light enough to see and be seen. When I got to Carnoustie, I peeped in through the windows as a precaution.

The ride home took me past five names.

Hume. Piker. Devereaux. Body Beautiful. Heidensohn.

In ascending order of priority.

I had discounted both Horton and Tanizaki and ruled out Vance Brymer because he, too, had not arrived in Scotland by Monday night. Stu Nicholson, a pensive New Zealander, was a non-starter in my estimation as well because there was no way he could expect to win the Open, even with Alan Saxon absent. Nicholson's safe and sound golf kept him in the money but out of the titles.

Hume. Piker. Devereaux. All possibilities. All strong personalities with blazing ambitions. But I could not see any of them committing a murder. Devereaux, perhaps. At a pinch.

Body Beautiful was a different question. He was the handsome stallion who had suddenly changed into a dark horse. It had clearly not happened overnight. He had been preparing for the Open for many months. Did his preparations entail sabotaging me?

Heidensohn was favourite. The miniature golfer linked him with the girl and his uncle might link him with a G3 rifle. Heidensohn was cold-blooded enough for anything. And what was his relationship with Ian Calloway? That was a new and disturbing element.

The light had faded when I reached the farm but the moon gave me enough guidance to park Carnoustie in the field and plug her in to mains electricity. I had begun to rig up the makeshift curtains when I had an intuitive feeling that I was being watched again.

While continuing to work away, I sneaked a look through the rear window and thought I glimpsed something behind the big hedge that ran across the top of the field, at an angle to the farm buildings. I needed no more encouragement. A claw hammer suggested itself as my best weapon and I tucked it inside my jacket before stepping out on to the grass. I carried a bucket and ambled off to the farmyard as if going for water. As soon as I made the cover of the buildings, I ditched the bucket, took out the hammer and sprinted towards the corner of the hedge. When I got there, I peered around very, very slowly.

He was by the tree, using it as a rest for his back.

I crept slowly over the grass, keeping low and staying tight to the hedge. The tree which helped him gave me shelter, too, and enabled me to come up on his blind side. I saw a dark, stocky figure in brown windcheater and trousers. There was no sign of any rifle but I was taking no chances. With surprise as my main weapon, I jumped at him and kicked hard at his legs. He went down in a ball but rolled over instantly and regained his feet with the ease of a trained fighter.

I raised the hammer and moved in.

'Now, go easy, Mr Saxon! I'm police.'

'We'll soon see . . .'

'Superintendent Ings sent me, sir.' He fumbled inside his windcheater. 'I've my warrant card right here.'

He *was* a detective. My fear became annoyance.

'I don't like being spied on,' I told him. 'Disappear!'

'It's more a case of protection, sir. Superintendent's orders, sir. I've to spend the night in that.' He indicated the enclosed cattle truck that stood on the edge of the farmyard. It had slits at eye level. 'I was only watching you from here until you turned in. Sorry, sir.'

I suddenly felt very sorry for him.

He had been quietly doing his job when the man he was trying to defend had attacked him from behind and threatened him with a hammer. For my sake, he was going to spend the night in a filthy cattle truck. He rubbed his leg where I had kicked him and forced a smile. He had a round, open face and looked ridiculously young. Or maybe it was just that he made me feel very old.

'How's the accommodation?' I asked.

'Stinks to high heaven, sir.'

'What do you do? Just stand there and train a pair of binoculars on me the whole time?'

'No, sir. We do it in shifts throughout the night.'

'There's two of you?'

He nodded. 'From midnight on. My mate'll be here directly.' He cleared his throat in embarrassment. 'Er, you'll not mention this to the Super, will you, sir? I mean, you're not supposed to know that we're about. I'd get a rocket if the Super found out that—'

'Don't worry. I'll say nothing.' A thought stabbed me. 'Were the pair of you on duty last night as well?'

'Yes, sir.'

'Then you saw who delivered my newspaper?'

'Of course. The paper lad.'

'Lad?'

'From Kingsmuir. He cycled up to the farm not long after seven. Delivered a paper there, then walked across to your motor caravan and left yours under the windscreen wiper. Then he cycled off. We assumed that you'd fixed to have it delivered.'

'Yes, yes, I did,' I said, covering. 'I asked the farmer.'

'Lucky to get a delivery this far out. That lad must cycle well over a mile from Kingsmuir.'

'What did he look like?'

'Scrawny kid with fair hair down to his shoulders. No more than fourteen or fifteen. But you'll see him for yourself tomorrow morning, if you want to.'

I intended to do just that.

'Right, well, I'm going to turn in,' I said.

'Good night, sir.'

'Good night. And – sorry about the leg.'

'My own fault for being seen. Er, you won't tell the—'

'Your secret is safe with me,' I promised.

After collecting my bucket from the farmyard, I went back to Carnoustie, catching a strong whiff from the cattle truck as I passed. While the idea of being under observation made me uneasy, it did mean that I was safe. At first I was peeved with the farmer for letting the police on to the premises without telling me but I soon came to see that he had little choice. Besides, he had been willing to let me stay on in my two-acre room. I decided not to tackle him about the police presence.

Supper was a cup of cocoa and another glance at Clive's article. Then bed. I had lain there for ten minutes or more before I realised that I was on the double bed. I flinched as I thought of the naked body of Veronica Willis with sand in her hair and a cigarette burn on her shoulder, but I resisted the urge to get up and put the bed away again.

Whatever crime had taken place in Carnoustie, it was still my home. I had to try to resume normality.

Like my two bodyguards in the cattle truck, the owl came out on night duty and broke the silence with its call. I listened to its wise old hoot until I fell gratefully asleep.

I was waiting for him early next morning a short distance from the farm so that our meeting would not be observed by the police. Rod Stewart came round the bend first and he followed, head down and feet pedalling hard. I recognised him at once from the description and he half-recognised me. Apprehension came into his urchin face as I waved him down. He switched off the transistor that was dangling from his paper bag and Rod Stewart stopped wailing. I tried to reassure him with a smile.

'Good morning.'

'Ah.'

'Did you deliver a paper to my motor caravan yesterday?'

He thought it over carefully. 'Aye.'

'Why?'

Another long think. 'Some fella gie'd it tae me.'

'Where was this?'

He pointed back the way he had come. 'Down there a wee way.' He seemed to be sizing me up. 'He gie'd me a quid.'

'There's another quid for you if you can describe him.'

'Aye,' he grinned as self-interest got the better of his fear. 'Big fella on a motorbike. Yamaha. Crash helmet and goaggles. Ah didna see his face.'

'What sort of age was he?'

The longest think yet. 'Old. Same as yerself. Mebbe more.'

'Is there anything else you can tell me about him?' I asked, ignoring the insult about my age. 'How did he speak? Was his voice rough or smooth? Educated or what?'

'Ah canny remember. Didna say much.'

'What kind of accent, then? Scots? English? American?'

'Oh, English . . . and sorta poash . . .'

I gave him the pound note and added a fifty pence piece.

'Bring me the same paper tomorrow and keep the change.'

He was pleased with the transaction. 'Aye!'

'Stick it under the windscreen wiper again – unless you remember anything else about the man on the motorbike. If you do, bang on the door for me. Okay?'

'Okay.'

'And don't breathe a word of this to anyone,' I ordered.

'Awright . . .'

He cycled off down the road and switched on his transistor again. Rod Stewart had been replaced by Culture Club and it was Boy George who led the way in through the main gate of the farm. I had my own newspaper tucked away in my pocket and brought it out to unfold it. As I went back to Carnoustie, I made sure that they would see it and assume that I had met the boy on my walk and collected my paper from him. If they saw me get a delivery one day and not the next, their suspicion might be aroused.

And I wanted to keep the motorcyclist to myself.

His age remained vague. To a boy of fourteen, everyone over twenty-five seems old. Again, my grey hair puts years on me so when he said the man was my age, he may have meant he was virtually pensionable.

My facts. He was big and he was English. His voice sounded posh to a Scots country boy. He rode a Yamaha motorcycle and got up early enough in the morning to read a newspaper, note an article of significance for me, and bring it to the farm by 7 a.m. Evidently, he could not live too far away. And he knew where I was staying.

Had he intended to deliver the paper himself and met the boy by accident? Or did he know that the farm was part of a paper round? I decided that he had come to act as his own paper boy but had stopped himself when he reached the farm.

He had sensed that the police were there to protect me.

He was dangerous. He knew more than I did.

White clouds filled the sky above St Andrews and the temperature had fallen. In the grandstands and among the galleries, there were more sweaters and fewer sunglasses than on the previous day. What was of crucial interest to the players was the fact that the wind had both softened and altered its direction. Instead of gusting down the first fairway into our faces, it was a firm but intermittent breeze at our backs. The Old Course had lowered its guard slightly. There was an opportunity to redeem the mistakes of the first round and respectabilise scores.

'Sure makes a change from last year, Alan.'

'That four-day heatwave, you mean?'

'Yup. Dried out the course till she was a beaut.'

'Hard, dry fairways and soft, watered greens. Royal Birkdale was just what the doctor ordered for you, Horton.'

'This ain't. Last year, I had that goddam course under the gun in every round. Not this one.'

'The bookies still have faith in you. You're still the 3–1 favourite. The punters are looking to you as the man to tame the Old Course and fill their wallets for them.'

'Well, that's why I'm here, Alan. To make dough for other folk.'

Horton Kincaid was angry. We were chatting as we walked out to the first tee and though his comments rolled off his tongue in a slow, Texan drawl, I sensed a rancour behind them. He was no longer as relaxed and imperturbable as he had always been before.

'On the tee – Yokuri Tanizaki.'

It was 1.30 p.m. Our second round began.

Whatever rage was smouldering beneath the surface, Horton did not let it affect his golf. He was the supreme professional who shut out everything else and brought his full concentration to bear on his game. His amalgam of raw power, nerve and instinct was soon paying dividends and he reached the End Hole three strokes under.

Tanizaki, too, was taking advantage of the milder conditions. His putting was superb. The greens of the Old Course are always a problem. Fourteen of them are double greens, immense stretches of close-cropped turf that roll and twist and curve at will. Even if you find a green with an approach shot, you may still have a huge putt left. Tanizaki gave a textbook performance. He drove carefully into prime positions, hit accurate iron shots near the flag, then putted with a blend of caution, confidence and sheer flair.

Inspired by their example and feeling much better in myself, I stayed in touch with them all the way to the Loop. At the tenth tee, I glanced up at the scoreboard and had an electric shock. Heidensohn, who was playing ahead of us, had completed the first nine holes in an astonishing 30. Six strokes under! If he could maintain that form on the back nine, he might even smash the course record for an Open Championship of '65.

I was galvanised into action. Heidensohn was charging to the top of the leader board with my lucky charm pinned to his sweater. He was riding on my share of good fortune and I wanted it back.

Horton and Tanizaki continued to play excellent golf but I somehow added another dimension to my game. Because the wind encouraged small, punched shots, I went down the grip on my 3-iron and, still using a full swing, got more control. I was sending the ball the same distance as before but it was flying lower with a reduced fade.

Nairn made his contribution, advising me on my line and steering me expertly past the unseen perils of bunker and rough. He revelled in my success and his little-boy features were aglow. An Open Championship is fought out between the caddies as well as between the players. The best British caddies tend to work for the Americans because they have a greater chance of success, but Nairn had always been loyal to me and that loyalty was now being rewarded as I went into a two-stroke lead over my playing partners.

Seeing that I was on a streak, the galleries got behind me and gave me the most wonderful encouragement on every shot. And there was another boost for me. As I prospered, Heidensohn was hitting problems up ahead and dropping strokes. Even the Road Hole was kind to me and the grandstands went delirious when I collected another birdie. The Tom Morris accorded me a long ovation when I sank my putt.

Alan Saxon – 67. Yokuri Tanizaki – 68. Horton Kincaid – 69.

Mine was the lowest round of the day so far and it caused a lot of activity in betting circles. From my starting price of 25–1, I now moved up to a flattering 4–1.

Nairn grinned like a schoolboy with an unexpected day off.

'Ye can do it, Mr Saxon.'

'There's still two rounds to go,' I reminded him.

'With me behind ye, man, ye could win!'

As well as a basic fee for his services, I had guaranteed Nairn ten per cent of my winnings. The first prize was £50,000 and he could buy a lot of his favourite bottled pastime with £5,000. No wonder he was giving the world his impression of the Cheshire Cat.

'Put it there, Alan,' said Horton, offering his hand.

'Cheers,' I replied as we shook.

'You really shot the lights out today.'

'Thanks. But you didn't play too badly yourself.'

'Aw, my touch is still not right. I missed birdies on the eleventh and the fifteenth. A guy can't expect to be in at the kill if he makes mistakes like that. No, I reckon I gotta put in some time on the practice ground.' He gave me a slow grin. 'Sure wish Yokuri would lend me that magic putter of his.'

'Yes. He was knocking them in with his eyes closed.'

We were in the locker room and Horton had come over for a brief word. Once again I sensed an unresolved anger in him but now it seemed to be tinged with sadness. We had known each other for many years and I decided to trespass on that friendship.

147

'Anything bugging you, Horton?'

'Bugging me?'

'I just get this feeling . . . I don't know . . . that something's on your mind. Is it?'

He glared at me as if he was about to hit me and I braced myself for the blow. But it never came. Horton's chest heaved as he took a series of deep breaths and a smile of regret touched his lips. He laid a hand on my shoulder.

'You ever had a manager, Alan?'

'Three of 'em.'

'What happened?'

'We fell out,' I admitted. 'Two were crooks and the other was something much nastier. So I decided to manage myself. I make a lot less money this way but at least I know it's all mine.'

He winced at the mention of money. 'I got no manager either.'

'What about Ed?'

'What about him?' he sneered.

'Well, I saw you arrive together yesterday . . .'

'That was yesterday!'

'Oh . . .' Anger was blazing in his eyes. 'Look, Horton, I'm sorry I spoke. Forget it.'

'That's okay. I guess I'm still sore about it. Mighty sore.' He walked away. 'Tell you about it some time.'

My brain started buzzing. Horton Kincaid and Ed Maserewa had been the leading double-act on the golf scene for years. It was inconceivable that they had split up. I ran through all the possibile reasons for the rift and came back to the obvious one.

Horton had at last found his manager out.

Further speculation was cut short by the fact that I had to give a press conference. My second round score had turned the spotlight on me and it had also vindicated Clive Phelps to some degree. For his sake, I was ready to face the interrogation.

Questions shot at me from a Gatling gun.

'How does it feel to be ahead of the Americans?'

'Was that eagle on the sixteenth the turning-point for you?'

'So what's your game plan for the next two rounds?'

'Have you altered the shape of your swing a little?'

'Why did you choose a 4-iron at the Long Hole when . . . ?'

'Who do you think will be in contention . . . ?'

'What went through your mind on the . . . ?'

'Are you as good a player as when . . . ?'

Clive Phelps finally got his question in at me.

'Can you win the Open Championship this year, Alan?'

'You tell me, Clive.'

Press laughter. Raucous, well-meaning, an in-joke.

I was glad when it was all over. Clive took me aside.

'Just like old times, Alan.'

'Yes,' I said, bitterly. 'Your colleagues will build me up in order to knock me down again.'

'Call your philosophy to your aid.'

'I tried but it won't come.'

He gave me a consoling grin. 'You made the mistake of winning the Open in your early twenties at the start of your career. Unless you'd gone on to bag other major titles regularly, it was bound to look as if Alan Saxon had gone into decline. Once you've climbed Everest, they expect you to do it again.'

'Whereas all I've managed since is Snowdon and Ben Nevis.'

'You won the Italian Open in May,' he reminded me. 'That must be almost in the Matterhorn class.'

I took his point. 'Have you done what I asked?'

'No.'

'Will you do it some time this afternoon?'

'No.'

'Clive, I need that information!'

'Find yourself another private dick.'

'It's vital to me!'

'Do you honestly think I'd neglect my valuable work on behalf of the great British golfing public in order to get you some addresses and count the heads on a German charabanc outing! My editor would have my balls off if I wasted my time doing that.' He thrust a piece of paper into my hand. 'So I didn't. Right?'

'Right.' He'd got everything I wanted. 'Now, one good turn deserves another . . .'

'This had better be good, Alan.'

'It could be dynamite.'

'Tell me more.'

'Kincaid is splitting up with Maserewa.'

Disbelief made him laugh. 'Aw, now, come on!'

'I had it from the horse's mouth. Kincaid himself. As opposed to the horse's arse, that is. Maserewa.'

'This has got to be some kind of a joke, Alan. Those two would never break up. They go together like Torvill and Dean. Or Little and Large. Or Marks & Spencer.'

'Not any more. I had it in the locker room. The happy couple have separated at last. It's true.'

'Scouts' honour?'

'Would I lie to you?'

His eyes glistened as he sensed an exclusive. 'I'll get on to this straight away. What do you think caused it?'

'That's what I want you to find out, Clive. And soon.'

'This smells good.'

'More than I can say for that bloody cigar.'

'If this tip-off is for real, I'll give up the cigars,' he said with alacrity. 'I'll even give up barmaids.' He considered this rash promise. 'Well, some barmaids, anyway.'

'Be seeing you, Clive.'

'And thanks.'

He went back to the press tent on air.

I glanced at the piece of paper he had given me. It contained all the addresses I had requested and a list of forty-five people who had come from Braunschweig to support the West German idol. I scanned the list quickly until I found the name I wanted.

Max Fleischner. It might not be his first visit to St Andrews.

Before I left the course, I studied the leader board once more. The main contenders for the title had all completed their second rounds and the results made pleasant reading.

LEADER BOARD

Holes	+Par–	Players	Score
36	–7	TANIZAKI	137
36	–6	HEIDENSOHN	138
36	–6	SAXON	138
36	–5	KINCAID	139
36	–5	HUME	139
36	–5	PIKER	139
36	–4	QUENTIN	140
36	–2	DEVEREAUX	142
36	–2	NICHOLSON	142
36	–1	BRYMER	143

The smallest man in the field was setting the pace but only three strokes covered the top seven names. It was still a very open Open. By moving up the leader board, I had surprised most people, delighted the British fans and boosted my own confidence. I had also made myself even more of a target for the man with the automatic rifle.

After accepting some more congratulations, I left the course and crossed over to the car park, attended all the way by two brawny stewards. As I walked towards Carnoustie, I saw something which stopped me dead. Coming towards me, his long hair showing below the crash helmet and his beard rippling in the wind, was Jeff Piker.

He was riding a Yamaha motorcycle.

When I had found a quiet place for a mid-afternoon snack and a scrutiny of my motoring atlas, I was ready to see a few sights. Working on the theory that if one of the players had committed the murder he must be staying within reasonable distance of the scene of the crime, I marked off the addresses on a map of the region and planned my itinerary. The police had already eliminated Horton Kincaid and Tanizaki because both had been out of the country at the time, and Vance Brymer could be discounted for the same reason. Nicholson, too, could be ruled out. He was staying in Kirkcaldy and it seemed unlikely that he would have driven all the way to St Andrews on Monday night and chanced on such a perfect place to leave Carnoustie in a ditch.

The person I wanted knew the area around Leuchars.

Both Heidensohn and Devereaux had booked into hotels in St Andrews itself. Jeff Piker had rented a cottage near Strathkinness, a village less than five miles west of the city. Orvill Hume, as befitted a man who had topped the USPGA money winners list the previous year with tournament earnings of almost $500,000, was living in the luxury of a country house just north of Anstruther. Tim Quentin, Body Beautiful, the surprise name on the leader board, had the most interesting address. He had a house at Rhynd on the edge of the Tentsmuir Forest.

About a mile from the lane where Carnoustie was ditched.

I drove south towards Anstruther and kept a strict note of the distance and time of the journey. Though I could not see Hume as a possible murderer, he was closest to my own accommodation and could have delivered a newspaper there most easily. On the other hand, he was too young and slight and American to fit the description given to me by the paper boy. Again. Jeff Piker, even if he had a Yamaha motorcycle, had to be ruled out as the man who gave the boy a pound. Jeff's long hair, beard and twanging Australian accent were too distinctive to miss.

The house Orvill Hume had rented was like something out of the National Trust handbook. It was a long, low Elizabethan building with half-timbering and mullioned windows, standing with rugged beauty in a couple of acres. It held an isolated position well off the main road and was screened by a rectangle of high trees. Fronted by expansive lawns that were fringed with flower beds, the house combined the twin attractions of country solitude and relative proximity to the coast.

As I approached on foot for a closer look at the property, I saw five cars in the drive and heard voices from the rear of the house. The sound of a tennis ball being whacked to and fro was joined by the laughter of a small child and by shouts of amusement from two women. Orvill Hume seemed to have brought his entire family along for a holiday in Bonnie Scotland. Distant splashes told of a swimming pool somewhere beyond the tennis court.

It was an advance on a motor caravan in the middle of a farm.

I was about to leave when Hume himself came out of the front door in earnest conversation with a guest. When I saw who it was, I felt a prickly sensation. The short, grinning, pug-faced old man who was moving towards a Daimler with his gangster strut was Ed Maserewa.

Since Hume already had a manager and as Maserewa had been more or less exclusively involved with Horton Kincaid, the sight of the two of them together was unusual, to say the least. A warm handshake was exchanged and then Maserewa got into his car. I stepped into the bushes and crouched low as the Daimler went past. Maserewa had a look of complacent malevolence and was obviously pleased with his visit.

On the journey to my next address, I reflected on what I had seen. The meeting could have been a harmless one between friends but somehow I doubted it. Ed Maserewa did not have friends. He divided people into enemies and business associates. If he was visiting Orvill Hume in private, it could be for one reason only and that reason might well be linked to his rift with the Texan. Maserewa was looking to sign up and promote a much younger player.

Horton Kincaid was about to be dispossessed.

By dint of keeping to the country lanes again, I avoided St Andrews and entered Strathkinness from the south. Jeff Piker's cottage was about a quarter of a mile from the village, standing towards the front of a sizeable plot of land. It was a solid, oblong, rather prosaic building in weathered grey stone but it ran to four bedrooms and offered comfort and privacy.

153

I hid Carnoustie behind some trees and worked my way around to the back of the property. The large, undulating lawn had been converted into a practice green and the turf was well-groomed. Because the flag-stick had been set on the lip of a small plateau, it posed a problem for any player. I could imagine Jeff spending hours on the green, practising putts from all directions. There was even a bunker.

The motorcycle was parked near the garage, next to a red sports car. Though I could see nobody about, I had the impression that Jeff was entertaining a visitor. Like Ulrich Heidensohn, the Australian was always popular with female fans and I had seen many on his arm over the years, but he differed from the West German in two respects. He was very discreet about his private life and he always put golf first.

I noted the number of the motorcycle and left.

Body Beautiful had the humblest accommodation of the three. It was a small, ugly house facing the Tentsmuir forest and its only notable feature was a well-established kitchen garden. While Orvill Hume could make a small fortune in a season and Jeff Piker never failed to take an appreciable income from the game, Body Beautiful struggled to make a profit out of golf. Of all the players on the leader board, he was the one who most needed the prize money.

Did he need it enough to kill for it?

Because the house was locked up and there was no sign of a car, I assumed that he was not at home. Again keeping an exact record of time and distance, I drove to the lane where we had been found on Monday night. Carnoustie's engine palpitated slightly as we paused near the ditch so I didn't keep her there long. I continued on down the lane, took the turning, went on past the clearing and headed towards the forest itself. Moving steadily north with the dark trees on my right, I eventually came to a narrow track that bisected the forest.

Curiosity made me swing down it but I was soon regretting the decision. Trees hemmed us in on both sides and an occasional branch tried to prod us for daring to intrude. Strange, unexpected noises came from the forest all around and none of them were welcoming. I kept going forward in search of a place to turn but the track got narrower and less hospitable. Fencing ran along either side of us and there were moments when we all but collided with it.

I was on the point of stopping Carnoustie to begin a long and difficult reverse when the track seemed to broaden. It encouraged me to press on further and I was relieved when the trees suddenly opened up to expose the sea and sky. High double gates rose up to bar our way and a large sign warned us to keep out of private property. I got out and looked through the mesh on the gates, watching the birds wheel above the waves or promenade along the shore. I must have counted thirty different species.

As I lifted a foot to climb back into Carnoustie, I noticed how much sand I had on my shoe. It had clearly been blown up from the beach and was quite thick in places. All four wheels were resting on it. I got in, swung her nose around to the left and then reversed slowly into a wooded alcove to the right of the gates. There was a grinding noise as we made contact with something sharp and vengeful. I braked at once and leapt out to investigate, leaving Carnoustie panting with indignation. Running along both sides of us but obscured by overhanging vegetation were strands of rusted barbed wire. Instead of being able to brush back a few bushes as we reversed, we were caught in a metallic bite.

At the same height as the existing marks on the bodywork.

I eased Carnoustie forward until she was free and got out. The mesh on the gate was just wide enough to admit a toe-hold and I was soon over. To the right and to the left of me were long stretches of sand washed by a placid tide. Birds were everywhere, paying no heed to me as they stalked about, conversed, hunted, landed, took off, or rose and fell in the wind above the sea. In the far distance to my right was the estuary of the River Eden and beyond that the Old Course.

Was this where Veronica Willis got sand in her hair?

I got back into Carnoustie and thought it all out. When I believed that I had reached some firm conclusions, I switched on the engine and rolled back down the track. The ground was too uneven and the trees too close to allow much speed and this was to help us. As we came around a bend in the track we slammed into a thick chain that was strung out in front of us. Carnoustie stalled and I was thrown forward slightly.

One end of the chain was wrapped around the metal fence to our left and locked into position but the other end was tied off around a tree to our right. Had we been travelling faster, the thick links of the chain could have done us real damage. As it was, Carnoustie had escaped with minor abrasions.

I looked all round to make sure that nobody was about, then got out of the cab and climbed over the fence on the right. It was the work of a few minutes to untie the chain and clear our path but it was not intended that we should drive away from the place.

As I dropped the chain, a rifle cracked; the bullet passed inches from my nose. It shaved the tree beside me so violently that splinters of bark shot up into my face and embedded themselves in my skin. I gave a yell of pain, brought my hands up to my face, and fell instinctively forwards. It all happened so quickly it must have looked as if the bullet had found its mark.

The noise had set off a great flapping and screeching among the birds and the entire wildlife of the forest seemed to join in. I lay quite still on the bare earth, feeling the blood oozing between my fingers, trying to work out the direction from which the shot came, listening above the cacophony for the stealthy tread of the killer.

But nobody came. Satisfied that he had hit me, the sniper had gone back to his car and I heard the engine start up. I also heard shouts of anger from the forest itself as a warden came to find out who was firing shots in the bird sanctuary. I did not stop to explain. Holding a handkerchief to my face, I ran to the fence, clambered over, jumped into Carnoustie and drove off as fast as I felt I could.

Only when I was well clear of Leuchars did I pull over to check my wounds in a mirror. They were not serious. When I had pulled the splinters out and washed my face, I only needed two pieces of sticking plaster. I looked as if I had been shaving with a blunt razor.

What frightened me most was the failure of my personal alarm system. On previous occasions when I had been watched, I had sensed it at once and been able to take action. This time there had been no warning. I had been followed to Tentsmuir Forest by someone who had set a trap for me with the chain. He knew I would have to get out and move the obstruction and he waited for his moment.

It was no warning shot. He had meant to kill me.

A car went past outside, slowed down, and reversed towards us. A horn beeped and I went outside to see who it was. Body Beautiful was behind the steering wheel of his white Volvo.

'Everything all right, Alan?'

'Fine. Just stopped for a bite to eat.'

'Meals on wheels, what?' He laughed inanely, then noticed the sticking plaster. 'What happened to your face?'

'I don't think you'd know her, Tim,' I said, tactfully.

He brayed copiously. 'Jolly good! Jolly good!' His mirth then vanished completely to be replaced by a knowing leer. 'Where is she now, then? Lying strangled on your double bed?'

'That's a pretty sick joke,' I protested.

'You're the one who picks up hitch-hikers, old boy.'

'Get stuffed.'

'I understand that she did.'

The temptation to throw a punch at him was very strong and I had to fight hard to control my temper. My predicament was bad enough and would not be helped by a brawl with another player. Body Beautiful had shed his normal affability and was trying to goad me. My only hope lay in staying calm and collected.

'A bit young for you, wasn't she?'

'You could be right,' I agreed.

'Good screw?'

'No comment.'

'Don't be shy. You're among friends.'

'I don't see any.'

He brayed again. 'Who *is* Alan Saxon? They're asking the wrong question. It should be – who *was* he?'

'Haven't you got somewhere to go?' I asked pointedly.

'Yes, old boy. Right to the top of the leader board.'

'Ah, that's it. Ideas above your station.'

'This is my year, Alan,' he asserted. 'I got fed up with being a good loser.'

'So you decided to become a *bad* loser.'

His jaw tightened, his eyes flashed and rancour came into his voice. 'You had your run as the darling of British golf. Time for you to move over. Make way for someone younger. And better.'

'Have you looked up at that leader board recently?'

'Two strokes are nothing,' he sneered. 'I'll claw those back from you tomorrow. You haven't got the stamina any more, Alan. You can't keep it up for four rounds.'

I forced a smile. 'Must be off. Nice meeting you.'

'You haven't told me what you're doing in this neck of the woods.'

'I wanted to look round the church in Leuchars,' I lied.

'Resorting to prayer now, are we?'

'Get lost.'

I got into Carnoustie and drove away, at once sad and angry. I was sorry to lose a friend and annoyed that I had gained another enemy. The old Body Beautiful had been the definitive good loser and I had liked him. Now he was determined to win. By fair means or foul.

Even though it meant picking my way through heavy traffic, I went back through St Andrews, believing that I had a better chance of shaking off anyone following me when there were plenty of other vehicles around. It was mid-evening when I got back to my own sanctuary at the farm. There at least I was protected. A thought hit me as I parked Carnoustie.

158

Had my meeting with Body Beautiful been a coincidence?

I cooked a meal and considered my narrow escape. I had been extremely lucky and couldn't expect to survive on that kind of good fortune indefinitely. It seemed certain that the two bullets had come from the same German automatic rifle and that the same finger had been on the trigger. Carnoustie's tyre and the bark of a pine tree. The third bullet would have my name on it and be delivered to the correct address.

My trip to the forest had brought reward as well as danger. I was convinced that Carnoustie had been down that track to the seashore before. The car park, the forest, the ditch. I marked the triangle on my map and stared at it. The killer knew the geography of the area well. Much better than me. That was worth remembering.

I went through it time and again but I still could not identify the marksman. Four or five names were possible but none of them seemed probable and there was always the chance that the man was someone I didn't even know. I drew up a mental list of people to see and questions to ask next day, then took out my clubs.

Two hours of practising in the field helped to rid my mind of fear and confusion. I didn't even stop to worry if I was being watched from the cattle truck or under scrutiny from the farm. Golf, as usual, took me into another world and I was happy there.

Back in Carnoustie, I took a shower, made cocoa and was in bed just after ten. I lay awake playing my guessing games for a long time and finally drifted off. It was not a lengthy sleep.

Bra-a-a-ark! Bra-a-a-ark!

I had forgotten to take the receiver off the hook.

Bra-a-a-ark! Bra-a-a-ark!

Telephone calls at that time rarely bring good news. I staggered across the floor and lifted the receiver.

'Mr Saxon?'

'Yes,' I mumbled.

'Ings here. We have some bad news for you, I'm afraid.'

159

Ginger Tom's voice had me completely awake. 'Bad news?'

'It's your caddie. Nairn MacNicol. He's had an accident.'

'What sort of accident?'

'A serious one, Mr Saxon. He's here at the hospital.'

It took me a split second to reach my decision.

'I'm on my way.'

Chapter Eight

As soon as I walked into the room, the smell of whisky hit me. It cut straight through the disinfected hospital odours and easily vanquished the stink of Ginger Tom's cigarette smoke. Nairn MacNicol was propped up in a bed in a sideward. His head was swathed in bandages, his neck was in a surgical collar, his right arm was in plaster, and there seemed to be heavy bandaging beneath his pyjama jacket. One side of his face was a deep purple bruise and a shiny lump had appeared on the bridge of his nose. He was evidently in some pain.

Ginger Tom and Robbie gave me welcoming nods. With a real effort, Nairn rose to a lopsided smile of apology.

'Sorry, Mr Saxon . . .'

'I'm the one who's sorry, Nairn. What happened?'

'Ah canny tell ye . . .'

'The details are not yet clear,' Ginger Tom chimed in. 'We're still trying to piece them together.'

I stood beside the bed and sniffed. 'You're supposed to drink the stuff not pour it over your head,' I said, kindly.

'Aye.'

'We think someone else did the pouring,' explained Ginger Tom. 'When our friend here was first brought in, his clothes and his hair were reeking of it.'

'Terrible waste of Glenfiddich,' said Robbie soulfully.

Nairn's bloodshot eyes rolled in agreement.

I had realised at once that the accident to Nairn had been set up in order to get at me. Having failed to shoot me out of the Open, they had now disabled my caddie. It was a body-blow to my chances.

'How much do you know, Superintendent?' I asked.

'Not enough, I'm afraid. It seems that Nairn left the course this afternoon, went back to his digs for tea and intended to stay there all evening. Thanks to you, he's been on the wagon all week.'

'I've not touched a drop since Sunday,' confirmed the patient.

'Until today,' reminded Ginger Tom before turning to me. 'Until he got your present.'

'But I didn't give him any present.'

'He knows that now, Mr Saxon.'

'What do you mean?'

'Earlier tonight, apparently, someone rang the bell at his digs. The landlady answered the door and found a bottle of whisky on the doorstep wrapped in tissue paper. This note was sellotaped to it.'

I took the scrap of paper from him and read the printed capital letters. HAVE A DRINK ON ME. YOU EARNED IT THIS AFTERNOON. My name had been scribbled underneath the message.

'I suppose we ought to have sympathy for Nairn,' continued Ginger Tom. 'Shut up in his bedsitter with a bottle of Glenfiddich on the table. He'd built up a rare old thirst in five days. The temptation must have been agonising. Quite irresistible.'

'Ah only meant tae have a wee dram, sir.'

'One dram leads to another with Glenfiddich,' sighed Robbie.

'So the bottle is soon half-empty,' said his colleague. 'Being a sociable man, Nairn decided he'd share the rest with friends. So he goes out into the night in search of company.'

'And he found it,' I guessed.

'I didna even see the fella, Mr Saxon.'

'Nairn remembers a bump on the head and being helped along the street. It was quite dark by then. The sight of a drunken man being carried home at night is not unusual up here during Open week.'

'Ah wasna drunk,' protested Nairn. 'Ah can handle ma whisky.'

Ginger Tom finished off the story. 'He was taken down to the castle ruins, doused all over, then shoved off the edge of

162

the north fortifications. It's a nasty drop on to a stone surface. Someone heard his groans and called an ambulance. Then we took an interest.'

Nairn was baffled. 'Who would do such a thing?'

I knew and so did the police. They would not be visiting a routine casualty in hospital at midnight unless the case had some bearing on the murder inquiry. Because of me, Nairn had been singled out for attack. My guilt stirred so much as I looked at him that I had to turn away. His injuries would take months to heal and by that time, the golf season, his main source of income, would be over.

He coughed. 'Ye'll have to get yourself a new caddie, Mr Saxon.'

'Any suggestions?'

'Try Craig Donaldson. Guid man . . .'

'Thanks, Nairn.'

'Feel Ah've let ye down . . .'

'Of course you haven't,' I told him, 'so don't give it a second thought. You just concentrate on getting well again.'

'They've a telly here,' he said, brightening. 'Ah'll be able tae watch you winning the title on Sunday.'

I forced a smile and patted his shoulder. Ginger Tom indicated that we should leave and we all muttered our farewells. Robbie was the first to speak when we had found a quiet place in the corridor outside.

'You played very well today, sir.'

I glanced back at the side-ward. 'Too well.'

'Yes, that was unfortunate,' he agreed.

'It shows just how desperate they are to stop you,' said Ginger Tom. 'According to the doctor, Nairn is lucky to be alive.'

He wasn't the only one but I didn't tell them that.

'Any chance of tracing that bottle of whisky?' I asked.

Ginger Tom frowned. 'We shall try, naturally. Check all the pubs and the off licences in the area for recent sales. But I don't hold out much hope. Fair amount of that stuff gets drunk around here, I daresay. Besides, our man may have bought his Glenfiddich months ago.'

'He certainly knew about Nairn's weakness,' I noted.

'Who doesn't?' said Robbie. 'Common talk among the caddies. Nairn MacNicol is an established piss-artist.'

Our conversation was interrupted as a nurse came down the corridor towards us, her flat heels clacking on the tiled floor. She gave us an all-purpose smile and went on into Nairn's side-ward. Ginger Tom led the way towards the main exit.

'So what do you have for us, Mr Saxon?'

'Have?'

'Gossip. Rumours. Evidence.'

'Oh well, take your pick . . .'

I retailed some of the chit-chat I had heard but held back the important details. They listened patiently but were not impressed. Ginger Tom stopped us near the doors.

'We've done better than that ourselves.'

'Oh?'

'Motives, that's what we've been after. Personal grudges against Alan Saxon. I'm afraid to say we've located quite a few.'

'Story of my life, Superintendent.'

'Orvill Hume, for instance. You've stolen his thunder a number of times over the last few years. He's not the type to appreciate that.'

'Orvill doesn't appreciate anything but money.'

'Then there's Jeff Piker. One way or another, you've been a real thorn in his flesh. We looked up the record books. Whenever you two have met in a big tournament, you've usually won.'

Robbie pointed a finger at me. 'In the past, you've beaten him in play-offs for the Tunisian Open, the Martini International and the French Open. A few years ago, you even had the temerity to go out to Victoria and take his Australian Open title off him. On his own patch.'

'So what?' I argued. 'Jeff's a pro. He knows that you win a couple and lose a lot. That's golf, Inspector. As you must have learned by now. And anyway, Jeff and I haven't played in the same tournament this year until now. He's been on the American circuit and I've stuck with the

European Tour. Oh, and another thing,' I added. 'If you looked up the record books, you'd have seen that Jeff earns an average of four times as much as I do each year. *And* he doesn't have my debts and back-taxes to worry about.'

Ginger Tom opened a door and took us into the car park. 'Let's turn to another player,' he said. 'Tim Quentin.'

'What about him?'

'He's never beaten you, has he?'

'He's never beaten anybody,' I laughed.

'Now, that isn't true,' corrected Robbie. 'He's been improving steadily in recent months. Even shaded into the top six in occasional minor tournaments. But never above you.'

'What does that prove?'

'He's got an extra incentive to win. To dislodge you as Britain's top golfer. Also, Tim Quentin is chasing a US Tour card for next year.'

'Most of us are, Inspector. The big pay days are over there.'

'So I understand,' said Ginger Tom with easy contempt. 'Though how people can earn so much for playing a game like golf . . .'

'We can't all be policemen,' I retorted.

His eyes flashed. 'Someone has to wipe the shit off society's arse, Mr Saxon. And I'm coming to see that my job is a lot cleaner than yours. At least I can trust my colleagues.'

'You sound like my father.'

'I take that as a compliment,' he said without sarcasm.

We had reached Carnoustie now. I jerked a thumb at her. 'When do I get my things back?' I asked politely.

'Call in at the station tomorrow,' he suggested. 'Er, if you're not doing anything important, that is . . .' He was disappointed that I did not rise to the bait. His tone normalised. 'The lab has finished with most of the items. You can sign for them and take them away.'

'I'll be there.'

He restrained me gently with a hand on my shoulder as I turned to go. 'Isn't there anything else you have to tell us?'

'Not as far as I know.'

'Still keeping things to yourself.'

'Just like you, Superintendent.'

'Why did you drive to Anstruther this afternoon?' he pressed.

'Because I felt like it.'

'What happened to your face?'

I fingered the sticking plaster. 'You wouldn't believe me if I told you,' I smiled. 'Any more questions?'

'Aren't you very keen to stay alive?'

'Yes.'

'Then you need us, Mr Saxon.'

'That's a matter of opinion.'

He released my shoulder and I got into Carnoustie. I lowered the window so that I could hear his parting remarks. He was bitter.

'I've never liked golf. And nothing that's happened so far this week has endeared the game to me. It's brought murder, assault, theft, and I don't know what else to a normally peaceful and law-abiding city. This evening alone, for instance, a chain was stolen from the Old Course, a gunshot and trespass were reported in Tentsmuir Forest, and a caddie was brutally attacked. Quite honestly, Mr Saxon, I'll be glad when the Open Championship is over and the whole lot of you fuck off back to where you came from.' He gave me a tight-lipped smile. 'I'm speaking off the record, of course.'

'It'll make me sleep sounder in my bed tonight,' I said.

'At least you'll get some sleep.'

All three of us muttered farewells and I drove away.

On the trip back to the farm, I was haunted by the image of Nairn MacNicol, sitting up in a bed that seemed far too big for his slight frame, nursing his terrible wounds, and trying to apologise to the person who had indirectly put him there. He was terrified that I would blame him when, in fact, he should have blamed me. I vowed to take revenge on his behalf. It was yet another score to settle.

What perplexed me was why the attack on him had been necessary. I was convinced that the man who had shot at me in the forest thought he had hit me and put me out of the Open Championship for good. That being the case, why did my caddie have to be set upon? The only explanation was that the marksman had later realised that I was still alive and kicking and able to play golf. But how? One person only had seen me leave the area.

Body Beautiful. The player who had never beaten me. Fairly.

I had ample food for thought as I lay in bed that night. My bid for the Open title had cost Veronica Willis her life, Nairn MacNicol a savage attack, and myself endless upset and danger. It had taken all the shine off the idea of winning and yet I had to stay near the top of the leader board in order to draw my enemies out of hiding. As long as I was a potential champion, the attempts to get at me would continue.

A new thought corkscrewed through my brain and made me sit up in bed. They would stop at nothing. If Nairn could be put out of action with such calculated ease, so could others close and important to me.

Nobody was safe.

Neither Clive Phelps nor Fiona Langley.

Not even Lynette . . .

'Alan, what the devil do you mean by ringing at this hour of the morning? It's so inconsiderate! Do you know what time it is? You'd better have a jolly good reason for waking me, that's all I can say.'

'I wanted to talk to you, Rosemary.'

'But you talked to me on Wednesday.'

'One can never have too much of a good thing,' I ventured.

Rosemary was not amused. She rid herself of a few home truths and my ear throbbed with embarrassment. But I weathered it and thought of her lying there in her silk pyjamas not a hundred yards from the Little Aston golf course. Rosemary had always liked silk pyjamas. When we were first married, I had liked them as well. On her. And off her.

A gap finally presented itself and I eased into it.

'I'm sorry to have rung so early but I have to leave soon.' It was not true and she would sense it. 'I simply wanted to ask you about Lynette. Have you heard from her yet?'

'We had a card yesterday. From France.'

'And where is she today?'

'I told you. In Germany.'

'But which part of Germany? Which city? Which hotel?'

'How should I know?'

'They must have given you an itinerary,' I argued. 'That damn school never stops sending out lists. How many towels and toothbrushes and pairs of knickers Lynette is supposed to have. Who will be giving her extra tuition in French and dance and elocution and tennis – and at what extra cost. Which colour shoes and socks and blouses and—'

'Alan, what *are* you on about?' she demanded.

'My favourite topic. Bills.'

'If you rang me up to complain about the—'

'I didn't, Rosemary,' I said, cutting her off before she got into full flow. 'All I want is the name of the hotel where Lynette is staying today. Do you have that information?'

She gave nothing away. She might have been playing bridge.

'Possibly . . .'

'Do you have a list?' I almost shouted.

'Not on me.'

'Well, can you find one, please?'

'Why should I?'

'Rosemary—'

'Is there something I should know, Alan?' she probed. 'It's most unlike you to ring me at all. Least of all at such a peculiar time. Now, what is it really about?'

I had my answer all worked out. 'You wouldn't understand,' I said with an exaggerated sigh. 'It's to do with golf.'

'Then I wouldn't understand,' she agreed, ruefully. 'I spent eight long years of my life not understanding about golf.'

'Let's skip the replay of our divorce,' I suggested.

'Willingly.'

'So will you get that list for me?'

'No.'

'Rosemary, please!'

She was firm. 'Not now.'

'But I need to speak to Lynette. Okay, call it superstition if you like but . . . I think it might bring me good luck.'

'You could certainly do with some of that,' she conceded.

'Then find the name of that hotel. I must talk to her.'

She kept me waiting out of sheer force of habit. 'I'll be in touch, Alan. This afternoon, maybe.'

She put the phone down without compunction.

A chat with Rosemary is always in the nature of a conversational cold shower and I felt at once abused and cleansed. I was also pleased that I had got through it all without communicating the dread that was lurking inside me. To tell Rosemary that I feared for the safety of our daughter would have been to alarm her, perhaps unnecessarily, and to set off a whole firework display of recriminations about the game by which I make my living.

Heidensohn. The miniature golfer on his sweater. Veronica Willis among his fans. The coach party from Braunschweig. His uncle from the army. The Heckler and Koch G3. A hard-faced man outside the golf shop. Ian Calloway's command of the language. Wartime photos. Max Fleischner.

All roads led to Germany.

For Lynette's sake, I hoped I had got it wrong.

'Hey, mister!'

I had forgotten the paper boy. He was banging on the door.

'Are ye there?'

'Just coming!' I called, pulling on some trousers.

When I opened the top half of the stable door, the boy was waiting on the grass, shifting his feet impatiently and slapping his thigh with a rolled-up newspaper. His transistor hung limp and silent.

He perked up immediately when he saw me.

'Ah remembered some more. About the fella on the Yamaha.'

169

'Well?'

'He'd a big nose. And a scarruf around his mouth. A tartan scarruf. So Ah couldna see his face proper. His goaggles was silver round the edges. And the crash helmet was black.'

'Anything else?'

'Aye . . .' His face puckered as he delved around in his memory. 'He'd a brown coat. Like sojers wear.'

'A combat jacket?'

'Ah think so . . .' He groped in his mind for more information like a hand desperately searching a pocket for a lost coin. Eventually, he found what he was after. 'The Yamaha. It was black and silver. About 500 cc. Aye, and it had these metal things on the back . . .'

'Panniers?'

He nodded enthusiastically and grinned up at me, hoping that there might be some reward. His grin intensified when I reached for my wallet but it vanished at once when I took out a slip of paper and handed it to him.

'Was that the registration number?'

He puzzled over it. 'Ah canny remember. Ah think there was a W but Ah couldna be certain. It was a new bike . . . that's all.'

I took the paper back and gave him a pound note in return. The grin came out like sunshine. Because he had been honest about the registration number, I felt that his other facts had been reliable. He was not just making it all up to coax more money out of me.

'Thanks!' he said and walked off across the field.

'Haven't you forgotten something?'

He stopped. 'Eh?'

Realising what I meant, he came bounding back to give me my newspaper. Then he switched on the transistor to full volume and ran off towards the bicycle he had parked up against the side of the cattle truck, blithely unaware that he was being watched by the detectives inside it.

The boy's description of the motorcycle tallied with the one I had seen Jeff Piker riding. Like the man who had brought the newspaper, Jeff had been wearing a black crash

170

helmet and silver-rimmed goggles, though not the tartan scarf and the khaki combat jacket. The new details were valuable but not conclusive. There would be dozens of Yamaha motorcycles in St Andrews.

Over breakfast I read Clive's article on the second round of the Open. He was preening himself slightly and reminding his readers that he had tipped Alan Saxon to emerge as a front runner in the Championship. He described me as the kind of player who thrives on adverse conditions and is at his best when his back is to the wall. What surprised me was that Clive had not revised the earlier forecast he had made to me. He was now repeating it in print.

Saxon, Kincaid, Piker. One, two, three.

What about Tanizaki and Heidensohn?

And Orvill Hume with the vital backing of Ed Maserewa?

There were still two rounds to go and anything could happen. While I was once again grateful for Clive's support, I was afraid that his article might invite another attack on me. Or, indeed, on him.

I was not due on the first tee until late morning and so I had plenty of time in hand. I decided to make full use of it. After washing up the breakfast things and putting them away, I drove Carnoustie out of her two acres. The farmer had finished milking and was just turning the herd out into a field with the aid of his yapping dogs. He gave me his one-fingered greeting and I responded with a toot on the horn. For him, at least, life had not changed. Even with detectives hiding on his premises and Alan Saxon trailing notoriety across his land, he went about his chores at the same unworried, unvarying pace. I admired him for it. There was a lesson to be learned from him.

Beth Gill was polishing the brass knocker on the front door when I rolled up at her cottage. She wore a pink overall and had tied a scarf around her head turban-style. I got a reflex smile but she was not at all pleased to see me. Reluctantly, she invited me into the living room.

'Just wanted to check the arrangements for the funeral . . .'

'Mr Reeman is taking care of all that,' she said.

'I know, but he's rather difficult to get hold of at the moment. Madly busy.' I tried to soften her with a friendly grin. 'Also, when I'm down at the Old Course, I do tend to have something else on my mind.'

She nodded. 'How is it going, Mr Saxon?'

'Oh, I'm still in there fighting.'

'Desmond always believed you could win it again.'

'I hope I can prove him right, Mrs Gill.'

There was a long, awkward pause during which she fidgeted with her cleaning rag and looked down. I was not going to be offered a cup of tea this time. Indeed, she was having to make an effort to be civil to me. She gestured towards the door.

'You'll have to excuse me, Mr Saxon. I have so much to do.'

'And the funeral?'

'Monday morning at eleven. St Leonard's Church.'

She took my elbow to guide me out but I held my ground.

'I know about Max Fleischner,' I said, quietly.

The effect was extraordinary. Her mouth gaped open and all colour seeped from her face. She dropped her cleaning rag, put her hands to her brow, and swayed about unsteadily. I helped her to the sofa and sat beside her. It was several minutes before she found the strength to speak. She was beyond tears.

'How?' she asked.

'He's back in St Andrews, isn't he?'

'Yes . . . But how did you find out?'

'The photograph in the R. & A. archives. That piece in the paper about the coach party from Braunschweig . . .'

'It's his home town,' she whispered fondly. 'Forty years, Mr Saxon. Just think of it. Almost forty years. Half a lifetime.'

'Desmond knew that he was coming, didn't he?'

'Yes . . .'

'That's why he got into such a rage. Over Max. The one

who smiled at you when you took that photograph on the Old Course.'

She bit her lip and nodded. 'You must have thought I was very cruel and heartless. The way I behaved when Desmond died . . . I couldn't help it. I was free at last. You've no idea how—' She checked herself and sat up, clasping her hands tightly. 'He hated Max so much. He never forgave him. Never.'

'Desmond didn't strike me as the jealous type.'

'Oh he was, Mr Saxon. Over the simplest of things. He liked to have everything his own way. And he was so possessive. It led to a lot of unhappiness over the years. Far too much.'

'Tell me about Max,' I suggested.

Beth Gill stared straight ahead and the years fell from her. She was a young woman again, not long married, settling into her new home in St Andrews, coping with wartime privations, making ends meet on her husband's meagre wage, and generally finding her feet.

'It meant so much to Desmond when the war was finally over and the Open Championship could start again. He worked all hours of the day and night to get the Old Course ready. It was like a mission to him. Nothing else mattered.' She heaved a sigh. 'Then they brought those men in from the camp and he didn't like it at all. The idea of Germans being allowed on *his* golf course! It made him furious. But they came and they did their share of the work. I got to know quite a few of them. They were rather sad people. I felt sorry for them. A friendly word was so important for them. I mean, the war was *over*. You can't go on and on fighting it.' She unclasped her hands to brush back her hair. 'Max was one of the men. His English was really very good, better than any of the others', so he was the person I . . . chatted to the most. Then I took my little box camera along to take some snaps of them. Just for a souvenir. I knew I'd never see any of them ever again and I thought it would be nice . . .'

The wan smile on her lips hardened into a grimace.

'Your husband caught you taking the snaps,' I guessed.

'Yes.'

'And he took his anger out on Max.'

'Yes.'

'By setting the dog on him.'

'Gip bit his arm, Mr Saxon. He jumped up at Max and sank his teeth into his arm. He had to have stitches and everything. It was terrible. Desmond had no need to do that. Max was a friend.'

The story was unfolding much as I had imagined it would and I was confident that my next guess would also be on target. 'Because Gip attacked him, Max got his own back. He killed the dog.'

'Oh no, Mr Saxon!' she exclaimed. 'It wasn't Max.'

'One of the other POWs?'

'No . . .'

'Then who?'

She lowered her head in penance. Instead of being the young woman of her memories, she was now an old lady with a guilty secret. Beth Gill had locked the truth away for so long that when it finally burst out of her it made her shudder. I put an arm around her.

'I killed him,' she said bitterly. 'I killed the dog. And not only because of what he did to Max. It was because of Desmond. He thought more of Gip than he did of me and I couldn't bear it! When we first met, it was different. It was me that he wanted. But after we got married, Desmond changed. Gip this, Gip that, Gip, Gip, Gip. He always put that dog first – even before his wife.' She suddenly became very calm. 'I know that it was a dreadful thing to do but I wasn't sorry. Desmond never had another dog after that. He noticed *me*.'

'And he blamed Max for the dog's death?'

'Yes. He was certain that it was Max.'

'So what happened?'

She shrugged and heaved another sigh. 'When the rough clearance was finished they went back to their camp. Months later, there was talk of them being released. And then, a year or so after that, quite out of the blue, I had a letter from Max. He was back home in Germany. It was only a short letter, really. He just wanted to thank me for . . . being nice to him. So I wrote back. That's how it started.'

'But your husband knew nothing about the correspondence . . .'

'He would have gone mad, Mr Saxon.'

'How on earth did you keep it from him?'

'I had a sister in Edinburgh. Max used to send his letters there and I'd pick them up when I visited. We didn't write often. Once or twice a year, perhaps, with a card at Christmas. We just . . . wanted to keep in touch.'

I was moved. 'For all that time?'

'Yes. Amazing, isn't it?' she said with a laugh. Bitterness flooded back. 'Last year, my sister died and so Max had to write to me here. Desmond found out.'

'I think I can guess the rest.'

'It ruined everything,' she said flatly.

After a long, ruminative silence, she got up and went into the kitchen. I followed her and we looked at the old snapshot she had framed and hung on the wall.

'What sort of a person is Max Fleischner?' I asked, gently.

'He's a good man, Mr Saxon, but he's very proud. He loves his country. It was one of the things that Desmond hated about him. After all that had happened, Max was still proud to be a German. Being a prisoner made him feel so ashamed.'

'Is that why he never came back to Britain?'

'Yes.' She turned to face me. 'And then this young German began to play golf and win tournaments.'

'Ulrich Heidensohn,' I sighed.

'Max didn't even live in Braunschweig any more. He's been in Kiel for years. But because this Heidensohn was from his home town, and because he's German and he *wins* . . . Max took an interest in him.'

'So that's what brought him back to St Andrews. He wants to see a fellow-countryman win on the course where he worked as a prisoner.'

She looked back at the photograph. 'Max is so proud,' she said, quietly. 'It's a little frightening sometimes.'

Another photograph popped into my mind. It showed Dubby Gill outside the golf shop, pointing his walking stick at

175

someone in futile anger. Not, as I had assumed, at Ulrich Heidensohn. The object of Dubby's surging hatred was a grim-faced old man who was keeping the female fans away from the West German golfer.

The old man was Max Fleischner.

'Does he believe that Heidensohn can take the title?'

'Max is convinced that he'll win. For Germany.'

'And what would Max do to help him win?'

She gazed at the smiling face in the framed photograph.

'Anything, Mr Saxon. Max would do anything . . .'

The station sergeant was a bluff, burly man with an acne problem. He made me sign a form, then got two uniformed constables to carry all the items released by the forensic laboratory back to Carnoustie. Everything was wrapped in individual plastic bags and I didn't bother to take it all out. I simply hung the curtains back, reinstated the carpet around the front seats, and screwed my television on to its fixture. After bundling the remaining items away in cupboards, I drove quickly away.

It was not difficult to find a replacement caddie at the Old Course. Only eighty competitors had qualified for the third round, leaving almost half of the original field out of the hunt. Caddies were going spare and I had several of them after me, scenting a chance to get up on the leader board now that Nairn had had to withdraw. I auditioned half a dozen before deciding to act on Nairn's advice and opt for Craig Donaldson, a short, chubby, willing character in his thirties with mutton-chop whiskers and snaggly teeth.

We agreed on a fee and a five per cent share of any prize money. I had already earmarked the other five per cent for Nairn, though it would be poor recompense for what he had suffered on my behalf. After a brief discussion with Craig about my general strategy for the third round, I went off to the locker rooms to get ready.

'Hi, matey. Nice day for it.'

'Can't complain, Jeff.'

'You going to shoot another 67, you lucky bastard?'

'Do my best.'

I had bumped into Jeff Piker as he was leaving the locker rooms to begin his game with Orvill Hume. He was his usual confident, smiling self and was wearing a sun visor.

'What have you done to upset Tim Quentin?' he asked.

'Nothing.'

'That's not the way he sees it, Alan. When I met him earlier, he was bad-mouthing you something rotten. What's eating him?'

'Ambition.'

He laughed drily. 'It figures. Well, I got to be going.'

'Hold on a tick, Jeff,' I said, barring his way. 'Did I see you on a motorbike yesterday?'

'Maybe. No law against it, is there?'

'A Yamaha?'

'Look, Alan, I'm due on the tee in a few minutes. Save it, will you?'

'Was it a Yamaha?' I pressed.

'Yes.'

'And where did you get it from?'

'Mind your own fucking business,' he snapped.

He pushed right past me and left me gaping. Why had such a simple question produced such a hostile and evasive answer? It was most unlike the Jeff Piker I knew. What had sparked him off like that?

I shelved speculation and got ready. Golf came first.

When Horton Kincaid and I began the penultimate game of the day, I was grateful that he was my playing partner once more. To have been paired off with Body Beautiful or even, after our recent exchange, with Jeff Piker, would have been something of a trial. With Horton, I could relax and get on with my game.

Because it was brighter and warmer, the sun had swelled the crowds and dried out the greens even more. With typical whimsicality, the wind had shifted yet again and now blew in off the sea. It was fresh enough to invigorate but not to pose any major problems. As I stepped on to the first tee, I felt that I was going to have a good round.

My instincts betrayed me. I faltered badly.

The trouble began at the fifth hole, the first of the only two par-5 holes on the course. I hit two fine wood shots down the fairway and was only a short iron from the green. My first birdie beckoned. Craig handed me an 8-iron and I sized up my shot, intending to lift the ball over the protective ridge at the front of the green. I thought I had struck it well but the ball swerved wildly and drew a groan of dismay from the crowd. It landed close to the flagstick – but on the thirteenth green! I was at least three putts from where I should have been.

From that point on, nothing went right. I sought out bunkers, I explored the whins, I even drove out of bounds and though I fluked a birdie at the Long Hole, the damage had been done. My round of 77 disappointed my fans, depressed me, agitated Craig and spent a fiver for Clive Phelps. As Horton rose higher, I fell by the wayside.

I was off the leader board and out of the running.

There was no way I could be Open Champion.

I signed my scorecard, had it countersigned, and handed it in. Then I walked swiftly to the locker rooms to be alone with my dejection. I had blown it. After 36 holes I had been tying for second place with Heidensohn; after 54 holes I was just one more golfer in the chasing pack. I had let a large number of people down. Myself included.

There was an overriding consolation.

I was safe.

In playing myself out of the reckoning, I had taken the enormous pressures off. I was no longer a marked man. There would be no more warnings, no more attacks, no more automatic rifles trained on me. I was free and the relief of knowing that was almost overpowering. I could live again. Thanks to one bad round on the Old Course, I could stop looking over my shoulder all the time.

'Hard lines, Alan.'

'That's the way the cookie crumbles sometimes.'

'You have my fullest sympathy.'

'Why? I played badly, Ian.'

'The surprising thing is not that you played badly but that you played at all. With all the stresses and strains you've been under, it's staggering that you reached the standard you did. Yesterday, your touch was masterly.'

'But today . . .'

'It all caught up with you,' he soothed. 'It was bound to, Alan.'

There was some truth in what Ian was saying. I had come to the clubhouse for a drink and he had made time for a word. He hid his disappointment more expertly but I could sense that it was there. Ian Calloway would have loved to see another British name on the trophy.

'Nil desperandum,' he said. 'There's always next year.'

I rallied slightly. 'Yes, I suppose there is.'

At least I would be around to compete in another Open.

'And you could still have a handsome wage packet this year,' Ian reminded me. 'Total prize money of £410,000. Good final round tomorrow and you'd pocket a sizeable cheque.'

'I hope so,' I confided. 'Nairn MacNicol is on a percentage of my winnings and he needs every penny he can get right now.'

Ian shook his head sadly. 'Yes, I heard about Nairn. Appalling business. I feel dreadfully sorry for the man. And, of course, you suffered as a result. Changing your horse in mid-stream, so to speak. Can't have helped your game at all.' He scratched his forehead in bewilderment. 'Nairn was such a harmless chap. Who could want to do a thing like that to him?'

'I'll let you know when I find out,' I promised.

'It was the final straw for Gordon.'

'Gordon?'

'He does take these things to heart. I mean, it's not *his* job to look after the caddies morning, noon and night but Gordon just feels responsible somehow. Seems to think the attack on Nairn was his fault. And coming as it did on top of the other incidents . . .'

'Other incidents?'

'A chain was stolen from here. The kind that's used to close off a car park. Disappeared yesterday afternoon in broad daylight. They found it in Tentsmuir Forest. Gordon was quite rattled. He thought it reflected badly on him and his security arrangements.' Ian sighed and his brow contracted into furrows. 'Then we had the news from Tanizaki . . .'

'What news?'

'Haven't you heard?'

'I've been a little out of touch this week, Ian,' I explained with a wry smile.

'Some of Tanizaki's clubs were taken.'

'When?'

'Last night. From his hotel room.' He nodded towards the window. 'He's staying at Rusack's. Right on our doorstep.'

'And what was stolen?'

'His driver, a couple of long irons and – the magic putter.'

'Oh no!'

My heart went out to the Japanese player. His putter had travelled the world with him for years and was the most effective weapon in his armoury. It had got him to the top of the leader board at the end of the second round. To lose it at this stage of the Championship would be a calamity for him.

'At first we thought it might be a souvenir hunter,' said Ian. 'Some of them will take anything they can lay their hands on.'

'Did Tanizaki report it to the police?'

'Fortunately, no. The hotel got hold of us first and, by the grace of God, we were able to sort it out.' He ran worried fingers through non-existent hair. 'Honestly, you begin to wonder what's going to happen next at an Open. At Royal Birkdale, we had the sixth green vandalised during the night. And now we've had practical jokes at the Old Course!'

'Practical jokes?'

'Tanizaki's clubs were found buried in Hell Bunker with just their heads showing above the sand. As you know, we have a small army of volunteers who clear up the litter off the course at the end of the day. One of them spotted the clubs. Thank goodness! Whoever put them there must have a very warped sense of humour.'

'But they weren't damaged?' I asked.

'No. Tanizaki is playing with them this afternoon. Though it remains to be seen if he's recovered from the shock of having them whisked away like that. He was extremely hurt about it last night.'

'Understandably.'

A member of the Championship committee signalled to Ian from the other side of the room. Before my companion could make an excuse and go, I blurted out the question I had been wanting to ask him.

'Is it true that you're interested in shooting?'

'Yes,' he replied, easily. 'I'm in the Wildfowlers' Association. Have been for years. Why do you ask?'

'Someone mentioned it, that's all,' I said. 'Seemed unlikely.'

He smiled warmly. 'I'm a very unlikely person, Alan. Or hadn't you realised that?' He glanced towards his colleague. 'I must go.'

'Cheerio.'

The stolen chain, the shot in the forest and the missing golf clubs were all the work of the same man. I was now convinced that he was not Ian Calloway. That fact reassured me.

I chatted for a while in the clubhouse, then went off towards the exit from the course. Someone intercepted me and he was not in his friendliest mood. He waved his notepad about in the air as he spoke as if giving a semaphore version.

'The line has got to be drawn somewhere, old son. I will be your Fairy Godmother. I will be your shoulder to cry on. I will even run your errands if you ask me nicely.' He slammed the pad into the palm of his hand. 'But I will not act as your messenger boy! Got it? *That* is where I draw the line. Got it?'

'I get it, Clive.'

'I'm a golf correspondent, not a village postman.'

'Everybody knows that,' I soothed.

181

'Your wife doesn't know it! Maserewa doesn't know it!'

'My wife?'

'Okay, your ex-wife. Why be so pedantic about it?' He puffed on his cigar and talked through thick smoke. 'There I am, sitting quietly in the Press tent, occupying my rightful place among the cream of the world's golf writers, addressing my mind to elevated thoughts, savouring a tee shot here, a bunker shot there, a perfect putt somewhere else, polishing the phrases for my next purple passage, doing, in fact, no bloody harm to no one, when my phone rings. Is it my editor? Is it my bookmaker? Is it the barmaid from the Scores Hotel? Is it anyone with a legitimate purchase on my attention?'

'What did Rosemary say?'

'No!' he bellowed, not even hearing me. 'It was Alan Saxon's wife. Ah-ah. Correction. His ex-wife. That leggy lady from the upper middle classes that he married in an ecstasy of social climbing . . .'

'She had a message for me, Clive?'

'Yes. So she gets Muggins here to deliver it! She rang you in that clapped-out caravanette but you were not at home. Guessing that I'd be in the press tent and knowing that I'd have nothing else to do but take calls for you, she gave me a buzz.'

'And where's Lynette staying?'

'I am not a go-between, Alan.'

'Which part of Germany? I need to know.'

'Munich. Now will you listen to me?'

'Did she mention a hotel? A phone number?'

'Stop treating me like a bloody answering service,' he wailed. He hurled his cigar to the ground and trod on it viciously, then put both hands on my shoulders. 'First things first, old son. You owe me five quid. That was lousy golf you served up today.'

'I'll make it ten quid,' I promised. 'Fifteen.'

'You went to pieces on me, old son. What am I going to tell my readers now? If I still have any, that is.'

'Clive,' I said patiently. 'What did Rosemary say?'

He let his arms fall to his sides. 'Relax. Your daughter is

safe and sound. Since I had the hotel number and the phone was in my hand, I rang Munich for you.'

I was overcome with gratitude. 'You did?'

'According to the manager, the girls are seeing the sights today. They should be at the art gallery by now.' He gave me a weary grin. 'The panic is over, Alan. Concentrate on your golf. Munich is a fair old way from Braunschweig.'

Clive had guessed at once why I was so anxious to make contact with Lynette and he had helped me in the most practical way. He had done me yet another important favour. A wave of relief washed over me. The danger was past. I was safe and my daughter was safe.

'Thanks,' I said simply.

'And while we're on the subject of Braunschweig, you can cross Uncle Werner off your list. Whoever looked at you down the barrel of a Heckler and Koch G3, it wasn't Ully Heidensohn's uncle. Poor old bugger's got arthritis in both hands.'

'You met him?'

'I met them all. They're quite a bunch. All shapes and sizes with an age range of eighteen to eighty. They're certainly here to give Ully their full support. Flags, banners, tee shirts with his name on, the lot. If he wins tomorrow, he'll be a national hero.'

'Did you manage to talk to any of them?'

'Yes. They were all too ready to talk about the local boy made good. Unlike Ully, his fans are nice people. Most of them, anyway . . .'

'Most of them?'

'There was this one old guy who was a real oddball. Wild look in his eye. Very bitter about everything. He had no time for me. In fact, he tried to prevent the others from chatting to me.' Clive gave a hollow laugh. 'For two pins, I think he'd have slung me out of the hotel. Even at his age. Never met anyone with so much anger in him.'

'Did you get his name?'

'No. The rest of the Kraut contingent were trying to avoid him. He was hardly the life and soul of the coach party. Typical loner. And so fanatical in his support of Ully.

183

To listen to that old character, you'd have thought Ully was about to win a replay of the last war.'

I was certain the man had been Max Fleischner.

'Clive . . .' I began.

'No!' he countered quickly.

'But you don't know what I'm going to ask.'

'Whatever it is, forget it. I'm signing off. I've been your bloodhound for long enough. I'm handing in my sniffer's badge.'

'Fair enough,' I agreed. 'In that case, there's no point in me asking you one last favour. I doubt if you could do it, anyway. It's a little beyond you.'

'What's a little beyond me?' he protested.

'I'd like to know about Jeff Piker's motorcycle, that's all.'

'Motorcycle,' he exclaimed. 'Why, for fuck's sake?'

'I'd just be interested to know where he bought it or hired it, that's all. Yamaha. 500 cc. British registration.' I patted him on the shoulder. 'But as you say, you've done more than enough for me, Clive. So let it drop.' I knew that he would help me again. 'Any joy with that story I gave you? Kincaid and Maserewa?'

He brightened. 'Something's definitely afoot there. Kincaid clammed up on me and Maserewa turned nasty. Two sure signs. So I poked about a bit – no jokes about barmaids, please – and found out a little more. The rift in the lute has come about because Maserewa is on the point of signing up a younger player and edging Kincaid into the background. I don't know who that player is yet but Ully has got to be favourite. Maserewa backs winners.' He remembered his second message. 'Oh, by the way, he wants to see you.'

'Maserewa?'

'Today. Like now.'

'What about?'

'I don't know, Alan, but you'd better not expect a tickertape reception. He's a mean hombre when he's aroused and I'm afraid that I roused him good and proper. Said he'd be in the tented village.'

The idea of being sent for annoyed me.

184

'Suppose I don't choose to go?' I asked defiantly.

Clive was serious. 'Then I think he'll come looking for you, old son. With that tame gorilla of his. In your place, I'd spare him a few minutes. What harm can it do?'

I thought it over and nodded. 'Okay, Clive, and thanks again. Oh, one small point. The player Maserewa is chasing is not Heidensohn. It's Orvill Hume. Keep it under your hat.'

I walked away and left him chuckling with glee.

'And we went to the Marienplatz, and the Deutsches Museum, and the Church of Our Lady . . . oh and Alte Pinakothek!'

'What's that when it's at home?'

'Old Pinakothek. It's an art gallery.'

'Of course. Been there many times.'

'Daddy!' she reproved.

'So where else have they taken you?'

'Everywhere. There's so much to see in Munich. The Palace, the Olympic Stadium, the English Garden, the Opera . . . everywhere! And tomorrow we're driving out to some zoo.'

I was making Ed Maserewa wait in the queue. Lynette came before everybody. I had managed to catch her during dinner at the hotel and although the line was a bad one, her excitement about the trip was coming through loud and clear. It was the perfect tonic for me.

'How's the food?'

'Marvellous! We've all been eating like pigs. I must have put on at least a stone! The pastries here are out of this world. Miss Aldritt says we'll all have to go on a strict diet when we get home.'

'Sounds as if you're enjoying yourself, anyway.'

'It's wonderful, Daddy.'

I let her tell me why for a few minutes and then worked the conversation slowly around to more serious matters.

'Things aren't going all that well here, I'm afraid.'

'But I thought you were playing at your very best,

185

Daddy,' she said with concern. 'Miss Aldritt bought an English paper today and it said Alan Saxon was among the leaders.'

'That was before the third round, Lynette,' I explained. 'But I wasn't talking about my golf, actually.'

'Speak up, please! I can't hear you!'

'Has Miss Aldritt – mentioned anything else about me that was in the papers?'

'No. Should she have?'

It was time to bite on the bullet.

'Lynette, I want you to listen carefully. And to trust me.'

'Of course . . .'

'Do I ever tell you lies?'

'All the time,' she giggled.

'Lynette, *please!*'

'Sorry.'

'This is important. Very, very important.' I moistened my lips with my tongue before continuing. 'I had a spot of trouble when I arrived in Scotland. I gave someone a lift. A hitch-hiker. A girl.'

There was a long pause. 'Well?' she pressed.

'The girl was murdered. In Carnoustie. We don't know yet who did it but the police are doing all they can to find out.'

'Murdered in Carnoustie! That's terrible.'

'I wanted you to hear it from me, Lynette, and I wanted you to know that I had nothing whatsoever to do with it. I dropped the girl off in Edinburgh. The next time I saw her was here in St Andrews. I have no idea how she came to—' I broke off as I heard a blubbering noise at the other end of the line. 'Now, darling, you must be very brave and grown-up about this. I need your help. I need you to believe me. Do you? Do you believe me, Lynette?' Another pause. 'Do you?'

'Yes, Daddy.'

'I'll explain everything when I see you. In the meantime, don't say a word about it to anyone. It's our secret. Okay?'

'Okay.' She had controlled the tears now. 'Does Mummy know?'

'Yes, darling. Mummy knows. As always.'

'Poor Daddy. It must be awful for you.'

'Fortunately, I've got the golf to keep me sane,' I said with a strained laugh. 'But don't worry about me. I'm fine.'

'Who was this girl?'

'I've told you all you need to know. The rest will have to wait.'

'If you say so, Daddy.'

'I do, darling.' I was close to tears myself now and wished I could reach out and hug her to me. 'I just hope that this isn't going to spoil your holiday for you. Don't let it, please. Carry on having a smashing time.'

'I'll try,' she said gallantly.

'Thank you.'

'Can I see you soon?'

'As soon as you get back.'

'Good.'

'And . . . you won't tell anyone about this, will you?'

'Not a soul. I promise.'

I needed to moisten my lips again. 'Well, I suppose I'd better let you get back to your grub. What was it?'

'Black Forest gâteau.'

'Sounds gooey and disgusting.'

'It is and I love it. If I don't go back soon, that Mandy Harrison will gobble up my share. She's so greedy.'

'Off you go, then. And take care.'

'Good luck for the next round.'

'Thanks. And Lynette . . . I love you very much, darling . . .'

''Bye, Daddy,' she whispered. Then she rang off.

I was so relieved that I had finally got through to her and broken the news of the murder. I had a feeling that she would have grown up a little bit more by the time she came home. Hearing her voice had both cheered and saddened me and I was ready to laugh and cry at the same time. I was grateful for one thing. She had forgotten to ask me about the little golfer. Somehow I would get it back before we met each other again. I made her a silent promise.

*

The tented village is a feature of every Open Championship but one about which I have mixed feelings. I had deliberately not taken too much notice of the huge acreage of canvas when I had driven into St Andrews on my first day because the sight tends to inflame me. I take the heretical view that a golf tournament should be solely about golf.

Adequate provision must obviously be made for the spectators and since upwards of 180,000 people are likely to visit the Old Course during the four days of the Championship, catering, banking, postal, telephone, first aid, left luggage and information services are essential on a large scale. Car parks are mandatory and toilet facilities an imperative. All this I accept.

What I do not find so easy to stomach is the commercial sideshow that is laid on in the tented village, where the golf equipment manufacturers' exhibition parades its wares alongside the general retail exhibition in an orgy of promotional gimmicks. But my real complaint is against the hospitality complexes where business concerns have their own private pavilions in which clients and friends can be wined, dined, entertained and kept well away from the course itself. For companies who do not have their individual retreat, there is an executive restaurant where they can treat their guests to highly expensive meals and keep an occasional eye on the scoreboard to remind themselves that an Open Championship is being played.

It all smacks too much of a brash, exploitative, I'm-only-here-for-the-champagne attitude and is an unwelcome step in the direction of the aggressive merchandising of some American tournaments. During the busier parts of the day when crowds throng through the tented village, there is a carnival atmosphere about and you might almost be strolling through a funfair. Golfers want people to watch golf. Simple as that.

My prejudices were given a field day as I headed for my meeting with Ed Maserewa. Although it was evening, there were still plenty of people about and laughter was coming from the hospitality tents. The designers had come up with the idea of naming the various thoroughfares after certain players and I winced as I read the results.

Kincaid Crescent. Piker Parade. Tanizaki Terrace. Devereaux Drive. Hume Halt. Nicholson Neuk. Inevitably, the route which I had to follow was called Saxon Street. I cringed inwardly.

'Looking for someone?' said a voice to my left.

'Not you,' I rejoined when I recognised Gordon Reeman.

'I see that you've blown it yet again, Alan.'

'One way of looking at it.'

'What's your version?'

'That's my business.'

He gave me a long hard look, then lapsed into his usual false joviality. 'This Open is turning out to have plenty of surprises, anyway. You never know what to expect next.'

'You'll have to excuse me, Gordon. I have an appointment.'

'With whom?'

'Somebody else,' I said and continued on my way.

His eyes followed me until I went into a tent at the very heart of the complex. I soon found the man I had come to see.

Ed Maserewa embodied all my objections to the place. He was sleek, well-fed and ever alert to the commercial potentialities of the game. Golfers were nothing more than products to him.

'Hi, Al.'

'You wanted to see me?'

'Sure. How are things?'

'Fine, thanks.'

'That's swell. Take a seat.'

I considered the offer, then sat down slowly. 'I'm not staying long,' I said firmly.

'Okay, okay. So what'll you have while you're here?'

'Nothing.'

'Aw, come on, Al!' he coaxed, opening both palms.

'Nothing at all, thanks.'

He nodded, sat back in his chair and looked me over. We were at a table in a private pavilion owned by a company in which he had a major stake. Over the years, he had used the name of Horton Kincaid to market the company's golf clubs and accessories with relentless success. Maserewa wore a hand-made lightweight grey suit over an open-necked silk shirt. There was a gold chain around his neck, another around his wrist and a cluster of rings on his right hand. He had an air of opulence that was almost intimidating.

His smile remained constant. 'You hit trouble out there today. I figured you would somehow. Tough, Al.'

'What did you want, Maserewa?' I asked, bluntly.

'I want us to be friends,' he answered, playing with a signet ring. 'I want us to understand each other.'

'The two don't necessarily go together,' I pointed out.

He laughed mirthlessly, then put a hand on my wrist. 'Why did you follow me yesterday?'

'I didn't follow you,' I replied honestly.

'Don't give me that, Al. You were hiding in the bushes when I went past in my automobile.' His smile ripened. 'True?'

I shrugged. 'Free country.'

'Nothing's free. You know that.' He tightened his grip on my wrist. 'So why did you do it?'

'Curiosity.'

'Bad habit.'

'So is carving up your business partner,' I retorted. 'Does Horton know that you're cooking up a deal with Orvill Hume?'

He released my wrist and toyed with the signet ring again. His smile was impregnable. 'Why did you set that crumby journalist on to me, Al? I'm the kind of guy that likes privacy. What happens between me and . . . anyone else is strictly our business.'

'Depends . . .'

'I'm telling you how it is. Just listen.' He washed his hands in the air, then leaned over towards me. 'Forget what you saw. That's what you gotta do. Forget what you saw and I forget that you saw it. Is it a deal?'

'No, it's not.'

190

'But it's my best offer, Al,' he urged.

I stood up. 'Goodbye, Maserewa. Thanks for the chat.'

'Did I say you could go?' he whispered.

His smile froze me to the spot. Ed Maserewa had always looked and sounded like a Mafia hit man but it was not until that moment that I realised why. There was something dark and compelling about him and I had to force myself to meet his narrow-lidded gaze. He enjoyed my discomfort.

'Know something?' he asked. 'You coulda been a real big shot in this game if you'd had the right manager handling you.'

'I never found one that I could trust,' I said pointedly.

'You needed an Ed Maserewa behind you.'

'Ready to stab me between the shoulder-blades?'

He was quite unruffled. 'I'm on the level, Al. You had a talent but you let it die on you.' He indicated my chair and I found that I was sitting down again. His voice returned to a whisper. 'Here's what you gotta do. Tell that jerk Phelps to get off my back. And forget what you saw. Now I'm sure a smart guy like you can do those two simple things to help out a pal. Thanks.'

He stood up and flicked his fingers to dismiss me.

Ed Maserewa had not even raised his voice and yet his threat had tremendous force. I was in the middle of a pavilion with several people around me and yet I felt more frightened than when a bullet had all but smashed my skull in the Tentsmuir Forest.

Maserewa had spelled it out for me. I had crossed him and found myself yet another enemy at St Andrews.

Perhaps the most dangerous of them all.

Chapter Nine

Crail is a delightful and much-photographed town to the south of Fife Ness. Visitors seek out its old Mercat Cross, its Tollbooth, the charming Kirk of St Mary, dating back to the sixteenth century, and the fascinating little museum set in an old house. Several of the elegant buildings have been honoured with preservation orders and the broad Marketgait, partly cobbled and tree-lined, an echo of the vanished splendour of a more leisurely age, sets off the whole community. In its time, Crail has been a medieval port, a royal burgh, a coastal market town and a popular holiday resort.

It had now become something rather different.

A rendezvous for two golfers under threat of death.

'Thanks for coming, Alan.'

'Thanks for asking me.'

'We got some figuring out to do.'

The house which Horton Kincaid had rented stood above the town and afforded a fine view of the harbour and the sea beyond. It was a big, gracious, three-storeyed Georgian building in the centre of a spacious garden and it was in an excellent state of repair. Horton liked to have his family around him. He had brought his wife, three young children, grandmother, grandfather and cook all the way from Texas and they fitted into the house without any difficulty.

I saw no sign of them as I was shown into the long, high-ceilinged lounge. Horton was clearly intending our conversation to be private.

'When did you speak to Ed?'

'This afternoon. He warned me not to contact you.'

'Sonofabitch.'

'That's putting it mildly.'

'Have a beer,' he said, passing me a pint canister.

'Cheers.'

We pulled the metal rings almost simultaneously and the beers frothed together as we poured them into our glasses. Horton saw off nearly half a pint in a first, long, guzzling drink. He looked tired and rather dejected.

It had not taken me long to shake off my fears about Maserewa. The fact that he had tried to gag me showed my information was both accurate and valuable and should be passed on to the person it most affected. After driving back to the farm and thinking it over, therefore, I had rung Horton and told him briefly that I had had a meeting with his former manager. There had been a lengthy, pained, pensive silence at the other end of the line and then he had asked if I could possibly call over later in the evening. I arrived in Crail in time to see the sun settling on the horizon like a giant yellow beachball.

'So what's the lowdown, Alan?'

'You're not going to like this, Horton . . .'

'I never expected to. From here on in, I ain't gonna like any goddam thing that's to do with Ed and I gotta get used to the notion. Why did he send for you?'

'Because I found out something he didn't want me to know. Quite by accident.' I took a sip of beer. It was refreshingly cool. 'I think I know who he's lining up to take your place.'

'Heidensohn?' asked the Texan with dull resignation.

'Orvill Hume.'

'Orvill? Holy shit. Are you sure, Alan?'

'I saw them talking together outside Orvill's house.'

'When?' He was on his feet.

'Late yesterday afternoon. Just north of Anstruther.'

He punched a fist into the other palm.

'I'm staying near there,' I added, not wishing to explain why I had been skulking in the bushes. 'Orvill and Maserewa came out of the house deep in conversation. Like close friends. They seemed pleased about something. Then they shook hands warmly.'

'Yeah,' he said, ruefully. 'I know all about those goddam Ed Maserewa handshakes.'

'That's really all I saw, Horton.'

'It's enough. Ed had no call to go visiting Orvill. It had to be business. With Ed, every goddam thing has to be business. That guy don't know any other way.'

'But Orvill already has a manager,' I argued. 'Lou Genky.'

'That won't bother Ed one bit. If he means to move in on Orvill, then he'll rub out Genky as easy as spittin'. Ed always gets what he wants.' He lowered his massive frame into a chair. 'Hadn't reckoned on Orvill, though. I'd have bet my bottom dollar it was going to be Heidensohn. That was what Ed was kinda hintin'.'

'Perhaps that's what he wanted you to think,' I suggested.

'Could be,' he agreed. He finished his beer in one go and stared into the empty glass. 'I've had a great life outa golf, Alan. A great life. And I owe it all to Ed Maserewa – the asshole. He picked me up when I was a raw kid workin' as a caddie at the local club. He took one hell of a chance on me but it paid off. And I was grateful. I was so goddam grateful I'da done anything for that guy. So he gives me a handshake and gets me to sign a contract and away we go.' He looked up at me, a wistful expression in his eyes. 'You know the rest, Alan. I got lucky. I hit a winning streak and I rode it all the way.'

'Don't be so modest,' I grinned. 'It wasn't luck, Horton. You won because you were the best golfer on two legs. You still are.'

He smiled lazily, then shook his head. 'It don't come so easy no more. When you're young, all you gotta do is to go out there and the shots come natural. As you get older, you start to slow down. Your rhythm goes, your distance shortens, your putts don't make the cup so often. You have to work on every goddam shot.'

'My game has always been like that.'

Horton opened another canister of beer and poured it into his glass. 'It ain't only that,' he confessed. 'I've had back problems. That's why my golf has been crap this season. I seen specialists all over the States but they can't

194

get me back in shape. One guy at this hospital in New York says there ain't nothing wrong with my back – it's all in the mind! Hell, it's my goddam back! And when I swing that club real hard and smack a ball the way I like, it hurts, Alan. I gotta have pain-killers after every round I play. I gotta have massage. In the mind! That doc was talking out of his ass.'

I was touched that he had chosen me to confide in. Back problems are an occupational hazard for golfers and they usually mean the end of a career at the top. Horton Kincaid had kept his troubles to himself and tried to play on. But Ed Maserewa had known. And it had made him look around for someone to take Horton's place.

'When did you find out?' I asked. 'About Maserewa.'

'Thursday night. He was sittin' in that same chair you are, talkin' big the way he always does, and . . . it kinda slipped out.'

'So you lost your temper . . .'

'That guy has earned over two million bucks outa me. He has a slice of everythin' that Horton Kincaid brings in. When I swing a club, Ed gets fifteen per cent of the divot. He doesn't miss a trick.'

I needed only a few seconds to reach a decision.

'It didn't slip out, Horton.'

'Hey . . . ?'

'Maserewa's timing was perfect. He *wanted* you to know that there was someone else waiting in the wings to take over from you.'

'But I shot a good round on Thursday,' he argued vehemently. 'I was sittin' up there on the leader board only two strokes behind Orvill. Why should Ed leak it out *then*? It don't make a heap of sense.'

'Yes it does,' I replied. 'He wants to sign up an Open Champion. And it would make a lot of difference to Orvill's chances of snatching the title if you weren't looking up his arse. Maserewa told you because he knew it would cause a big upheaval. He hoped it would poison your game.' I tapped his knee. 'Any other player but Horton Kincaid would have fallen apart in a situation like that.'

It had obviously never occurred to him. As the truth dawned, his jaw opened and his eyes glazed. His own manager, the person he had relied on totally for the whole of his career, was actually trying to sabotage him so that the heir apparent could win. He rubbed a hand across his chin and nodded gently.

'I'm gonna go out there tomorrow and play the best goddam golf of my life,' he promised himself. 'I'm aimin' to leave Orvill Hume spread all over the fairway like cattle shit.'

I finished my beer and got up. 'We both need an early night, Horton. Rest that back of yours.'

'Hold on there, Alan. There's somethin' else . . .'

He stood beside me and weighed it up in his mind. It was a long while before he was certain that he could trust me. He crossed to an antique desk in the corner and took an envelope from one of the drawers.

'What d'you make of this?'

He handed me the sheet of paper from inside the envelope and I read the message that had been printed in capital letters. IF YOU WIN TOMORROW, YOU WILL BE SHOT. The paper was identical to that used for the note to Nairn MacNicol and the bold letters looked as if they had been written by the same hand with the same pen.

'Have you shown this to the police?' I asked.

'I hate cops,' he said, dismissively. 'And I ain't playing in the Open with a posse of detectives all around me.'

I didn't tell him I had been doing just that for the last three days. The threat was a serious one, but I wasn't sure I should tell him that either. Even Horton Kincaid might quail if he knew an automatic rifle was trained on him as he played. Besides, I needed him. He had replaced me as the target. If he looked like winning on the next day, he would force the hand of the person I wanted. It seemed cruel not to tell him the truth but I felt it was necessary.

He grabbed the note from me and tore it up.

'Just some screwball having fun,' he decided.

'I hope so.'

'Happens all the time, Alan,' he said, throwing the bits of

paper into the empty coal scuttle. 'Whole goddam world is full of nuts. I been threatened with just about everythin' before now and I've still lived to tell the tale.' He smiled confidently and thrust my glass back into my hand. 'I'll get you another beer.'

Night was falling as I left Crail for the short journey back to the farm. Horton had talked himself into a frame of mind that would help him in the final round. He was calm, determined, defiant and more than a little arrogant. He intended to hang on to his crown and refused to abdicate in favour of a young pretender. Scorning back problems and managerial betrayals, he would go out on the Old Course and win.

Not even a death threat could stop him.

I admired Horton's attitude tremendously because it chimed in harmony with my own but I still feared for him. Someone's name had been written on the Open Championship trophy long before the event had got under way. Players who might have replaced that name with their own had been put under pressure. I had been shackled from the very start. Tanizaki's challenge had been undermined by the theft of his clubs. Horton Kincaid had been warned.

The man behind it all had gone too far to draw back now.

I swung Carnoustie into a side-road for the last leg of the journey. Overhanging trees on either side of me created a long dark avenue and the sky was blotted out completely. We were only a quarter of a mile from the farm when it happened. Around a bend ahead of us came a car with its full beam on, blinding me with its dazzle and forcing me to put an arm up to shield my eyes. With a continuous and aggressive beep on its horn, it headed straight for us on our side of the road. I braked, swung hard on the steering wheel, felt Carnoustie judder beneath me and ran into the overhanging boughs on the opposite side of the road.

The trees acted as an auxiliary brake and slowed us to a halt as we ploughed through branch after branch. My tyres skidded on the grass verge and we finished up twisted at an angle across the camber. Behind us, no longer sounding its horn, the car had vanished. The attack had been so unexpected that it had jolted me badly and I was fortunate to have escaped any injury beyond a few bruises. When I walked around Carnoustie with a flashlight, I counted several more wounds and blemishes on her bodywork and saw that one of her windows had been scored all over. The final indignity was the leafy branch which had been snapped off its tree and which now lay across her roof. Carnoustie looked hurt, helpless and quietly despairing.

She was as battered and woebegone as Nairn MacNicol.

I flung the branch off her, checked for more damage, then drove her at a gentle pace back to the farm. Like me, she had thought we were safe from further attack. It had knocked the wind out of her. Over a cup of cocoa, I pondered over what had happened but could not make up my mind who had been driving the car. Had it been the man who had fired at me and put Nairn in hospital? Or was it Ed Maserewa taking his revenge because I had ignored his warning? Neither possibility brought me any comfort.

When I let down the double bed and started to make it, I recalled the sheets which had been taken away by the police. I retrieved them from a plastic bag in a cupboard and opened them out. They smelled reasonably clean but one of them had a small hole burned in it. I remembered the cannabis that Veronica Willis was supposed to have smoked and the cigarette burn on her shoulder. Fitting the sheet on the bed so that the hole was near the pillow, I lay down and tried to work out the sequence of events.

If she had been smoking when she had been attacked, the cigarette might have rolled on to her shoulder, burned her flesh, then fallen on to the sheet and singed it. I experimented with a pencil and saw that there was a more likely explanation. The man in bed with her had been smoking. As he reached over to strangle her, there had been a struggle and the cigarette had fallen from his mouth on to her shoulder and then rolled on to the sheet where it had been extinguished as they threshed about on top of it.

I went through it a number of times until I was convinced

that I was right. While I had lain unconscious in my motor caravan, the couple had had intercourse on the bed and then smoked pot. When the girl was at her most defenceless, she had been murdered by her lover. I toyed with the pencil and the cigarette suddenly came alight again to burn an idea into my brain.

She had been in Carnoustie all the time.

When I left the Scores Hotel and walked back to the car park, Janie, as I knew her, had been waiting for me with the man. She knew about the security devices inside the vehicle because she had seen me flicking on the switches when we had stopped near Dalkeith, and had asked what I was doing. If her accomplice could get the two of them into Carnoustie, she would know how to switch off the devices and make her safe to drive away.

I had been knocked out, Carnoustie had been taken to Tentsmuir Forest, and they had adjourned to bed. It was her way of getting back at me for refusing her. She had been a compliant lover; no force was needed. Until afterwards. In trying to strike back at me, the girl had unwittingly turned herself into a murder victim. She had connived at her own death. Carnoustie had then been taken to the quiet lane outside Leuchars and I had been draped across the bed beside her. The police had then been tipped off.

The most obvious fact about the man was the one that I had so far missed. He *had* to be a golfer. Nothing else would have done for her. The world of professional golf had a glamour for her that was irresistible and she had made the long journey to St Andrews to be part of its most famous event. If she could talk her way into a lift from me, then she could certainly have got close enough to another golfer to use her blandishments.

But which one?

I glanced at my watch, then lunged at the television to push down the start-button. Highlights of the day's play were being shown and I was just in time to catch the tail-end of the programme. The set purred as it warmed up, then sound and vision came on together. They were giving a round-up of disasters and I saw myself on the fifth fairway taking a short iron from Craig Donaldson.

The commentator was droll and rather superior, but then it's easy to play brilliant golf behind a BBC microphone.

'. . . But once again Alan Saxon flattered to deceive . . . climbed to the top of the leader board only to dive off again . . . He hits the ball well but his direction is completely cock-eyed and – yes – there it is, rolling towards the flag on the thirteenth green. Ah well, unlucky for some, I suppose. With that shot, Saxon effectively played himself out of the reckoning . . . our best British golfer . . . wayward genius . . .'

Tanizaki now came on the screen and missed a simple putt at the End Hole. He then compounded the felony by missing an even simpler one at the next hole and dropping another stroke. Vance Brymer was also having a torrid time, trying to dig his way out of the Road Hole bunker. It took him four attempts to get the ball on to the green and the commentator watched him with wry amusement.

The last victim hauled in for Mistakes of the Round was the beaming and confident Body Beautiful. He was shown on the tee at the High Hole, trying to take an adventurous and direct route to the flag. The producer cut from the unassailable grin as Body Beautiful watched his shot soar down the fairway to an agonised search for the ball in the gorse bushes. Another British challenger had faded into oblivion. Body Beautiful had recorded a round of 77.

The programme ended with a still and credits rolled over it. I craned forward to read all the names.

LEADER BOARD

Holes	+Par–	Players	Score
54	–9	HEIDENSOHN	207
54	–8	KINCAID	208
54	–7	HUME	209
54	–7	PIKER	209
54	–5	TANIZAKI	211
54	–4	NICHOLSON	212
54	–4	DEVEREAUX	212
54	–3	CONELLI	213
54	–3	MEEK	213
54	–3	OSBORNE	213

One of those players had murdered Veronica Willis in my motor caravan. I suspected that he might be perched at the top of the leader board with my miniature golfer pinned to his sweater. Body Beautiful's traumatic third round had eliminated him from my list. He had no chance whatsoever of winning the title now and therefore no reason to send a warning note to Horton Kincaid.

As I looked at the names and sighed at the absence of my own, I felt a sharp stab as I realised why I had been forced off the road earlier that night. I was no longer a threat as a player but they were now after me for another reason.

They were worried. I was getting close.

Sunday morning is usually the best time to visit St Andrews. Its three main streets which converge on the ruins of the cathedral are comparatively empty and it is possible to enjoy to the full the medieval beauty of a city that was once the ecclesiastical capital of Scotland. Only the church bells disturb the cloistered calm.

When the Open is held there, Sundays are very different.

The main thoroughfares are jammed with traffic and crawling with pedestrians and it is impossible to recognise anything medieval about a city that has become the golfing capital of the world. Not even church bells can be heard above the droning hubbub at the Old Course. The faithful are attending their own religious service and separate congregations flourish around each of the eighteen sacred areas to hear the gospel.

'Good morning, Mr Saxon.'

'Hello.'

'How are you feeling?'

'Glad to be alive,' I said, ironically.

'Have no fear. We shall be around and about.'

'That's what I'm afraid of, Superintendent.'

Ginger Tom greeted me as I came out of the competitors' car park. He was wearing what looked to be his Sunday-best suit of mottled blue serge and he had stuck a red rose in the lapel. He surveyed the teeming crowds with candid distaste.

201

'The Gadarene swine.'

'They've paid their money and they're entitled to be here.'

'Well, they don't make our job any easier,' he complained. 'It's going to be like searching for a needle in a haystack.'

'I usually find a needle wherever it's hidden. It has a habit of sticking itself in my arse.'

He gave me a supercilious smile. 'Message from your father.'

'I don't want to hear it.'

'He said you wouldn't.'

'So you're going to tell me anyway.'

'It was short and sweet,' he said. 'Good luck.'

He reproduced my father's sarcastic tone so perfectly that he made me jump. It was the last voice I wanted to hear on the final day of an Open Championship. My father's view of golf matched my view of the police force. It was an unnecessary evil. Because he was a policeman, I ran away from home; because I was a golfer, my father condemned the game out of hand. We were each as bigoted as the other. That was the problem. In some ways, I was horrendously like him.

Ginger Tom was mind-reading again.

'Why do you hate your father so much?'

'Because he's a bully. In or out of uniform.'

'Yes,' he countered, smoothly. 'He warned us that you couldn't cope with discipline. But we've found that out for ourselves.'

'If you'll excuse me, Superintendent . . .'

'Of course, Mr Saxon. I just wanted to jog your memory about something, that's all.'

'I haven't forgotten. Today would have been her birthday.'

'Twenty-one. She deserves a present.'

'Two,' I promised.

Then I turned on my heel and strode quickly away.

The weather was fine but the wind was at its most mettlesome. It gusted in from the north-west so strongly that it was bound to blow away the hopes of many players. For the first time ever, I was delighted to see a high wind at the Old Course. Even a trained marksman with a GE3 would have difficulty in those conditions. He would have to judge and allow for the wind and that fact might be the saving of Horton Kincaid.

'On the tee – Alan Saxon.'

The huge crowds gave me a cordial welcome. It put extra yardage into my opening drive and reminded me that I still had an important job to do out on the course itself. I was playing for pride. I was chasing a reasonable share of the prize money so that I could help out Nairn MacNicol. I was trying to cheer up my supporters and rally my friends. I was getting back at my father. I was making my living.

The wind dictated the style of play and I obeyed. Safety first and no heroics. Keep to the left, avoid the bunkers, never let up. It was controlled rather than inspired golf but it eventually prospered. I picked up a couple of birdies at the Loop and another at the Corner of the Dyke Hole. With the utmost caution, I managed to get a par 4 at the Road Hole and then found myself marching down the eighteenth fairway to the sort of applause that told me why I love the game of golf. Two careful putts on the final green and I was home and dry.

My round of 69 was an achievement in those conditions and it took me back up on the leader board. There were still six names above mine but they were all still playing and I was safely back in the clubhouse. At the very least, I had won a substantial amount of money and regained a lot of self-esteem.

There was no time for self-congratulation. I had a very special friend to help. He and his playing partner had been the last of the sixty golfers to begin their final round and it was assumed that the title would go to one of them. Kincaid or Heidensohn. America or Germany. Experience or flair. Friend or foe.

I went straight back to Carnoustie from the locker rooms and put my clubs inside. I took out binoculars, locked the door and turned to move away. A big, square, impassive face stared into mine. It was Maserewa's bodyguard and he needed no words to tell me why he had come. He eased me around to the other side of Carnoustie so that we were largely out of sight and then he took something from his pocket and slipped it over his knuckles.

It happened so quickly I was taken by surprise.

The first punch caught me in the solar plexus and knocked the breath out of me. Instinct for survival told me that I mustn't take a second punch or I was finished. As the first aimed itself at my chin, therefore, I swung my head sharply and the knuckleduster rammed into Carnoustie's bodywork, rocking her violently. I lunged at my attacker with the binoculars and caught him a glancing blow on the temple. As he raised the metal fist to strike again, I grabbed at his wrist and held it back. His other hand got to my throat and forced me hard up against Carnoustie.

I got in a kick to his leg and jerked a knee up into his groin but he didn't release me from his grip. His superior strength was beginning to tell and I knew that I couldn't keep him at bay for more than a few seconds. My throat was on fire, my eyes were filming over. He wrenched his right fist free, held the knuckleduster under my nose, and drew back his arm for the decisive punch.

But it was not delivered by him.

At the very moment when he was about to fell me, something hit him so hard behind the ear that he was sent sprawling on the ground where he lay dazed and moaning.

Tim Quentin grinned hopefully at me. 'Okay, Alan?'

His Body had never looked quite so Beautiful as just then.

'Thanks,' I gasped. 'I owe you.'

'It's the other way around, old boy. I'm afraid I've got a lot of apologising to do. Things went to my head. I got carried away.' He gave a rueful shrug. 'I'm back where I belong now. Among the good losers.' He offered me his hand. 'Are we still friends?'

'For life,' I promised him, pumping hard.

The man on the ground was starting to get up. Tim pushed me back and dropped into a boxer's crouch, ready to tackle my assailant again. But the man had had enough. Cursing under his breath, he lumbered morosely away between the parked vehicles. Thanks to Body Beautiful I had escaped any serious damage.

Gordon Reeman came hurrying up with two security guards.

'What's going on?' he demanded. 'Someone reported a fight.'

'All over bar the shouting,' I said. 'You're too late. As usual.'

'Wasn't that Maserewa's heavy sloping off?'

'It was,' I conceded.

'What did he want?'

'To deliver his boss's calling card.'

'Luckily, I was on hand to dissuade him,' beamed Body Beautiful.

Gordon bristled. 'If he was threatening you, we should inform the police. I'm not having these hoodlum tactics on my patch.'

'Forget it,' I said. 'I don't think he'll be back.' A question was forming on Body Beautiful's lips and I killed it dead. 'Don't ask why he should want to thump me, Tim. It would take far too long to explain. The important thing is that you did your Superman act when it was most needed. And most welcome.'

'All part of the service,' he grinned.

'Now why don't we go and watch some golf?' I suggested.

Gordon stayed close to me as we headed for the clubhouse. 'I want you where my chaps can look after you, Alan. We need you in one piece.'

'How many of Ginger Tom's men are about?'

'I've counted a dozen or more so far. He's here himself and so is Inspector Robbie.' He gave a mirthless laugh. 'All riding shotgun on Alan Saxon.'

'Only they weren't around just now when I needed them.'

'Don't worry. I'll take care of you from now on.'

It was more of a veiled threat than a reassurance.

Back inside the clubhouse, I detached myself from

Gordon and thought out what I had to do. Horton Kincaid's life depended on how well he was playing in the final round and the scoreboard showed that he was not yet dominating the field. It was very much a four-horse race. Playing ahead of him, Orvill Hume and Jeff Piker had each clawed back the two strokes that separated them from Heidensohn. All three players were now nine under for the Championship, with Horton just one stroke in arrears. It was going to be a close finish and that fact was sending extra charges of electricity through the galleries.

Horton began his charge at the fourteenth, the Long Hole. News of his birdie flashed up on the scoreboard and my heart began to pound. He was making his bid and inviting attack. Without knowing it, he was taunting the man with the automatic rifle. What I had to work out was where it would be fired. At Cartgate, coming home? At the Corner of the Dyke? At the Road Hole? Or on the hallowed green of the Tom Morris?

Which would be the Bullet Hole?

It had to be either the seventeenth or eighteenth.

Only then would it be clear if he was the likely winner. Until he reached the Road Hole, he was safe but he might be treading on borrowed time after that. I left the clubhouse and worked my way past the grandstand and in front of the file of buildings that runs alongside the final fairway. Thick, jostling crowds impeded me at every stage and I had to endure endless back-slapping and comment. Eventually I got within sight of the seventeenth tee and let my binoculars take over.

There were so many possible places for a sniper that it was difficult to know where to start but my scrutiny was soon drawn down the fairway slightly to the Old Course Hotel. I remembered what Clive had told me. Ulrich Heidensohn was staying there. The balconies that front the building command a magnificent view of the course and they were packed with guests enjoying a privileged vantage point. I ran the binoculars past face after face until at last I locked them on one that I could identify. On a top floor balcony, standing beside another man and glaring down at

206

the seventeenth tee with grim concentration, was Max Fleischner. He and his coach party were staying in a hotel on the other side of St Andrews. There seemed to be only one explanation for his key position high above the course.

Heads got in my way and I had to wait a few seconds before I could focus my binoculars again. This time I saw something else. At Fleischner's side was a long metallic object glinting in the sun.

He was in Heidensohn's room. With a rifle.

To get from where I was to the Old Course Hotel – or the Old Course Golf and Country Club, as it has been restyled – took a lot of pushing and shoving and apologising. It was many minutes before I arrived panting and dishevelled at the entrance. Behind me, the roars of approval signalled that somebody had just triumphed at the Road Hole.

I dashed into reception and found it almost deserted. On the final day of an Open Championship, only one side of the building exists and both staff and guests had gravitated towards it. The girl behind the counter looked surprised when I rushed up and demanded the number of Heidensohn's room.

'He's not in at the moment, sir,' she explained.

'Give me the number, please,' I insisted.

'I'm not sure that I ought to—'

'What's the bloody number, for God's sake?'

Under duress she gave it to me but I could see she would call the manager the moment I disappeared. I didn't care. I ran to the lift and sent it climbing. Every second was precious. I stood there urging the machine to go faster, banging on the wall with my fist. I was mortified when it stopped at the second floor and a grey-haired old lady in a flowered dress stepped in beside me, smiling sweetly.

'Going down, are we? Good.'

'I'm going up,' I told her.

'Oh, but you can go down first,' she said, easily, putting a hand on my arm. 'I'm in rather a hurry, you see.'

The doors tried to close. I stuck my foot out to trigger them open, and dashed into the corridor, leaving the old lady gasping. I raced to the stairs and took them in threes. When I reached the top floor I was panting worse than ever.

I hurried along the corridor until I found the right room, then paused to get my breath back and decide what to do. A close and valued friend was in danger. I could help him. No time to delay. I grasped the door handle and tried it gingerly. It was locked. Panic threatened. I had to get inside the room as quickly as possible. There was only one way.

Another great roar from the course gave me my cover. When the sound was at its peak, I raised my heel and kicked hard at the lock several times. Then I retreated to the other side of the corridor and launched myself with full force. My shoulder took a bruising, but the door gave way. I tumbled into the room, ready to tackle Fleischner and wrest the rifle away from him.

'Mr Saxon! What are you doing here?'

Beth Gill was pouring tea into three cups. Beyond her, on the balcony, Fleischner turned to face me. What I had taken to be a rifle was a metallic walking stick belonging to his companion.

Fleischner recognised me and his face contorted with fury.

I stood there and cringed at the enormity of my mistake. The old man on the balcony, a trim, erect figure in slacks and polo neck sweater, subjected me to a stare of disapproval.

'*Was ist los?*' he snapped.

'Out!' snarled Fleischner, indicating the door.

Beth laughed nervously to hide her embarrassment. 'Max invited me to join him. Mr Heidensohn has kindly loaned us his room so that we can watch the golf.' She gestured deferentially towards the man on the balcony. 'This is Mr Heidensohn's uncle . . .'

Ecstatic applause from outside sent the two Germans to the edge of the balcony where they joined in the clapping. Down below them, Heidensohn had arrived on the seventeenth tee with Horton Kincaid.

I mumbled an excuse and got out of the room quickly. As I ran down the stairs, I realised I had been looking for the wrong pairing. It was not Heidensohn and Max Fleischner, after all.

Could it possibly be Orvill Hume and Ed Maserewa?

'Get off this fucking line!'

'I want some information, Clive.'

'Don't tempt me.'

'That thing I asked you to find out . . .'

'For crying out loud, Alan. I'm watching the climax of an Open Championship and you want to hear tittle-tattle.'

I had rung the press tent from a hotel booth. Clive Phelps was preoccupied with other matters. Once again, I was coming between him and his job at a crucial moment. He unloaded his rage in choice phrases. I stuck it out and then got in my question again.

'*Please*, Clive. It's the last thing I'll ever ask you. Where did that motorcycle come from? I must know.'

'Jeff Piker borrowed it from Gordon Reeman.'

I let the receiver fall from my hand and sprinted off. Clive's irate voice continued to swear down the line as he dangled in space but I was soon out of earshot.

Jeff Piker and Gordon Reeman. The nearly man and the head of security. The plausible Australian with the mask of affability and the trained organiser with unlimited access to all data relating to the Open. The foreigner and the local man. Between them they were a formidable team and if I had been frightened off at the start, there might have been nothing to hinder their plans.

It all came back to Clive's initial forecast.

Saxon, Kincaid, Piker. One, two, three.

We were the men to beat. Jeff Piker did not fear Hume and Heidensohn. I was his jinx player with a consistent record of victories against him and Horton Kincaid was the defending champion. If he could eliminate me and disturb Horton, Jeff Piker might at last get his hands on a major title.

As I struggled through the maelstrom of spectators to get back to the clubhouse, I tried to apportion their roles. Jeff had been in Carnoustie with the girl and throttled the life out of her. Gordon had fired the rifle and brought the newspapers on the Yamaha and lured Nairn MacNicol out of his digs. With Saxon and Kincaid accounted for, Piker could keep ahead of the field; with his police contacts and military training, Gordon Reeman could keep ahead of the murder inquiry. When an unforeseen danger threatened, such as Tanizaki's purchase on the lead, it could soon be blunted.

Resounding cheers up ahead acclaimed Jeff Piker's putt on the eighteenth green. His name leapfrogged to the top of the leader board. He had finished with ten under, two strokes clear of Orvill Hume. Still to play on the seventeenth green, Heidensohn was three strokes behind the leader and Horton Kincaid was one. Only the defending champion had any hope of catching Jeff Piker but almost none of overtaking him. If Horton could sink his putt at the Road Hole and birdie the Tom Morris, he would tie for first place and force a play-off.

Somewhere in the clubhouse, Jeff Piker was now receiving the congratulations of friends and colleagues; somewhere overlooking the eighteenth green, Gordon Reeman was waiting with an automatic rifle to make certain that the Australian could not be beaten. An affectionate and sustained outburst of applause behind me confirmed that Horton had putted successfully to keep himself in contention. That also meant he was in danger. My priority was to find Gordon Reeman.

Fighting my way through the crowd lining the eighteenth fairway was like swimming against the tide but I kept going. I scanned the rooftops ahead for possible vantage points and saw dozens. Gordon could be anywhere. The scoreboard and the distant applause told me that Heidensohn had put his ball dead and that the two players were now making their way to the eighteenth tee. Time was running out.

'What on earth are you doing, Alan?'

'Where's Gordon?' I gasped.

'Get your breath back first, old chap.' Ian Calloway looked at me with concern. 'Are you sure you feel altogether well?'

I had made it to the clubhouse after circling it and coming

in from the rear. Ian had almost caught me as I rushed to him on the terrace. Members and officials thronging around also wondered why I was in such a state.

'Where's Gordon?' I repeated. 'I must find him.'

'He's taken his wife away,' explained Ian.

'His wife!'

I thought of the handsome woman I had seen in the wheelchair.

'The excitement was too much for Helen, I'm afraid. Should never have come, really, but the woman is so game. She'll be fine when she's had a lie down for an hour.'

'Where?' I asked.

He chuckled to himself. 'Gordon covers all eventualities. He had an idea that this might happen so he arranged to borrow Yokuri's room over at Rusack's. Means that Gordon can tend his wife and watch the climax of the Open at the same time.'

I didn't tell him that Gordon intended to watch that climax down the barrel of an automatic rifle. I was about to leave when a hush of expectation fell on the crowds all around. On the eighteenth tee, Horton Kincaid was taking off his sweater for a monster drive. It would be a risky shot. A slight error of judgement would send his ball on over the fence and out of bounds. But Horton had something to prove and made light of the risk. After a few practice swings, he took his stance, glanced at the target, then down at the ball, moving his feet, adjusting his grip, getting really comfortable.

Then the club swept back over his shoulder, a trigger seemed to click, and his entire body uncoiled in a display of flashing power. The ball stayed low and straight but carried well beyond Granny Clark's Wynd before hitting the turf, rolling down into and then up out of the Valley of Sin, and on to the green itself some twelve feet from the pin.

It was the shot of a great player and it brought everyone to their feet. The applause reverberated and Horton casually acknowledged it by raising a gloved hand. How much pain in his back the shot had cost him I didn't know, but I was certain it put his life in danger. He had reached the Bullet Hole.

I was off again at speed.

211

Rusack's Marine Hotel, a fine Victorian building, is diagonally opposite the clubhouse but it took me an age to burrow my way to it. My frantic journey gave me time to reflect on the thoroughness of Gordon's planning. The wheelchair was an ideal way to transport a rifle that could be taken to pieces. Without realising it, Helen Reeman had helped to conceal a lethal weapon – a souvenir of her husband's army days. Gordon had no scruples about using his invalid wife as an accessory to murder.

Heidensohn had played his tee shot and the two golfers were striding down the last fairway to a crescendo of cheers. I pushed my way into the hotel and ran to the receptionist. She told me that Mrs Reeman was resting in a room on the ground floor but that her husband had gone upstairs. I asked the room number, then bullied the pass key off her. As I tore upstairs, I realised that I would be getting a bad name among hotel staff in St Andrews.

When I burst into the room, Gordon had just finished assembling the rifle. He swung it to cover me and I wasn't sure whether it was loaded. His manner was as briskly calm as ever.

'Sorry you got caught up in it, Alan, but there was no choice. You just happened to come in useful. You and Carnoustie.'

'Tell me more,' I encouraged.

'We *have* to win, you see. It was a bargain. I need the money and Jeff needs the glory. Together, we can get what we both want.'

'Stop kidding yourselves.'

'Jeff thought this year would be his last chance. It was make or break. He was determined to get his name into the record books. Win an Open Championship and it's the key to a million pounds. That's what they say, isn't it? The money doesn't mean that much to him. So he was prepared to give me a sizeable chunk of it.'

I tried to edge nearer but he ordered me back with the rifle.

'You had enough warnings, Alan. You should have heeded them.'

212

'Not my style.'

'Kincaid was warned as well. He's another man who doesn't know what's good for him. He'll have to be taught. So will you.'

He aimed the rifle carefully at my forehead. Before he could pull the trigger, however, there was such a roar of wonder from outside that he automatically turned to see what had caused it. I needed no prompting. Hurling myself at him, I pushed the barrel of the rifle up into his face and twisted the butt out of his hand. When he tried to grapple with me, I kicked hard into his crotch and sent him groaning to the floor. I lifted the weapon to bring it crashing down on his head but a voice checked me.

'Leave him to us, Mr Saxon.'

Ginger Tom had come into the room with a couple of uniformed policemen. I tossed the rifle to him and raced out. I was in search of the second birthday present for Veronica Willis.

Jeff Piker was sneaking away from the exit as I approached. Horton Kincaid's astonishing eagle at the eighteenth had robbed the Australian of the title and he had elected to cut and run. He was pulling on the black crash helmet as he crossed to the car park. I found extra speed and got to Carnoustie before I heard the motorcycle revving up at the far end of the car park. He had to ride past us to get out. After all she had suffered at his hands, Carnoustie deserved the opportunity to get her own back.

The motorcycle came hurtling along between the lines of parked vehicles and I judged my moment to perfection. When he was thirty yards away, I jabbed my foot down hard on the accelerator and we shot out into his path. He braked, swerved, lost control and smashed into a Datsun. I was out of the cab and at his throat before he could get up. He fought back fiercely and rolled me over.

'She asked for it, the stupid little cow. It was *her* idea to do it in your motor caravan. She was a tramp, that's all.'

'That girl was sick,' I urged.

213

'She asked for all she got.'

He butted me on the forehead with his crash helmet and I was dazed for a few seconds. As he felt my grip relax, he jumped off me and ran back across the car park. I was soon after him, vengefulness putting more urgency into my stride. When he turned left and sprinted along the Scores, I overhauled and brought him down with a rugby tackle. He lashed out at me but I had the advantage now. I sat across his chest and began to pummel his face. The pent-up fury of the last week at last had an outlet and he gave way under the onslaught.

The police had to pull me off him.

Jeff Piker was helped to his feet. He was gasping for breath and his face was running with blood. His eyes raked me and he spat into the air as a gesture of defiance.

'I nearly won! I nearly did it!'

'Nearly doesn't count,' I said.

'We had it all sewn up until you came along.'

'There's only one way to win the Open and that's to play better golf than any other man in the field. Nobody gets to be Champion unless he's the top golfer. You're not, Jeff. You never were.'

He broke free from the policemen holding him and grappled with me for a moment but they soon plucked him off again. Another policeman had to hold me back from retaliation.

'Are you all right, sir?' asked Robbie.

'No,' I snarled. 'I hadn't finished with him.'

Ginger Tom stood over me to deliver his reprimand. 'I told you to let us handle it, Mr Saxon. Whatever made you think that you could do it alone?'

'Ask my father.'

While Jeff Piker was taken off to the police station, I staggered back to the clubhouse for the presentation of the Open Championship trophy. First, however, I wanted to put my mind at rest about another presentation. I cornered Ulrich Heidensohn and pointed to the miniature golfer pinned to his sweater.

'Where did you get that?' I demanded.

214

He shrugged. 'From a friend.'

'What was her name?'

'I did not ask, Alan. Lots of girls give me little gifts. Why are you so worried about this one?'

'Because it happens to be mine.'

Before he could protest, I grabbed the lucky charm and unpinned it. A shock awaited me. It was not mine at all. Though almost identical, it lacked the telltale scratches that my golfer had managed to acquire.

'If it means that much to you, Alan,' offered the West German, 'you keep it. I can soon get another.'

'Another?'

'The golf shop on the corner has dozens exactly like that.'

I stood there with egg on my face and mumbled apologies. He enjoyed my discomfort, then took the object from me and pinned it back on his sweater. Officials were rounding everyone up.

'Come on,' said Heidensohn. 'We're needed out there.'

Now that the engraver had had time to put Horton Kincaid's name on the trophy, the presentation could begin. We took our places in front of packed stands and the huge gallery of spectators. They were still ignorant of the drama that had just taken place off the course and that was as it should be. Nothing should be allowed to disturb the supreme moment when a new Open Champion is acclaimed.

Horton Kincaid came down the line to shake hands with the players whose names were behind his on the leader board. As he squeezed my hand tight, his grin had a fund of gratitude in it.

'I reckon I owe you a helluva lot, Alan.'

'Keep the trophy clean for me,' I said with a confidential wink. 'I'll want it back from you next year.'

St Leonard's Church was full on the Monday morning for the funeral of Dubby Gill. It was touching to see how many players and caddies had stayed on to pay their respects to the old greenkeeper. Beth Gill wept genuine tears, the

215

priest delivered a short but moving speech about the deceased and we all filed past the grave with lumps in our throats.

As I tossed earth on to the bare coffin, I glanced around at the churchyard. It was well tended. Dubby would appreciate that.

'It's nice to remember him as he was,' observed Ian.

'Yes,' I agreed. 'It would have been wrong to let recent events sour any memories of him. He was a good friend to me, Ian. That's what he'll stay.' I lowered my voice to a whisper. 'Do you know what his wife's plans are?'

'She's changed her mind about leaving. Staying on at the cottage. I daresay you'll find her down here of a Sunday putting flowers on the grave.'

'And Max Fleischner?'

'Went back to Germany in the coach yesterday. I don't think we shall be seeing him in St Andrews again somehow.' There was a twinkle in his eyes. 'We don't need Herr Fleischner now. We have you to do our rough clearance for us.'

'Tell that to Ginger Tom.'

'I will, I will . . .'

We shook hands and exchanged thanks. After a final word with Beth Gill, I walked over to where I had parked Carnoustie. My thoughts were still very much with Dubby Gill as I unlocked the door and got up into the driving seat.

I was not alone.

'Surprise, surprise!'

'Fiona!'

'I've decided to give you another chance.'

'How the hell did you get in?'

She held up my spare ignition key. 'You left this in my flat. It was the one thing I didn't throw through the window.'

Fiona looked stunning in a white dress that hugged her like a doting lover and I could have just sat there and stared at her. But something else had caught my attention. Hanging from the driving mirror was the miniature golfer.

'Where did that come from?' I gasped.

216

'In the cupboard. You were a hell of a long time at that funeral, Alan, so I decided to spruce Carnoustie up for you. Everything was wrapped up in plastic bags in a cupboard. I put it all back where it should be.' She smiled happily. 'You've got a home again. Pleased with me?'

I laughed as I realised what must have happened. When we had the collision on the Edinburgh ring road, the golfer had obviously been knocked from his perch. He had dropped to the floor and been hidden behind the curled edge of my little carpet. When the police had stripped Carnoustie for examination, the lucky charm had been taken off to the laboratory. It had not been stolen at all.

'Are you laughing at me?' she chided.

I kissed her cheek gently. 'Fiona, I love you.'

'That'll do for openers,' she giggled. 'I knew it would be worth my while to come up on the sleeper.'

'I love you very, very, very much.'

She was the practical type. 'Prove it.'

'I will,' I said, switching on the engine. 'I'm taking you off to South America.'

'South America! Wonderful.'

'I'll show you South America and Jockie's Burn and Plantation and Southward Ho and Luckyslap and all the rest of them,' I promised. 'They're holes on a rather special golf course.'

Carnoustie headed north towards Carnoustie.

With two lingering stops on the way.